W9-DDW-838

Date: 12/21/15

LP MYS ANDREWS
Andrews, Donna,
Six geese a-slaying

Six Geese A-Slaying

This Large Print Book carries the
Seal of Approval of N.A.V.H.

SIX GEESE A-SLAYING

DONNA ANDREWS

THORNDIKE PRESS

A part of Gale, Cengage Learning

Farmington Hills, Mich • San Francisco • New York • Waterville, Maine
Meriden, Conn • Mason, Ohio • Chicago

GALE
CENGAGE Learning·

LIBRARY OF CONGRESS CATALOGING-IN-PUBLICATION DATA

Andrews, Donna.
    Six geese a-slaying / by Donna Andrews. — Large print edition.
       pages cm. — (Thorndike Press large print mystery) (A Meg Langslow mystery)
       ISBN 978-1-4104-7599-2 (hardcover) — ISBN 1-4104-7599-9 (hardcover)
    1. Langslow, Meg (Fictitious character)—Fiction. 2. Women detectives—Fiction. 3. Large type books. 4. Christmas stories. I. Title.
PS3551.N4165S59 2015
813'.54—dc23   2015020686

Published in 2015 by arrangement with St. Martin's Press, LLC

Printed in Mexico
1 2 3 4 5 6 7 19 18 17 16 15

To Caroline Willner,
Mother of Mayhem

ACKNOWLEDGMENTS

To the folks who made this possible:

At St. Martin's Press, many thanks to Ruth Cavin, Hector DeJean, Andrew Martin, Toni Plummer, and Pete Wolverton. More thanks to Ellen Geiger, my agent, the crew at the Frances Goldin Literary Agency, and to Dave Barbor and others at Curtis Brown.

My writing groups provided moral support and manuscript reading — the Rector Lane Irregulars (Carla Coupe, Ellen Crosby, Laura Durham, Peggy Hanson, Val Patterson, Noreen Wald, and Sandi Wilson) and the Hellebore Writers (Erin Bush, Meriah Crawford, M. Sindy Felin, Barb Goffman, and C. Ellett Logan). And thanks once more to the friends and family who kept me relatively sane while meeting a tight deadline: Stuart and Elke Schlager Andrews, Aidan and Liam Andrews, Kathy Deligianis, Suzanne Frisbee, David Niemi, and all the Teabuds.

Special thanks to Dina Willner for allowing me to borrow the Mother of Mayhem, and to the late Caroline Willner for a decade of friendship.

CHAPTER ONE

December 23, 8:30 A.M.

"We wish you a merry Christmas
We wish you a merry Christmas
We wish you a merry Christmas
And a happy New —"

"Bah, humbug," I said.

Under my breath, of course. As Caerphilly County's reigning Mistress of the Revels, I didn't dare let anyone hear me badmouthing Christmas or showing less than the brightest of holiday spirits. I took a deep breath and straightened my holly wreath headdress before saying anything aloud.

"Could you please tell the drummers and pipers to stop drumming and piping immediately?" I finally said. Shouted, actually, to be heard above the din.

"They won't like it, Meg," my brother, Rob, shouted back. "They're having a

9

competition to see who can make the most noise."

"I never would have guessed," I muttered. But I kept smiling as I said it. And I reminded myself that muttering wasn't particularly inconspicuous in weather so cold your breath smoked.

If only someone had warned me beforehand that "Mistress of the Revels" wasn't an honorary title. It meant I was in charge of organizing Caerphilly's annual holiday parade.

This year's theme was "The Twelve Days of Christmas." The twelve drummers drumming were represented by twelve members of the Caerphilly College fife and drum corps, while the pipers piping were eleven assorted bagpipers — currently playing in at least eleven different keys.

The drummers outnumbered the pipers, especially since they'd also brought along twelve matching fifers. But the bagpipers seemed quite capable of holding their own in the noise department. They were definitely going to win if this turned into an endurance test. The drummers were already showing signs of fatigue, and the bagpipers hadn't even hit their stride yet. And while "Silent Night" and "The Little Drummer Boy" are both lovely Christmas carols when

10

played separately, they didn't work well when played simultaneously by dueling groups of musicians.

None of which would have bothered me if they'd been doing it farther off — say, down in the cow pasture where they'd been asked to muster. Why did they insist on hovering right across the street from our house, all too near the spot in our front yard where I'd stationed myself, clipboard in hand, to check in the arriving parade participants?

"Go and tell them —" I began, and then stopped. Rob looked at me expectantly. He was quite dashing in one of the medieval costumes we'd borrowed from the Caerphilly College drama department. The blue brocade tunic matched his eyes, and unlike some of the volunteers, he was skinny enough to get away with wearing tights. As one of the ten lords a-leaping he was going to be a smashing success.

But as an enforcer, Rob would be a disaster. I knew what would happen if I sent him over to quell the riotous music. He'd ask them politely. They'd ignore him — if they even heard him. A little later, I'd go over to see why they hadn't shut up and find Rob taking bagpiping lessons or practicing his leaping in time with the fife and drums.

11

Some things you have to do yourself.

"Never mind," I said, as I turned to head in the direction of the musical duel. "Go make sure none of the other leaping lords have hopped off anywhere. And can you check the Weather Channel and get the latest prediction on when the snow will start? I'm going to — damn!"

I'd stepped in something squishy. I remembered that the eight maids a-milking had recently strolled by, leading their eight purebred Holstein milk cows.

"Please tell me I didn't just step in cow dung."

"Okay, you didn't just step in cow dung," Rob said. "I'm pretty sure the cleanup crew has been by at least once since the cows came through here."

"That's a relief," I said. Though I was energetically scraping my foot on the gravel anyway.

"So that's almost certainly camel dung."

As if that made a difference. I lost it, briefly.

"Can't those stupid wise men keep their beastly camels out of the road?" I snapped. Rob had turned to go and either didn't hear me or pretended not to. It occurred to me that perhaps I shouldn't be so harsh on the wise men, since Michael Waterston, my husband of six months, was one of them.

"Don't blame the stupid wise men," came a voice from behind me. "It was my fault."

I turned around to see an enormous, bushy-bearded figure clad in a peculiar feathered garment. One of the six geese a-laying, I realized — I'd have recognized that immediately if he'd been wearing the goose head and had been waving wings instead of a pair of brawny arms covered with thick hair and a colorful collection of biker- and wildlife-themed tattoos. But never mind the incomplete costume — I was just glad to see its wearer.

"Clarence!" I said. "You made it!"

"Wouldn't miss it for the world," he said, giving me a bear hug.

"So this is one of the six geese a-laying?" said a nasal voice with a hint of a Southern drawl. I glanced over to see who was talking and saw a tall, cadaverously thin man in jeans and a faded brown parka. And he wasn't just tall compared to my five feet ten — he even looked tall standing beside Clarence, who was six and a half feet tall and almost as wide.

Brown parka was scribbling in a pocket notebook. Around his neck he wore a small silver digital camera and a lanyard with a laminated badge.

13

"You must be the reporter from *The Washington Star-Tribune*," I said.

"Are you —" he paused to look into his notebook. "Meg Lansdowne? The parade organizer?"

"Meg Langslow," I corrected.

"J. Ainsley Werzel," he said. He stuck out a hand and I shook it, somewhat awkwardly, since he was still holding the ballpoint pen in it.

"So, one of your geese, I presume?" he repeated. He stuck his pen behind his ear and grabbed his digital camera, apparently intent on getting a festive holiday shot of the ferrets inked up and down Clarence's arms.

"And also one of our vets," I said. "This is Dr. Clarence Rutledge. He'll be helping look after the welfare of the many live animals appearing in today's parade."

I winced inwardly at how stilted I sounded, like something out of a press release from the town council. But better stilted than dimwitted.

Clarence shook the reporter's hand with a great deal less caution than I had. He was so used to enduring the teeth and claws of his more recalcitrant patients that a mere ballpoint pen wound meant nothing to him. Werzel was the one who winced.

"Damn," Werzel said, as he continued to gape at Clarence. "I wish my photographer would get here already. You haven't seen him, have you — short guy with a big Nikon?"

I shook my head.

"Damn," Werzel repeated. "He said ten minutes half an hour ago. Ah, well."

He stood looking around with an odd expression on his face, as if tracking down the source of a bad smell. I checked my foot again. No, it was clean. And when I took a deep breath, the icy air held only the tantalizing odors of the coffee, cocoa, and spiced cider at a nearby refreshment stand. I could hear sleigh bells jingling in the distance, and strains of Christmas carols drifting from various parts of the yard. A brace of cousins hurried by pushing a cart loaded high with poinsettias, and several small children dressed as elves were handing out candy canes, courtesy of the Caerphilly Candy Shop. What could possibly be causing that sour face?

"Quaint," Werzel pronounced.

"Quaint what?"

"Clearly that's going to have to be my angle on this story. Quaint."

He nodded as he said it, and a satisfied expression replaced the frown. He couldn't

15

have been here more than five minutes, the parade itself wouldn't start for hours — and he'd already decided on his angle?

"Pity I can't think of something more sexy," he said, shaking his head.

Not that he'd tried.

"I've never really considered Christmas all that sexy," I said aloud.

"It's all a big conspiracy by the stores," he said.

I hoped that wasn't going to be the theme of his story. But then, I didn't have high hopes about the story anyway. The Caerphilly Town Council members might have been thrilled when they heard that the *Trib* wanted to cover our event, but I was far more pessimistic about how much could go wrong today. Not to mention more cynical about how ridiculous an unsympathetic reporter could make us look if he wanted to.

And why was the *Washington Star-Tribune* sending a reporter to cover our parade, anyway? Caerphilly County and the town of Caerphilly were in rural Virginia, two hours south of Washington, D.C., and the *Trib* rarely mentioned their one claim to fame — the small but prestigious college where my husband taught in the drama department. Our parade drew good attendance each year, but mainly from the county itself and from nearby counties even more rural than we were. Why wasn't Werzel covering more glamorous sights closer to home, like the national Christmas tree and whatever holiday parades and festivals the greater metropolitan Washington area had to offer? He could have written a clichéd story about our quaint country parade without leaving his desk. I was convinced Werzel had an ulterior motive — to make us look not only quaint but ridiculous. Unfortunately, if that was his plan, I couldn't think of any way to stop him.

The ten lords a-leaping danced past, with Rob in the lead. They had all strapped sets of Morris dancing bells onto their shins, and their procession sounded like "Jingle Bells" on steroids. I couldn't help smiling as they passed. Werzel didn't even look their way.

"I mean, what's so special about yet another Christmas parade?" he asked, when he could make himself heard again.

"Holiday parade," I corrected. It was a reflex by now. "We've decided to make this year's parade as diverse and multicultural as possible."

"That's nice," he said. "Of course, in a place like this, I guess multicultural means you've asked both the Baptists *and* the Episcopalians."

He doubled over laughing at his own joke.

"Not exactly," I said.

Just then a large, mud-spattered truck eased to a stop near me and an elderly woman wearing a large, jewel-trimmed turban stuck her head out of the passenger side window.

"So where do the elephants go?" she asked.

"Anywhere they want to," I said. "But see if you can convince them they'd like to wait in the sheep pasture across the street."

"No problem," she said, as the driver eased the truck over in the direction I'd indicated.

"Elephants?" Werzel asked, looking slightly wide-eyed.

"For the Diwali part of the parade."

"Diwali?"

"The Hindu festival of lights," I said. "It's their major winter holiday. Elephants are customary, I understand. Why don't you go watch them unload?"

Werzel nodded and stumbled after the truck. I smiled. Maybe the elephants would save us from the quaint stereotype. And if not — well, we could live with quaint.

"Nothing like elephants for human interest, is there?" Clarence said.

"For some kind of interest," I said. "I wouldn't necessarily call it human, with just the elephants and this Werzel fellow involved. But with any luck, he'll have so much fun photographing the elephants that he'll be in too good a mood to be snide."

"I should go over and check out the pachyderms," he said. He sounded quite matter-of-fact — but in addition to being one of the town veterinarians, Clarence was the official veterinarian for the Caerphilly Zoo, so he had treated elephants before. "That reminds me — sorry about the camel dung, but one of them was limping, and I was taking him for a walk to check it out."

"Please don't tell me we have an injured camel," I said, clutching my clipboard anxiously. "The zoo's only got the three camels. It just won't have the right effect at all if the wise men come riding in on two camels and a ten-speed bike."

"Oh, don't worry —" Clarence began.

"Meg, dear," I heard my mother say.

CHAPTER TWO

I tensed and reminded myself that Mother wasn't necessarily reporting a problem or making a complaint. Still, I took a deep breath as I turned to see what she wanted. She was standing behind me, dressed in an elegant cobalt blue velvet Victorian party dress, complete with a matching parasol.

"You look lovely," I said. Which was true. Rob had inherited his aristocratic blond looks from Mother, whose hair, in her sixties, was still a rich if implausible shade of gold. As usual, I felt dowdy by comparison. Years of practice helped me refrain from patting at my own wayward brunette mane whenever I saw Mother's sleek coif. And was it fair that well short of forty, I already had to fight to keep my figure from turning matronly, while Mother was still as slender as she had been in high school?

I could tell she was eyeing my costume with dismay. I'd dressed for warmth and comfort, and then thrown on one of the county-issue shepherd's robes — cheap, one-size-fits-all garments that some past parade organizer had had made several decades ago so volunteers who didn't have their own costumes could throw on a robe and blend in. Since no one had bothered to launder the robes for years — if ever — the only people who ever wore them were those like me, who didn't remember till the last moment that they needed a costume. I suspected that once the parade was over, Mother would have a few words to say about my appearance.

Of course, I had no idea what her own stunning costume had to do with Christmas, but at this point, I didn't much care.

"I'm glad you like the costume, dear," Mother said, beaming a gracious smile at me and smoothing a bit of the dress's black lace trim.

"By the way," Clarence said, "the house looks lovely."

"Thanks," I said. "But it's all Mother's doing."

Mother beamed widely.

"Really?" Clarence said. "It's fantastic!"

Of course, Clarence already knew Mother had done the decorations. But he'd come to know our family well enough to guess that nothing was more guaranteed to put her in a good mood than a compliment to her decorating skills.

The house really did look fantastic. The exterior of our once-dilapidated three-story white Victorian was now in immaculate condition, thanks to the Shiffley Construction Company and Michael's and my depleted checkbook. Left to my own devices, I'd have stuck electric candles in the front windows and a tasteful wreath on the door and called it quits. In fact, and given how busy I was with the parade, I'm not sure I'd even have managed that. I'd assumed that Mother would expend her holiday decorating energy on their summer cottage — actually a farmhouse that she and Dad had bought, on the next farm down the road from Michael and me. But when she realized that hundreds — perhaps thousands — of holiday tourists would be seeing our house with its minimalist holiday décor, she'd immediately offered to take care of the decorations and had enlisted a small army of helpers from the ranks of the Hollingsworths, her vast extended family.

Every single stretch of roofline, including all the dormers and gables, was trimmed with a three-inch fringe of icicle lights. Every shutter, window-frame, and doorway was outlined with evergreen garlands trimmed with red bows. Every window had been painted to look like stained glass and behind each set of brightly colored panes glowed not only a flickering electric candle but a small constellation of prisms to reflect and scatter the light. Fortunately, Mother's taste didn't run to reindeer on the roof, but she had sent a team up to drape it with a giant banner that read "Peace on Earth." A pair of Christmas doves the size of turkeys hovered over each end of the banner, pretending they were holding it up, though in reality that function was performed by a sturdy cable around the chimneys on either end of the main house. A wreath the size of a truck tire obscured most of the front door, and more evergreen garlands made a festive path down to the mailbox. As we watched, the cousins were arranging the cartload of poinsettias into a bank of red and green on the front porch.

It wasn't exactly my taste, but considering that I hadn't lifted a finger to bring it about, I wasn't going to complain. I just had to remember not to fetch the paper in my bathrobe for the rest of the holiday season — in the three days since Mother's crew had finished it, the house had become a minor local tourist destination.

Even as we spoke, another family group flagged down a passerby to take their picture on our front steps. All in all, the decorations were a smashing success, and boded well for the interior design business Mother had announced she'd be opening in the spring.

"Thank you, dear," she said. "I just stopped by to ask where the Dickens are."

"Where the dickens are what?" I asked.

Mother allowed a small note of exasperation to creep into her sigh.

"The Dickens *characters,* dear," she said. "For the *Christmas Carol* float. You know — Scrooge, Tiny Tim —"

"Oh, right." I checked my clipboard. "Front yard, to the left of the walkway. Who are you, anyway?"

"You can tell she's having a bad day when she can't recognize her own mother," Clarence said, almost managing to keep a straight face.

"I'm playing Mrs. Cratchit," Mother said. She floated off toward the front yard, pausing briefly to straighten the evergreen garland decking one of the trash barrels. As Mother was fond of saying, it's those little details that really make a design.

"I thought the Cratchits were paupers," Clarence said.

"They were. Poor as churchmice. Mrs.

Cratchit is described as 'dressed out but poorly in a twice-turned gown, but brave in ribbons, which are cheap and make a goodly show for sixpence.' "

"Have you memorized the whole book?" he asked. "I'm impressed."

"Only parts of it," I said. "The abridged version. Michael's rehearsing for his one-man *Christmas Carol* show, so by the time he's ready, I'll have the whole thing down pat."

"Oh, wonderful! When?"

"Six P.M. tomorrow night at the college auditorium; tickets ten dollars at the door; proceeds to benefit the Caerphilly Children's Fund," I rattled off.

"What a lovely way to spend Christmas Eve," he said. "I'll be there. Meanwhile, don't worry about Larry. He's fine."

"Larry?" I repeated. My glance strayed down to my clipboard. Was I missing a Larry?

"Larry the camel."

"Oh, that's right. Trust Dr. Blake to name his zoo's camels after the Three Stooges."

"A wonderful sense of humor, your grandfather."

I made a noncommittal noise. Less than a year ago we'd learned that Dr. Montgomery Blake, the world-famous conservationist and animal welfare activist, was Dad's long-lost father. I was still working on thinking of him as "Grandfather" instead of "Dr. Blake." I hadn't yet begun learning to appreciate his odd, curmudgeonly sense of humor.

"Anyway," Clarence was saying. "Larry always fakes a limp when he wants attention. I've got them feeding him some camel treats, and he'll be fine by parade time. By the way, you do realize that you sent the elephants to unload in the pasture where the drummers and fifers are rehearsing, right?"

"Yes," I said. "If you're heading there anyway, see if you can convince the drummers and fifers that all that racket they're making could spook the elephants."

"It would if they kept it up," he said, frowning. "Where do you want them to go instead? The musicians, that is."

"In the cow pasture behind the house. It's farther away — and downwind."

"You don't really intend to inflict a dozen bagpipers on a herd of defenseless cows?" Clarence said, with mock fierceness.

"There are no cows in the cow pasture at the moment," I said. "It's too full of Boy Scouts — they had their annual pre-parade campout there. And good luck spooking them — Rob was out last night helping ride herd on them, and he reports that they laughed at all his scariest ghost stories."

"This modern generation," he said, shaking his head. "Well, I'm off to cope with the camels and elephants."

Of course the moment he left, I wondered what he meant by camel treats. Did one of the leading pet food companies manufacture such a thing? And if not, what did you use to bribe a sulking camel back into good humor?

I could ask him later. I looked back at my check-in sheet. I was using a tiny self-inking stamp of a holly leaf to mark everyone present and accounted for. I smiled with satisfaction at the almost unbroken garland of leaves marching down the right-hand side of the page.

I accepted a piece of peanut brittle from a small angel with red pigtails, and a cup of eggnog from a passing cousin. I waved at a local farmer who strolled by herding a small flock of white turkeys with red bows around their necks. Evidently they were marching in the parade — which meant, I hoped, that they wouldn't be anyone's dinner this holiday season. Someone in the front end of a reindeer costume, complete with a battery-powered flashing red nose, wandered by scanning the crowd as if he'd lost something. Probably whoever was playing the hind legs.

"Aunt Meg? We're here."

My twelve-year-old nephew, Eric McReady, appeared at my elbow, at the head of a swarm of brown-clad shepherds around his own age. The Boy Scouts. Eric had recruited the local troop, who would be earning credits toward the next rank by performing public service. They'd be acting as mobile cleanup crews, with groups marching in the parade behind the camels, the elephants, the horses, and all the other large animals. Had the bagpipers evicted the Boy Scouts from their campground already? Or had Eric succeeded in getting his volunteers to show up on time? Either way it was good news. I smiled as I stamped them as present.

"Are we really going to have a white Christmas?" one of them asked.

I glanced up at the sky again. I'd been doing it so often all morning that I was getting a crick in my neck. The latest forecast I'd heard called for a small storm to dump two to six inches of snow on us sometime today. Normally two to six inches would have constituted a fairly large storm by central Virginia's standards, but the meteorologists were almost ignoring it to focus on the massive storm system currently pummeling the Midwest and scheduled to unload another six to twelve inches on Christmas Eve.

"Yes," I said. "I just hope it waits until the parade is over." Or at least until the tail end of the parade was closer to town than our house. I had no desire to be snowbound with half the population of Caerphilly. Or with the dozens of animals we'd recruited for the parade — for this evening, I'd arranged quarters for the animals in town, in the barns belonging to the Caerphilly College Agricultural Sciences Department. I only hoped the snow would hold off long enough for them to get there.

"Snow! Snow! No school tomorrow! No school tomorrow!" chanted a dozen voices, as the Scouts capered around me in what I assumed was a snow dance.

Yes, two to six inches were more than enough to cancel classes. In their enthusiasm, they seemed to have forgotten that the schools were already closed tomorrow for the Christmas Eve holiday. In my school days, we'd have called this a wasted snow. But that didn't seem to bother the exuberant flock of miniature shepherds.

"Ten-hut!" Eric called.

Behind him the rest of the shepherds fell

29

into formation, saluted in unison and then clanged their shovels against their buckets.

"Cleanup patrol reporting for duty, ma'am," Eric said.

"Thank goodness you're here," I said. And thank goodness they'd stopped calling themselves the Dung Fu Fighters and other worse names. "We just had a camel incident over there," I added, pointing to the offending spot.

Most of the troop scurried over toward the small pile of camel dung and began squabbling to see who got to shovel it up.

"It's okay if Cal helps us, isn't it?" Eric asked.

I glanced down at the small form at his side — much smaller than any of the other shepherds. A round brown face peered out of his hood, and I recognized six-year-old Calvin Ripken Burke, the youngest grandson of our Baltimore-born chief of police.

"As long as it's okay with his grandfather," I said.

Cal grinned, and ran over to join the rest of the crew.

"His brother is home sick with a cold," Eric explained. "So Chief Burke asked me if I'd look after him. Otherwise he'd have to stay with his grandmother and march with the choir. Cal would much rather shovel . . . um . . . dung."

"You're a good egg," I said. "Here — I made a list of the animals that are marching today. It would be great if you could assign a squad to follow each group."

"Roger," he said. "I'm going to do the elephants myself!" With that he ran off to organize his troops.

All by himself? Well, he'd learn. Then again, as the youngest of my sister Pam's six children, Eric was always running as fast as he could to keep up with his siblings, and was doomed to become a teenage overachiever. The parade cleanup was in good hands.

And it sounded as if Clarence, reinforced by the threat of stampeding elephants, had finally resolved the piper and drummer problem. Now I could return to checking in the remaining participants and keeping them from causing too much trouble before the parade started. Which would be in . . . a little over three hours.

I glanced up at the sky. No snow yet, thank goodness. Cold as it was, any snow that fell would undoubtedly stick around.

"What's wrong?"

I turned to see my husband, Michael, tall and resplendent in his wise man's costume.

"Just fretting over the weather again," I said, giving him a quick kiss. "You look very dashing. Have you got your myrrh?"

"Yes, ma'am," he said, giving a deep, elegant salaam that went well with the vaguely Middle Eastern costume. "Not with me, of course; it's on the prop table in the barn with the frankincense and fake gold. Your grandfather's giving a lot of the kids camel rides, so I thought I'd see if you needed any help. So nothing's wrong?"

"Nothing," I said. "Well, except for the fact that they keep changing their minds about when the snow will start, but there's nothing you can do about that. Most of the participants are already here, and it's not even nine."

"Which means we have to put up with them for the next three hours," Michael said, frowning.

"Cheer up," I said. "That gives us plenty of time to send out a posse for anyone who doesn't show."

"Or better yet, plenty of time to round up a replacement," Michael said. He waved at a brace of tuba players in Caerphilly High School band uniforms. "No one is irreplaceable."

"Except possibly the camels," I said, as I pointed dramatically to the left to steer the tuba players toward the rest of their band. "There are just two people left that I'm at all worried about."

"Who?"

"The Virgin Mary," I said. "For the nativity scene float."

"The one who's nine months pregnant."

"Only eight," I said. "Maybe eight and a half. The costume's bulky. No one will notice."

"Tell me again why we cast her as Mary?"

"Her father-in-law owns a flatbed truck," I said. "The only one we could find large enough to hold the nativity scene."

"She's perfect for the role, then."

"It's really the truck I'm worried about," I said. I glanced down the road again, hoping to spot it. "We can replace her, but if the truck doesn't show up, the Holy Family will have to walk all the way to Caerphilly. And then there's Santa. He's only a couple of miles away, and what do you bet he'll be the last to show up. Of course, on the bright side, at least we won't have to put up with him for too long. Frankly, if there's anyone I'll be happy to see the last of when the parade's over, it's him."

CHAPTER THREE

"Oh, Mr. Doleson's not so bad," Michael said.

"Compared to whom?" I asked. "Scrooge? The Grinch? W. C. Fields with a hangover? Attila the Hun?"

"I admit he's a total grouch and can make 'Good morning' sound like a mortal insult," Michael began.

"Not that I've ever heard him say anything as polite as 'Good morning,' " I muttered.

"But at least he's a reclusive grouch, so we don't have to see him more than once or twice a month."

"Wish we could say the same for some of my family," I grumbled. "I can't remember the last time we had dinner for two. But Ralph Doleson's not my idea of a proper Santa."

"I don't think he's anyone's idea of a proper Santa," Michael said. "But he's practically the only guy in town with the requisite white beard and round belly who's also short enough to fit into the existing costume. You know how cheap the town council is — they would never pay to replace a perfectly good costume that's only used once a year."

"Well, at least it's only once a year," I said. "And — speak of the devil."

The short, round, rather toadlike figure of Ralph Doleson was slouching our way. He was lugging a garment bag and a battered canvas duffel that I assumed contained his costume. He'd obviously made an effort for the occasion. He had on a clean pair of overalls. And in an unprecedented fit of vanity, he appeared to have shampooed his beard. Though not his long, stringy hair — a good thing he'd be wearing the Santa hat. His face wore its usual surly expression.

I glanced casually at my watch. Nine o'clock on the dot. He might be lacking in social graces, our Santa, but at least he was punctual. Anyone who arrived from now on was officially late, and would receive the faint frown, the stern scowl, or an actual lecture, depending on how late they were and how penitent they seemed.

"Morning, Mr. Doleson," Michael said.

Doleson looked up, scowling as if Michael had hurled a string of insults at him.

"Do you expect me to get dressed in that barn of yours?" he snapped. "It's full of children and animals."

A Santa who hated children and animals? I was about to snap back that the barn was the only men's dressing room we had and he could change in plain sight if he liked, but fortunately Michael stepped in.

"Of course not," Michael said. "We've cleaned out one of the more private outbuildings for you. Wouldn't do for the kids to spot Santa changing into uniform, now would it? Here, let me help you with your luggage."

Doleson snorted, but surrendered the garment bag and the duffel and shambled off in Michael's wake.

"One of the more private outbuildings?" I repeated. Maybe elegant estates had outbuildings. We had sheds, in various states of disrepair. Though they looked better than usual at the moment. Mother's decorating crew had gift-wrapped the more disreputable-looking ones for the season, with green plaid paper and perky red bows, and decorated the rest with wreaths, evergreen garlands, and fake snow that would soon become superfluous.

I managed not to break out laughing when Michael bowed and gestured grandly toward the door of the pig shed. Michael must have done a good job of charming the old reprobate. Mr. Doleson peered through the door, nodded brusquely, and stepped in. Trust Michael to save the day and restore my good mood.

The pig shed was the perfect place for Santa. We didn't have any pigs, so the shed was rarely used. We'd stashed Santa's sleigh there overnight in case the snow started slightly earlier than the weatherman predicted. The sleigh was an old horse-drawn wagon with boards nailed along both sides to hide the wheels. The boards were painted to look like runners, and I'd spent several hours the night before scraping off peeling paint, touching up the design, and then literally watching the paint dry — I'd had to run several space heaters to get the air warm enough for it to dry, and I didn't think it was safe to leave them untended.

Most years having a fake sleigh on wheels worked better than a real one, given how rarely we got a white Christmas in central Virginia. But how well would our ersatz sleigh work if the snow got very deep before the end of the parade? I shoved the thought out of my mind. The Shiffley Construction Company was on call for snow removal duty, standing by with snowplow attachments on all their trucks and tractors. If that wasn't enough — well, there was nothing more I could do now.

With the sleigh crammed into it, the shed wasn't exactly palatial quarters but it was extremely clean — I'd made sure of that before we shoved the freshly painted sleigh inside. Mr. Doleson would have enough room to change in privacy, and he could spend the rest of the time until the parade began in the relative comfort of the sleigh's padded back seat. Since Michael reappeared without him, I assumed Mr. Doleson was satisfied, and I stamped a particularly heavy-handed holly leaf beside his name on the participants' list.

"Mission accomplished," Michael said, reappearing at my side. If —"

"Professor Waterston?"

Michael turned to see a short, plump, elderly woman dressed in a Mrs. Claus outfit, holding something wrapped in red foil and trimmed with green ribbon.

"Merry Christmas, dear," Mrs. Claus said. She handed him the parcel and tripped away.

"Who's that?" I asked.

"The dean's wife, I think. More to the point, what's in this?"

"Another fruitcake," I said. "Do you like

fruitcake?"

"Not particularly," he said, frowning as he teased open one end of the foil to verify its contents. "Why?"

"Someone has it in for you, then. There's a rumor going around town that you do."

"Oh, no," he said. "I know how that got started. Professor Braintree's holiday tea."

Dr. Edith Braintree was the chair of the committee that, in a few months, would decide whether to offer Michael tenure at Caerphilly College. If they turned him down, he'd have a choice between settling for a lower-paid adjunct position for the rest of his career or looking for someplace else to start another seven-year tenure quest. Thus the committee had much the same power over our future as the jury has over the defendant in a criminal trial — though at least no one expected accused felons to have tea with the jurors, lose to them at racquetball, and buy cases of Girl Scout cookies from their daughters.

"She seemed so pleased when I took a slice," Michael went on, "I got a little carried away and said it reminded me of my mother's fruitcake. And before you ask, no, Mom never made fruitcake that I can remember. I don't know what came over me."

I knew perfectly well — tenure fever. I hadn't told Michael, but tenure fever was the real reason I'd gotten stuck with organizing the parade. If the mayor had called up and tried to charm me into the job, I could have managed to keep saying no until he gave up and went looking for another victim. But when Dr. Braintree called, full of flattery and enthusiasm, implying that not only the town but the college would be so grateful if I'd agree to take the post . . .

"I suppose we can manage to eat up a fruitcake eventually," Michael was saying.

"Can we eat up seven of them?" I said. "Apparently there's a large hidden cult of fruitcake bakers in town, all eager for new converts."

"Oh, dear," he murmured. "Probably not. Don't any of your family like fruitcake?"

"Good idea," I said. "We'll regift them to out-of-town relatives."

"What a devious idea," he said. "I like it. I'll leave this one with you, then, and if you don't need me for anything I'll go help your grandfather with the camels."

"Have fun," I said. "And —"

Just then we heard a shout from the pig shed.

CHAPTER FOUR

Michael and I both started running toward it, as did several other people nearby, but before any of us reached the door, it slammed open and a small black and white furball sailed out, propelled by the toe of Ralph Doleson's boot.

"Keep that damned rodent away from me or I'll sue!" he bellowed. "I'm bleeding, dammit!"

Yes, he was bleeding ever so slightly. Nothing that wouldn't stop in a few seconds if he held his wounded finger up and wrapped something around it instead of holding it down and waving it around vigorously.

The rodent in question was our family dog, Spike — eight and a half pounds of pure meanness wrapped in a deceptively cute and furry exterior. He'd landed outside with a yelp, and took a few seconds to catch his breath, but then he launched himself toward Mr. Doleson, who swore, and slammed the door so hard the wreath fell off. Spike barked furiously at the door for a few seconds, then retreated so that it wouldn't hit him in the face when it opened, and lay down with his head on his paws to wait for his enemy to emerge.

It would have been cute if I didn't know how serious Spike was about revenge. And if I hadn't been so tempted to help him. I strode over and knelt down to check him for wounds — wondering, as I did, who had been brave or foolish enough to decorate Spike's collar with a red-and-green velvet bow the size of his head.

"What a jerk," Rob said. I was so focused on Spike that I started at his voice.

"Spike might have bitten him first," Eric said.

"You know he hardly ever bites strangers unless they bother him first," I said. "And even if Spike started it, Doleson seriously overreacted."

"I think we should report him for cruelty to animals," Michael said, in what someone who didn't know him might think was a calm and unemotional voice. I could tell he was furious.

"Wait till after the parade," I said. "Then we'll get him."

"I'll talk to the chief about it," Michael said.

I nodded. Spike seemed okay, so I began jotting down the names of the potential witnesses in my notebook-that-tells-me-when-to-breathe, as I called my giant, spiral-bound to-do list. Apart from Rob, Michael, and me, at least half a dozen respectable citizens of Caerphilly had witnessed Mr. Doleson's act. Not to mention Ainsley Werzel, who was staring at the door of the pig shed with an outraged look on his face. Maybe Werzel and I had just gotten off on the wrong foot. I made a resolution to be particularly friendly and helpful next time I talked to him.

"It's my fault," Rob said. "I put Spike in there because I thought it would be safer than the barn, and you know how he hates being confined. I'll put him in his crate."

"Get Clarence to check him out first," I said. "I didn't see any blood or obvious injuries, but it's possible he's broken a bone or two and is so fixated on his prey that he just hasn't noticed yet."

"And don't be silly," Michael said to Rob. "Your failure to crate the small evil one does not give Ralph Doleson the right to drop kick him across the yard. I'll find Clarence and send him over."

I returned to my post to continue check-ing in stragglers, though I kept walking over to look at Spike until Clarence arrived. He examined the patient, and gave me a thumbs up before leading Spike off to the safety of his crate in the kitchen.

I breathed a sigh of relief. Spike wasn't technically our dog. Michael's mother had dumped him on us several years ago when her doctor advised her to see if a trial separation helped her allergies. We'd become resigned to the fact that he was with us for the long haul. But I knew Mrs. Waterston would have a fit if she heard that anything had happened to Spike.

For that matter, I'd developed a grudging fondness myself for the small evil one, as we'd nicknamed Spike. He had more guts than sense, and was not only capable but fond of biting the hands that fed him. On at least one occasion, though, he'd accidentally saved my life. Ralph Doleson had not heard the last of this.

"Let me know if he tries to file charges," a voice said. I looked up to see the tall form of Jorge Soto, one of the programmers who worked at Mutant Wizards, my brother's computer game development company.

"Thanks — I've already got you on my list of witnesses to the dog-kicking."

"Not the first time he's done something like that," Jorge said. "I live at the Pines, you know."

I nodded. Ralph Doleson owned the Whispering Pines, a former hot sheets motel that was now a grungy garden apartment building. Rob technically lived there, too, although for the last couple of months he'd been spending most of his time in one of the unused bedrooms on the third floor of our house.

"He doesn't like dogs," Jorge went on. "We've had a couple of cases at the Pines where people who had dogs found out Doleson was teasing and mistreating them till they tried to bite him, and then calling the police on them."

"What a jerk!" I said.

"Yeah. I mean, if he doesn't like dogs, he should just put in a no-dogs rule. He owns the place; no one could argue with him. But I think he likes causing trouble."

"I wish we could fire him as Santa," I said. I tucked my notebook away and headed for the refreshment stand. The adrenaline charge induced by Spike's encounter with Doleson had faded, leaving me feeling suddenly tired and in need of warmth and caffeine.

"Why don't you fire him?" Jorge asked,

falling into step beside me.

"Hard to find a replacement on short notice," I said. "Especially one who can fit into the tiny costume."

"Can him anyway," Jorge said.

The lady at the refreshment stand smiled and handed me a black coffee without my even asking for it. Maybe I'd been hitting the coffee a little too often this morning.

"How can we possibly have a Christmas parade without Santa?" I asked.

"Holiday parade," he said, with a grin. Obviously he'd heard my knee-jerk correction to other people.

"Holiday, yes; but still — without Santa?"

"In my country, Santa's optional."

"Santa doesn't bring you presents?" I took a deep gulp of my coffee.

"No, in Costa Rica, Baby Jesus brings the presents."

"So you don't have Santa at all?"

"No, we have him," Jorge said. "Santa — St. Nicholas, that is — brings Baby Jesus. He's like the chauffeur."

"I never knew that."

"When my parents were little, they didn't have Santa at all. But once we kids started seeing a lot of American Christmas movies, they had to have some way to explain to the kids what the fat guy in the snow suit was all about. Not sure if it's just my parents or if it's widespread in Costa Rica, but that's how I was brought up."

"I wish we were having a Costa Rican holiday parade, then, but I think around here the kids would be heartbroken if we didn't have a Santa."

"Yeah," Jorge said. "I guess they don't know that behind that beard is the meanest man in town."

With that he waved and wandered off. I finished my coffee and could already feel my energy level rising. I'd crash later — I'd been running on four or five hours of sleep a night for the past week — but for now, I was okay. I squared my shoulders and turned back just in time to see the long-awaited arrival of the flatbed truck for the nativity scene. Our heavily-pregnant Virgin Mary waved cheerfully at me from its passenger window. Things were looking up.

Clarence had even stopped the piping and drumming, thank goodness. I could see the musicians straggling across the road in small groups, heading for the cow pasture. Followed by several tourists with cameras. Well, the musicians were a picturesque sight — the drummers and fifers in their red, white, and blue Revolutionary War uniforms and nearly every one of the bagpipers wearing a different plaid with his full-dress kilt. Given the temperature, all of them probably had matching blue knees by now — should I have someone check them for signs of frostbite?

"There you are!" My father bounced into view, his round face beaming. His exuberance erased whatever last bits of stress I'd been feeling. Dad adored Christmas — adored holidays generally in fact, and was in seventh heaven at being able to help with the annual holiday parade. No present I could possibly have given him would have made him happier. Well, okay, maybe announcing the prospect of another grandchild would have beat the parade, but Dad was one of the few family members who took it on faith that Michael and I had been working on that project since our Memorial Day elopement, and he had never demanded periodic updates on our progress.

He was carrying his black medical bag. I hoped this meant that he was prepared for any emergency that might need his medical skills, and not that we'd already had one.

"Where do you want the boom lift?" he asked.

"I don't know that I want a boom lift at all," I said. "Who brought it, and why? Does one of the floats need repairing or something?"

"It's going in the parade, of course!" he exclaimed, and from his expression I could see that he was clearly astonished at my lack of enthusiasm for the boom lift. "The Shiffleys brought it. Don't you have it on your list?"

I flipped through the pages of my checklist, baffled. Had I, in a moment of mental derangement, approved the addition of a boom lift to the parade? Perhaps decked in holly, evergreen, and red ribbon, and carrying a banner saying "Merry Christmas from the Shiffley Construction Company"?

"There it is," Dad said, pointing to an item on my list. "The Clayville Congregational Church Choir."

"I thought they were just marching and singing," I grumbled.

"They're calling it 'Angels We Have Heard on High.' They're all wearing angel costumes, and they're going to have the soloists up on the platform, scattering confetti. Biodegradable confetti, of course. Don't you remember?"

"Silly me," I said, although this was the first I'd heard of the Congregationalists' plans. "How about putting the boom lift over there by the side of the road? Just beyond the elephants."

"Elephants? We've got both of them, then? Splendid! That means I get to ride one!"

Dad scurried off, and a few minutes later, I saw the boom lift chug slowly by, with Dad twenty feet in the air on the platform. It appeared to be driving itself, unless the person standing up on the platform with Dad was the driver. I'd been wrong about the holly and red ribbon — they'd covered up as much of the boom lift's industrial orange frame as possible with sky blue crepe paper, and stuck several giant cotton clouds to it at random intervals.

The choir members followed in the boom lift's wake in twos and threes, most of them already wearing white choir robes, white wings made of cotton batting and silver glitter, and glitter-coated halos.

And there went Werzel, the reporter, stumbling along in pursuit of the choir, snapping away with his tiny camera. So much for our image as an erudite, cosmopolitan community. Maybe I should be glad he'd already pegged us as quaint. Quaint was an improvement over barmy.

Since Werzel's camera looked like the same inexpensive model that I used to take family snapshots, we could always hope that his photos didn't turn out good enough for the *Trib* to use. Where was the promised professional photographer, anyway?

I double-checked my participants list to make sure I had the waiver from the choir absolving me, the Caerphilly Town Council, and the immediate world of responsibility for anything that might happen to the high-flying angels during the parade. Reassured, I stamped the choir in as present and accounted for.

"Not bad for a small town."

Ainsley Werzel had returned. I had to smile — the reporter was clearly struggling to maintain his former air of cool superiority. Score one for the elephants.

I waved and just nodded to him — at the moment, I was busy welcoming Miss Caerphilly County. Werzel stood by with surprising patience while I admired the beauty queen's hair, earrings, nails, makeup, dress, and shoes and gave her directions to the women's dressing room — the living room and library in Michael's and my house.

"So how far is Tappahannock from here?" he asked.

"Forty-five minutes to an hour," I said.

"You're an hour away," he shouted into his cell phone. "I said west of Tappahannock, not in it." He snapped the cell phone closed.

"Photographer's still lost," he said. "So how come you guys have this shindig only two days before Christmas? Most towns have their Santa parade at the beginning of the shopping season so the parents can hear their kids' gimme lists. And the stores can make more sales."

"Caerphilly's parade started out as an event to give presents to the town's poor children."

"You mean poor as in economically disadvantaged?" Werzel said.

"A hundred years ago, when the parade started, people mostly just said poor," I answered. "But yes. And then when the Great Depression came, everyone was economically disadvantaged, and they started the tradition of giving every kid in town a present. So that's what has happened for the last eighty years or so."

He nodded and scribbled some more. I considered telling him that while our curmudgeonly Santa was handing out small presents to all the children, regardless of economic status, in the public ceremony, many of the families who were quite genuinely poor would be picking up additional presents, not to mention food and warm clothing, from stations set up by the various churches and community service organizations.

I decided against telling him. If he bothered to use the information, it would make Caerphilly look good, but I doubted he would mention it. And more important, most of those proud, struggling country families were embarrassed enough at having to accept handouts. It would be the last straw to have some reporter from a big city paper taking intrusive pictures of them doing so.

"And there's a big festival," I said instead. "Baked goods, barbecue, craft sales, lots of raffles, judging the quilting and cooking contests, performances from many of the local musical groups and church choirs — sort of like a big church bazaar and a county fair rolled into one."

I could see his eyes glaze over. Good; we were safely back in quaint again. Maybe he'd skedaddle back to Washington after the parade and the county's unemployed and working poor could collect their turkeys and warm coats in privacy.

I turned to greet the delegation from the nearby clown school, which involved receiving multiple joy buzzer handshakes and having innumerable coins pulled out of my ears. I heard Werzel's camera clicking, and cringed.

But when I'd dispatched the clowns to their staging area, I turned and found that Werzel was snapping pictures of the Dickens float. Mother and her fellow Victorians certainly were elegant. I smiled approvingly as Werzel snapped shots of the float from various angles. Another triumph for Mother's decorating skills, not to mention her ability to appear completely impervious to both summer heat and bitter cold like today's weather.

Unfortunately, when Mother saw I was free, she furled her parasol and came over.

"Meg, dear," Mother said, "we have a little problem."

CHAPTER FIVE

"What little problem?" I repeated. I braced myself — Mother had once described the presence of a black bear in the living room of our vacation cabin as a little problem.

"Those SPOOR people are at it again."

"At what, Mother?"

"SPOOR people?" Werzel echoed.

"Stop Poisoning Our Owls and Raptors," I said. "They're a local environmental group. They specialize in bird-related issues. What are the SPOOR members up to now, Mother?"

"They've brought those protest signs," Mother said. "The ones with the depressing pictures of dead birds on them. I thought you told them they couldn't bring their placards. If they're going to be marching with those signs . . ."

"I did, and they're not," I said. "Where are they?"

"Over by the barn."

"I'll talk to them," I said. "While I do, why don't you show Mr. Werzel the camels?"

But Mr. Werzel wasn't interested in camels, or assumed he could see them anytime between now and the start of the parade. He trailed behind me as I went to straighten out the SPOOR delegation.

They were already dressed in their costumes — SPOOR members would be playing the six geese a-laying. They'd been trouble from the start. Shortly after dawn, I'd had to lay down the law and forbid the entire SPOOR membership from marching in goose costume.

"It's *six* geese a-laying," I'd said. "Not thirty-seven."

"Thirty-eight counting Mrs. Markland," one of them had put in, and the others had nodded approval, as they always did when anyone mentioned their late founder and first president.

"Mrs. Markland died last year," I'd countered. "You're not planning to bring her along, I hope?"

"She's always with us in spirit," one of the members had said.

"That's fine," I'd said. "You can have as many people with you in spirit as you like, whether they're still on this plane or have gone to that giant protest march in the sky.

56

But I only want to see six of you marching in costume in the parade, or I'll get six of the Boy Scouts to replace you."

They'd sulked at that, but had started drawing lots to see who got to wear their elaborately feathered Canada goose costumes and who would simply march along behind in plain clothes, carrying the SPOOR banner. I'd also had to discourage them from including an offputtingly realistic reenactment of egg-laying in their routine. I'd had a private word with Clarence, whom I considered one of the more sensible of the SPOOR members, and he'd promised to keep them in line.

And yet, in spite of everything, here they were blatantly trying to ignore the ban on carrying political signs in the parade.

When I arrived, the six lucky members who would be portraying the geese were doing a Rockettes-style dance number. I had to admit, it was pretty funny, seeing their giant webbed feet kicking into the air in unison, and even funnier when they bent over and waggled their fake tail feathers. I realized I was grinning at the sight, so I paused a moment to settle my face into the kind of stern look that would tell them I meant business. And to see if I could have a word with Clarence. Even in costume, I should be able to spot him, thanks to his towering height.

No tall geese in sight, unfortunately. But I did notice that a dozen other SPOOR members were scuttling around furtively behind some shrubbery. They seemed to be carrying something.

I strode over, parted the bushes, and frowned at them. They were all hovering over a pile of placards. One of them had taken off his coat and was trying to conceal the contraband. The dancing geese broke ranks and came trailing after me.

"I'm confiscating the signs," I said. I began picking up the placards and tucking them under my arm. Something poked me, and I realized that they'd trimmed the placards for the occasion with little bits of holly and evergreen.

"But it's for such an important cause!" one of the costumed geese said.

"Yes, and that's why I asked SPOOR to represent the geese," I said. "Giving you a key, highly visible role in the parade. But you're not going to win over anyone, marching in the holiday parade waving pictures of dead birds."

"They don't all show dead birds," one SPOOR member said. "We've got some with birds that are victims of an oil spill."

"Oh, and that's so much more cheerful than dead birds," I said. "Look, the dancing's great — it should get SPOOR a lot of attention, and then when you are in a forum where it's appropriate to protest, everyone will remember you favorably."

Some of them seemed content with that idea, but the rest were muttering mutinously.

"And if you insist on carrying the placards —"

"We know — you can always replace us with Boy Scouts," one said. "Of course the Boy Scouts don't have costumes."

"They're always prepared, remember?" I said. "I'm sure they could come up with something on short notice."

They nodded, most of them rather sullenly, and didn't try to stop me from taking the rest of the signs.

Werzel fell in step with me as I headed toward the house with my armload of placards. He even nudged a couple back into place when I began to lose my grip on them. It would have been nice if he'd offered to take a few, but he had his notebook out and he was scribbling madly.

"So, you don't approve of this SPOOR thing?" he said. He'd probably taken a few shots of the SPOOR rebellion. I made a note to see if I could borrow his camera, once the parade was over, and accidentally delete anything really embarrassing.

"I thoroughly approve of SPOOR," I said. "It's a wonderful organization. My father's the current president, and I've joined in some of their protests myself. They're doing good work to protect the bird population. But I told everybody from the start that we weren't allowing any political signs or gestures as part of the parade. Not even for political causes I agree with. It's a holiday parade."

Just then, I noticed that one of the geese had followed us and was hovering nearby, clearly waiting for a chance to talk. A very tall goose — Clarence? I looked around for someone to handle the placards and spotted my brother.

"Rob," I said. "Put these somewhere. In the safe room."

"Sure thing,"

"Safe room?" Werzel repeated.

"Our pantry," I said. "It's got a lock on the door. We have a lot of strangers wandering around the house and grounds today, so anyone who wants a safe place to leave a purse or a laptop can check it in the safe room."

"Good idea," he said. "There's always a

klepto in every crowd."

Especially if the crowd included Mother's side of the family. We had several relatives who suffered from what Mother referred to as "a little problem." Michael liked the phrase "insufficiently developed under-standing of the concept of private property," but I suspected in at least half the cases in my family the so-called kleptomaniacs were actually drama queens with an unquench-able thirst to be the center of attention. Not that I was going to mention this to a reporter.

"And while you're in the house, give Spike a bathroom break, okay?" I said to Rob.

"Roger."

Jorge Soto came up to help Rob with the placards and I turned back to the goose.

"Can I help you?" I asked.

The goose took its head off, revealing Clarence's shaggy mane.

"Sorry about that," he said. "I've been telling them repeatedly that signs were completely inappropriate. Not that they've been listening."

"I understand," I said.

"It's just that —"

He glanced at Werzel, who was holding his pen poised over his notebook as if wait-ing to take dictation.

"Can we have a little privacy here?" I asked.

Werzel cocked his head as if he didn't quite understand what I was saying.

"Beat it," Clarence said, his voice an octave lower than usual. He scowled at Werzel, and tried to cross his arms to assume a menacing posture. Of course, the goose costume wasn't designed for arm crossing, and it looked more as if he was trying to fold his wings in prayer, but Clarence still looked remarkably menacing. Werzel got the message and hurried off. Clarence turned back to me.

"Look," he said. "I just wanted to give you a heads up about something. Feeling is running rather high among some of the SPOOR members."

"About the protest signs? Don't they understand —"

"No," he said. "About Santa."

"Is there something environmentally unsound about the concept of Santa?" Staying politically correct seemed to get harder every year.

"Not Santa in general, just your Santa."

"You mean the Santa the Town Council foisted on me," I said. "I would never have cast Ralph Doleson as Santa."

"No, you've got more sense," he said. "But

remember what happened with him this summer? Oh, wait — it was while you and Michael were on your honeymoon, so I suppose you didn't hear. Well, in late June — oh, look!"

I turned to see what he was pointing at. The wise men were taking their camels for a test ride. The camels alone would have been worth staring at — they were stately and majestic and wore the most elaborate and brightly colored leather saddles, bridles, and other accoutrements I could ever remember seeing. They were even more impressive with the elaborately robed wise men riding them. I looked around, but Ainsley Werzel had wandered off someplace. Ah, well — with luck, none of the photos he took would be used for the article anyway, and the camels would still be around when the photographer eventually showed up.

Michael, at the head of the procession, looked as if he had been born in a camel saddle — partly because he was fairly good at riding horses, and partly because he was too good an actor to let anyone know that he wasn't quite at ease with Larry's oddly swaying gait. Behind him rode Dr. Montgomery Blake, my grandfather, who had spent so many of his ninety-some years roving various wildernesses for zoological projects and environmental crusades that he was perfectly comfortable riding a camel, horse, donkey, elephant, or any other steed or vehicle you could think of. He had one leg hooked around a protrusion that was the Bedouin equivalent of the saddle horn, and was turned around nearly backwards, shouting instructions at our local police chief, who was portraying the third wise man.

"Chief Burke doesn't look altogether happy," Clarence said, with a frown.

That was an understatement. The chief's normally calm, brown face wore a fierce scowl that would ordinarily have reduced his officers to abject terror lest they be the ones who'd screwed up. Under the circumstances, I suspected the scowl was a deliberate attempt to hide absolute panic. But I had to hand it to him — he hung on gamely as the procession lurched and swayed its way past the house and headed down the road.

"Aren't they going the wrong way?" asked a child's voice at my side. Cal Burke stood, shovel and pail in hand, staring anxiously at the camel procession as it disappeared around a curve in the road.

"They're just taking a practice ride," I said.

"Hmph!" Minerva Burke, the chief's wife, had appeared, wearing the maroon satin choir robe of the New Life Baptist Church. She shook her head as she watched her husband's progress. "At this rate, the old fool will break his neck before the parade even begins. But there's no stopping them when they get a crazy idea in their heads, is there? Cal, go keep an eye on your grandfather."

Cal nodded and scampered off behind the camels. Clarence frowned — was he still worried about Larry's limp? — and followed.

Ainsley Werzel sauntered up. He'd thrown on one of the county-issue brown shepherd's robes and was stuffing his press pass inside it.

"Getting into the spirit of things," he said, when he saw me eyeing the robe.

More like trying to fool people into thinking he was part of the parade and catch them off guard, I suspected.

"So Chief Burke's one of the wise men?" he asked. "Is that okay?"

"More than okay, it's useful," I said. "In the unlikely event of any trouble, we'll already have the police chief and a number of his officers on hand to deal with it."

"Yeah, but isn't that carrying this whole multicultural thing a little too far?" Werzel asked. "I mean, were any of the original wise men African-American?"

Was he making a joke? No, he sounded serious. I was still trying to figure out a tactful way to answer when Minerva Burke spoke up.

"African-*American*?" she said, with a snort. "Not hardly, since it wasn't till fifteen centuries after the Nativity that Columbus discovered what the Indians had already found and a while after that before people started calling it America. Not to mention a couple of centuries till the slave trade brought Africans to this side of the ocean. So, no, there weren't any African-American wise men."

"However," I said, "there's a tradition dating back to the Middle Ages that one of the wise men, Balthazar, was African."

"Just African," Minerva Burke said. "No hyphen required."

"And we've asked Chief Burke to be a wise man to honor that tradition."

"Great, great," Werzel said. He backed off, smiling nervously, until he was about ten feet away — at which point he pretended to become fascinated with one of the musical acts — a barbershop quartet dressed as Christmas trees — and loped off as fast as he could.

"Sorry," Minerva said, shaking her head. "Don't know why, but that man just brings out the mean in me."

"Don't apologize," I said. "You're welcome to chase him away any time you see him hovering near me. I really don't want to have to deal with a reporter on top of everything else."

"I'd have thought you'd be pleased to see he was here," Minerva said. "After all, we've been trying for years to get someone other than the local rag to cover it. And you snagged the *Star-Tribune* — it's a fabulous coup."

"I didn't snag him," I said. "He just showed up. And if that's a coup, it's one that could backfire, big time," I said. "Have you read any of Werzel's articles?"

She shook her head. Not surprising — I hadn't either before the *Trib* called to request directions and a VIP pass. But a quick Google search told me all I needed to know.

"He wants to be Woodward and Bernstein for the new millennium, and they've got him stuck in the Style section, writing human interest stories. So he tries to turn every assignment into a new Watergate."

"But there's no possible scandal he can find connected with our parade," Minerva said. "Is there?"

"No, but that just means he'll drive us crazy trying to find the smoking gun, and when he fails he'll sulk and try to make us look like lunatics."

"Oh, dear," Minerva said. "Yes, we'd be all too vulnerable on the lunacy angle."

"You should see the article he did on a group of little old ladies up in Loudoun County who make bears for sick children in disasters. He spent most of the article making fun of their accents and their clothes and then toward the end made it sound like he suspected they were using the bears to smuggle drugs or launder money or something. He's trouble with a press pass."

"We can't let him stay!" she exclaimed. "It'll kill Henry if we have more negative publicity. His stomach was in knots for weeks after that nasty business over the summer."

Nasty business? Rather a mild term for a murder and the breakup of a major drug smuggling ring. But perhaps her years in Baltimore, where Chief Burke had been a homicide detective, had made her jaded about the crime level in our more sedate rural community.

"We can't very well chase a reporter away," I said aloud. "The parade's free to the public, as I had to explain several times to that ninny who asked us to give Werzel a VIP pass. And if we tried too obviously to shoo him, he'd get suspicious and really make our lives miserable."

"We'll just have to keep an eye on him, then," she said, and strode away — probably to enlist the rest of the New Life Baptist choir in the surveillance. I wondered if it would make Werzel nervous, being constantly under the stern eyes of at least a dozen dignified black women in majestic burgundy choir robes. I hoped so.

I was, for the moment, blissfully unbothered. Slightly chilled, but unbothered. No one was standing in front of me, demanding private dressing rooms, complaining about their unsatisfactory place in the marching order, or asking where to find the rest of their party. Most of the people with nothing better to do were either lining up to get elephant rides or staring down the road waiting to see how many wise men were still in their saddles when the camels returned. I glanced around to see if Clarence had come back, but either he hadn't or he'd put his goose head back on — I couldn't tell which of the far more than six identical geese was him. His height should have been a clue, but either many of the SPOOR members were unusually tall or the goose heads added a lot of height. I made a mental note to drop over there before too long to find out what SPOOR had against Santa and whether it was likely to cause any problems during the parade. And possibly to confiscate all the surplus goose costumes, just in case.

Maybe I could channel the SPOOR members' energies into fixing up the two bird-themed Christmas trees flanking the front walk. When Mother had given Dad and his SPOOR comrades leave to decorate them, I think she'd envisioned the ten-foot spruces festooned with artificial birds, feather garlands, and perhaps a wee tinsel nest or two. It never occurred to her that the SPOOR thought of the trees as for the birds rather than about them. The garlands of nuts, berries, and popcorn were decorative enough, and the little seed balls were not unattractive, but no amount of red ribbon could possibly make large, droopy net bags of suet look festive. And since the SPOOR members had finished decorating them two days ago, the birds had been demonstrating their appreciation by systematically eating the trees clean. They now had that ratty, picked-over look of store counters on the last day of a really good sale. Yes, I should definitely enlist the SPOOR members to replenish the trees. Maybe I could even donate our surplus fruitcakes to the cause.

But not now. For now, everything was under control. I glanced over at my clipboard and saw that only a few bit players had yet to check in. I stuck my clipboard under my arm, stuffed my chilled hands in my pockets, leaned gratefully against one of our front fence posts, and drank in the fantastical sights and sounds around me.

And they were fantastical — even at my busiest, I realized that. I could have been enjoying it all so much more if I didn't have to feel responsible for it. I felt a brief twinge of resentment at that, and banished it with the thought that by nightfall, my term as Mistress of the Revels would be over. And surely, armed with the memory of this year's experience, I could gather the gumption to refuse if they asked me again. So next year I could take a small part and enjoy the festivities. Maybe I'd learn to juggle or at least get a medieval costume and march with Michael's colleagues who attended every year as jesters. Or help Mother's garden club friends with their traditional flower-themed float. Or maybe just stand at the roadside and be part of the audience.

Yes, everything was going splendidly, and before too long I could return to my own plans for Christmas, which included not only the giant potluck family dinner at Mother and Dad's farm on Christmas Day, but also a quiet Christmas Eve with Michael after his one-man show was over. We'd fended off several dozen invitations from friends and family alike, and were planning to spend the evening in front of the fireplace with a glass of Shiraz and soft carols and —

"Aunt Meg!"

Eric came running up, followed by Cal Burke. They both looked wide-eyed and ashen-faced.

"What's wrong?" I said, nearly dropping the clipboard in my alarm.

Eric swallowed hard.

"I think something's wrong with Santa."

CHAPTER SIX

"Where is Mr. . . . Santa?" I asked.

"In the pig shed," Eric said.

"Do you know what's wrong with him?"

Eric glanced down at Cal, then shook his head.

"Not really," he said.

But from the look in his eyes, he knew, and it wasn't good news.

"Wait here," I said. "If anyone shows up looking for me, tell them I'll be right back."

Eric nodded.

"And don't either of you say anything to anyone," I added. "Promise?"

Cal nodded.

"We won't," Eric said.

I handed him my clipboard to hold so he'd look more official, and hurried over to the pig shed.

"Meg, would you like some Christmas cookies?" someone called out as I passed.

"Later, thanks," I said over my shoulder.

What could be wrong with Mr. Doleson?

Whatever the problem, I was grateful Michael had thought to give Mr. Doleson the pig shed. It was not only private, it was somewhat out of sight of the rest of the yard, so if there was some kind of problem, perhaps we could deal with it quietly.

The shed door was closed. I heard no sounds from inside, so at least he wasn't having another of his cursing fits.

"Mr. Doleson," I called, as I rapped on the door.

No answer. I straightened the wreath on the door and waited another token few seconds before turning the knob.

Yes, there was definitely something wrong with Santa. He was sprawled on the back seat of the sleigh with one boot on and one held in his left hand.

His right hand clutched what appeared to be a stake stuck in the middle of his chest. From his fixed, staring eyes and the amount of blood inside the sleigh and on the dirt floor below, I had no doubt he was dead.

I stood there staring for what seemed like an hour — partly out of shock and partly out of morbid curiosity. I felt guilty about it, but I couldn't help the impulse to drink in every detail while I could. After all, in another couple of seconds, I would call the police and Chief Burke would banish the prying eyes of civilians like me.

I glanced at my watch. Nine thirty-five. Only a little over half an hour since I'd seen him enter the pig shed. I pulled out my notebook-that-tells-me-when-to-breathe and jotted the time down.

Then I stepped out, shut the door, and looked around in all directions for someone I trusted to guard the shed while I went for help. I saw two choir members, assorted shepherds, and a very tall goose, but no one I knew well enough to guard a murder scene.

Then my luck changed. I spotted two figures strolling past. One was a wearing a bulky snowman suit while the other was my cousin, Horace Hollingsworth. At least I assumed it was Horace. All I could see was that the figure was wearing a ratty gorilla suit, but Horace came in his ape costume not only to costume parties but also whenever he could get away with pretending he thought costumes were called for.

"Horace!" I called. The gorilla turned around and stumbled in my direction while the snowman waved and continued on his way.

"Hi, Meg."

Even muffled as it was by the gorilla head,

I could tell that Horace's voice was flat and depressed. I made a mental note to ask him later what was wrong. For now, Horace was the perfect person to stand guard. Back in my hometown of Yorktown, where Horace still lived, he was a crime scene technician for the sheriff's department, so he of all people would understand the importance of keeping everyone out of the scene until someone competent could examine it.

In fact, he'd probably be the someone. Since Caerphilly was too small to have its own crime scene technician, York County often lent them Horace when they needed forensic help. Particularly if he was already here, as he so often was these days.

"I thought you were guarding the safe room," I said.

"I locked it up so Sammy and I could have a snack," he said.

"Was that Sammy in the snowman suit?" I asked. Sammy was one of Chief Burke's deputies. "Damn, we could have used him, too."

"What's wrong?"

"Someone killed Santa — Mr. Doleson," I said.

"Have you called 911?" he asked.

"Not yet," I said. I decided not to mention that I hadn't yet pulled myself together enough to even think of it.

"I'll do it, then," Horace said. He pulled a cell phone out of his pocket — well, that was new. The gorilla suit never used to have pockets. Unless Horace had learned to sew, perhaps someone with sewing skills had been helping him improve it. That could be good news — Horace's love life lately had been even worse than usual.

"Great, and don't let anyone in the shed," I said. "I'm going to find Sammy, or Chief Burke, or one of his officers."

Horace nodded.

"Debbie Anne?" I heard him say. Good, he'd reached the police dispatcher. I strode off toward where I'd last seen the camels.

I was in luck. The wise men were returning in stately procession. Ainsley Werzel was busily snapping pictures, and several amateur videographers were following the procession's path with their hand-held cameras.

I felt bad about ruining the photo op, but they still had the whole parade to go. I ran out to meet the wise men and fell into step beside the chief's camel.

"I have bad news," I said.

"Something I'm going to have to get down off of this fool camel to deal with?" he asked. He sounded eager.

I nodded.

"Hang on a minute, then. Dr. Blake, how the blazes do you park this thing again?"

"Tell him to s-t-a-n-d," Dr. Blake said.

"Stand!" the chief barked. Curley stopped, and Dr. Blake pulled up beside him.

"Stand, Moe. Now tell him to 'Hoosh!' And lean back while you do."

"Hoosh!" the chief shouted.

The chief's camel stood motionless, while Dr. Blake's beast obediently began the awkward-looking process of folding first his front legs and then his back legs.

"Blast it!" Dr. Blake grumbled. "Moe's rather badly trained, and Curley's a little too eager. Try it again. And lean back, hard."

I began to wonder if I should have told the chief my news while he was still on the camel. Ralph Doleson's rigor mortis would probably have set in by the time the chief finally got back on solid ground.

"Hoosh! Hoosh, dammit!" the chief shouted, and leaned back so far I thought for a moment he'd fall off. But when Moe's front legs abruptly folded, I realized the chief had, accidentally or on purpose, gotten it right. Now that Moe was kneeling, the chief was upright.

"Now lean forward again, quick!" Dr. Blake ordered.

The chief leaned forward, grabbed the front of the saddle, and hung on for dear life as Moe's back end hit the earth with an audible thud.

"Meg, put your foot on his front leg," Dr. Blake said. "Moe's front leg, that is, not the chief's." I complied, a little nervously, because I couldn't remember if Moe was the one who bit.

"Put some pressure on it!" Dr. Blake said, as he reached for Moe's reins. "The idea is to discourage him from trying to get up again while the chief is dismounting."

I leaned on Moe's leg, and the chief slid off.

"I'm good," he said. "You can take your foot away if you like. Now what's the problem?"

I glanced around. Plenty of people were watching us, most of them either videotaping the camel dismounting demonstration or pointing their fingers and laughing. But only Dr. Blake and Michael were within earshot, so I decided this was as good a place as any to talk.

"Someone's murdered Ralph Doleson," I said.

"You're sure?"

"If he's not dead, he's a hell of an actor, and I don't think he could possibly have

79

done it to himself," I said.

The chief closed his eyes for a second as if gathering strength, then sprang into action.

"Right," he said. "Where?"

"In our pig shed."

"You didn't just leave him there?"

"I found Horace and left him to guard the scene," I said.

He nodded grudgingly.

"Show me."

"Okay," I said. "You might want to look a little happier. Or at least more nonchalant. I don't see him right now, but odds are that reporter's still lurking around here somewhere, and I bet you don't want him to figure out something's wrong and follow us."

The chief frowned for a moment, as if trying to decide whether I had an ulterior motive or not. And I did, of course, but he quickly deduced it was the same one he had: not letting Ainsley Werzel make Caerphilly look completely ridiculous. His face broke into a slightly forced smile.

"Great idea," he said, rather loudly. "Let's just go and do that while I'm thinking of it." In an undertone, he added, "I'd appreciate it if you could find some way to distract that damned newshound when he turns up."

"Roger," I said.

I strolled over to where Dr. Blake and Michael were standing, holding the camels' reins and posing for the photographers.

"Go away," Dr. Blake said. "You're spoiling the pictures."

I ignored him.

"Bad news," I said to Michael. "Santa's dead."

"Who?" Dr. Blake asked.

"Santa," I repeated. "Though I assume Ralph Doleson was the intended target."

"Oh, dear," Michael said. "No bite marks on him, I hope."

"No new ones, anyway. He was stabbed — no way they can blame it on Spike. Look, both of you — keep it under your hat for now. And the chief would really appreciate it if we could keep anyone from finding out for as long as possible. Especially that reporter."

I had spotted Werzel now. If he'd donned the brown shepherd's robe to be unobtrusive, it was a miscalculation. He was so thin that he could almost have wrapped the robe around him twice, but it barely came below his knees, revealing an awkward two-foot expanse of blue denim and a pair of ratty anachronistic brown shoes. And, damn it, he seemed to be watching us.

"We could offer him a camel ride," Michael suggested. "Good publicity for the zoo, you know. He's from *The Washington Star-Tribune.*"

"Excellent idea!" Dr. Blake exclaimed. Bashfulness was not one of his failings. He strode over toward Werzel and stuck out a deceptively gnarled hand. He seemed to consider shaking hands a competitive sport — if not a form of hand-to-hand combat — and I'd seen stronger men than Werzel wince after Dr. Blake had greeted them.

"Lovely to see you!" he was saying, as he mauled Werzel's hand. "Meg tells me you might be interested in a camel ride!"

I rejoined Chief Burke and led him over to the pig shed.

"Hey, Chief," Horace said as we strolled up. "We've got a bad one."

"You've been inside?"

"Just far enough to see if he needed medical assistance," Horace said. "And Meg's right — he's definitely dead. No pulse, no respiration, eyes open and fixed."

The chief opened the shed door, peeked inside, and nodded.

"We'll need the medical examiner to pronounce before we can proceed, of course, but I have no doubt you're right. Any chance you can help us out with this one?"

"Be glad to," Horace said, nonchalantly, though I could tell from his expression that he was dying to work the case. Perhaps because he was still relatively new at forensic work, and enjoyed working what he called a "nice, grisly crime scene." After twenty-five years with the Baltimore Police Department, Chief Burke looked as if he'd rather see anything else.

"Meg," the chief said. "Keep an eye open and let me know if anyone's heading this way. Any thoughts on whether he was killed here or just stashed here?"

The last bit, I realized, was directed at Horace.

"Almost certainly here," Horace said. "If he'd been killed elsewhere and brought in here, where's the blood trail?"

The chief nodded.

"Another interesting thing —" Horace began.

"Trouble," I said. "Ainsley Werzel's riding his camel this way."

Chapter Seven

"I thought you had someone distracting him," the chief grumbled.

"So did I," I said. "But I guess Michael and Dr. Blake underestimated the power of the press."

"Are there any other doors to this shed?" the chief asked.

"No, but I suppose someone could try to get in or out through the windows," I said. "In's more likely; they're shuttered on the outside."

"Go in and guard the crime scene," the chief said to Horace. "And can you call Debbie Anne and tell her to send Dr. Smoot over?"

Horace nodded and slipped inside.

Ainsley Werzel appeared around the corner of the barn and reined in his camel about ten feet away from us.

"What's going on?" he asked.

"I'll have to ask you to leave," the chief

said. "And take the camel with you."

"What right have you —" Werzel began.

"You're about to contaminate a crime scene," the chief snapped. "Now take that thrice-blasted beast someplace else."

Werzel's eyes grew large, and he opened his mouth. Then he shut it again.

"Hut-hut!" he said, kicking the camel. They disappeared around the corner of the barn.

"That was too easy," the chief said.

In the distance, we heard Werzel shouting, "Hoosh! Hoosh!"

"He's not going away," I said. "He's just dumping the camel."

The chief muttered something indistinguishable.

Sammy Wendell, one of the chief's deputies, appeared from the other side.

"Debbie Anne paged me and said to meet you here," Sammy said. "What's up?"

"Homicide," the chief said. "Keep that damned reporter at bay while we work the scene, will you?"

Just then Werzel appeared from around the barn, notebook in hand.

"I'm sorry, sir, ma'am," Sammy said. "You'll have to watch from behind this line."

Sammy held out his hands to define an imaginary line about twenty feet from the

85

shed door. The ma'am, I realized, was directed at me. I went over and stood behind Sammy's line, with an ostentatiously cooperative look on my face. Werzel didn't like it, but he followed suit. For now, at least — if I were the chief, I'd keep my eye on him.

"What happened?" Werzel asked.

"Homicide," the chief said.

"Whoa!" Werzel exclaimed. "Someone offed Santa?"

"The name of the deceased is being withheld, pending notification of next of kin," the chief said. "What makes you think Santa Claus is involved?"

"Stands to reason," Werzel said. "That's the shed where I saw Santa kicking the dog."

"What do you mean by 'kicking the dog'?" the chief asked. From his frown, I realized he thought "kick the dog" might be a hip, new synonym for "kick the bucket."

"Santa had a close encounter with Spike," I said.

The chief closed his eyes and shuddered. He'd met the small evil one before. Then he opened his eyes again.

"We need Smoot, damn it," he said.

"You need what?" Werzel asked.

The chief frowned but didn't answer him.

"It's a who, not a what," I said. "Dr.

Smoot is the county's medical examiner."

"Acting medical examiner," the chief said. "Any idea where he is?"

"He's over there on the Dickens float," I said, pointing.

The *Caerphilly Clarion,* our local weekly, was taking its turn at photographing the Dickens float. Not surprising — thanks to Mother's decorating skills, it was one of the highlights of the parade. It featured an enormous Victorian Christmas tree at one end and a London street scene, complete with mountains of fake snow, at the other. Mother and the rest of the improbably well-dressed Cratchits were seated in a pair of velvet sofas at the foot of the Christmas tree, toasting each other with plastic champagne flutes and pretending to open elaborately wrapped presents. At the other end stood Scrooge, surrounded by the Ghosts of Christmases Past, Present, and Yet-to-Come. The Cratchits may have gone upscale, but the ghosts' costumes more or less matched the book — Christmas Past was a tiny blond child in a choir robe; Christmas Present was an enormous robed figure with a crown of holly, and Christmas Yet-to-Come was a specter whose face was hidden in the shadows of his hooded black robe. Okay, the text did say that Yet-to-

Come was "shrouded in a deep black garment, which concealed its head, its face, its
form, and left nothing of it visible save one
outstretched hand." But couldn't Dr. Smoot
have found a way to look a little less like the
grim reaper? I'd always thought the costume
at odds with the holiday spirit of the parade
— though strangely appropriate for our
present problem.

"I don't see Smoot," the chief said.

"In the hood," I said.

"Oh, good grief," the chief muttered and
strode over toward the float.

"What's wrong with him?" Werzel asked,

"We don't get a lot of crime in Caerphilly,"
I said. "Chief Burke takes it very seriously
and very personally when someone breaks
the peace in his county."

I didn't see him taking notes.

"Right," he said. "I mean what's wrong
between him and this Dr. Smoot?"

I shrugged and tried to look puzzled by
the question. I knew exactly what was
wrong. The chief was a very by-the-book
guy, and Dr. Smoot had recently developed
an active interest in the supernatural. There
was no way the chief or the town council
would offer a permanent appointment to a
medical examiner who, in addition to
determining the manner and means of

death, would occasionally venture an opinion on the likelihood of the deceased's return as a ghost, vampire, or zombie. But since the job paid almost nothing, none of the county's other medical personnel had shown the slightest interest in doing it. The way things were going, the chief could be stuck with Dr. Smoot as acting medical examiner for the rest of his career.

And the chief was still mad about what happened when Dr. Smoot, hearing that one of the New Life Baptist deacons had a severe garlic allergy, took it on himself to determine if the deacon was one of the undead. Apparently Dr. Smoot had seen too many movie vampires cower from a single drop of holy water. Unfortunately, the New Life church wasn't equipped with holy water fonts and the closest equivalent was the pool used for full immersion baptism. The chief might have forgiven Dr. Smoot a little sooner if the *Caerphilly Clarion* hadn't printed a picture of the would-be vampire slayer and his victim being rescued from the watery deep.

Still, the chief was polite enough as he conferred with the sinister, hooded figure at the snowy end of the Dickens float. Then the Ghost of Christmas Yet-to-Come climbed awkwardly down from the float and headed our way at a brisk trot.

"That's just wrong," Werzel said, shaking his head as his gaze followed the running figure. "Phantoms should glide."

Yes, scurrying didn't exactly enhance a sinister ghost's image, but what unsettled me more was the undignified sight of the chief trotting after him. Clearly the chief didn't trust Dr. Smoot not to say something the press shouldn't hear. At any rate, he beat Dr. Smoot to the door of the pig shed. After a brief whispered exchange of words, he held open the door.

"In here," he said.

"Oh, dear," Dr. Smoot said. "Inside?"

The chief closed his eyes, and if I could have read his mind, I bet I'd have heard him counting to ten.

"Yes, in there," the chief said. "That's where the body is."

"It's just that it's a very small shed," Dr. Smoot said. He crept a few inches closer to the shed and peered into the door. Which anyone who knew him would realize was incredible progress. At one time his claustrophobia would have sent him running away at the mere thought of being forced to look into an enclosed space.

"It's bigger than it looks," I said. "And if you like, we could open up the windows.

You'd hardly know you were in a building at all."

"I don't see why we can't have more outdoor homicides," Dr. Smoot said. He turned sideways to the door and began inching toward the shed door in crab fashion.

"You might want to leave the robe out there," came a voice from inside the shed. Only Cousin Horace's voice, but at the sound, Dr. Smoot let out a loud shriek, jumped a foot, and then turned and fled.

"Damn the man," Chief Burke muttered.

"I'm sorry," Horace said, emerging from the shed. "I didn't mean to startle him."

"What is he afraid of — ghosts?" Werzel said.

"No, he likes ghosts," I said. "He's afraid of small spaces."

"A claustrophobic medical examiner," Werzel said, with a chuckle.

"Claustrophobic *acting* medical examiner," the chief repeated. "Horace, what —"

Then he looked at Werzel, frowned, and leaned over to whisper in Horace's ear.

They made quite a picturesque tableau — the gorilla and the wise man. Werzel grinned and reached inside his brown shepherd's robe — for his camera, no doubt. He frowned, took his hand out, and began patting his pockets, while leaning over to whisper to me.

"Why is he dressed as a gorilla?" he asked.

"I've forgotten offhand," I said. "But I'm sure it's connected with one of the floats."

I mentally crossed my fingers as I said it. Maybe Werzel would buy the parade excuse and not keep asking other people the same question until he found out that we had cousins who didn't know what Horace looked like as a human.

"Damn," Werzel said. "Where's my camera? I had it right here."

A wave of impatience suddenly seized me.

"I'll go bring Dr. Smoot back," I said, turning to go.

"Good luck," the chief said. "The fool is probably halfway back to town by now. We won't find him for days."

"I'll manage," I said over my shoulder.

I had a sneaking suspicion where I could find Dr. Smoot. I checked my clipboard and wound my way through the crowd of participants to the sheep pasture across the road from our house, where the shepherds keeping watch by night had been assigned to abide with their flocks until parade time.

Clustered near the fence where they could observe what was going on were about thirty prize Lincoln sheep belonging to Seth Early, our neighbor. I also spotted Ernest, the llama I'd given Michael for Christmas. I wondered if Michael was still trying to sneak Ernest into the parade with the sheep. If I had time, I'd have a word with Seth. He could care less that there had been no llamas within five thousand miles of Bethlehem at the time of the Nativity, but if I even hinted that Ernest would take the spotlight off his beloved sheep, that would do the trick.

First things first, though. Finding Dr. Smoot was more important than preserving the historical accuracy of the parade.

The shepherds were all seated on the ground, just as the carol described, except for Seth himself, who was standing in the midst of his flock, wearing a brown homespun shepherd's robe, holding a rough-hewn shepherd's crook, and staring over the fields, seemingly unaware of the dozen tourists snapping his picture. I couldn't blame them — he was attractive in a weathered, forty-something way, and he certainly had his shepherd act down cold, possibly because he was a full-time sheep farmer in real life.

I just wasn't sure it was such a good idea, his planning to march in the parade with a flock of thirty sheep.

"Can't you just bring a couple of sheep?" I'd suggested when I heard about his plans.

"And there were in the same country shepherds abiding in the field, keeping watch over their flock by night," he'd said. I couldn't tell if that was supposed to be a yes or a no.

"Right," I'd said. "But couldn't you just keep watch over two?"

"Two? We're not reenacting Noah's ark. Two sheep are not a flock."

"How about three, then?"

Of course he'd ignored me. He'd learn. Seth's sheep were an adventurous lot. Even when he left them in the pasture, they spent a large portion of their time finding ways of slipping past the fence so they could roam the countryside. And he wanted to take them traipsing halfway across the county? He'd be hunting down stray sheep for days.

But that was his problem, not mine. I glanced in the direction he was frowning and spotted my cousin Rosemary Keenan, or Rose Noire, as she now preferred to be called. She was also dressed in a homespun shepherd's robe — doubtless handwoven out of sustainable organic cotton, since Rose Noire had become a leading light in Caerphilly's environmental and New Age circles. She was patting what at first looked like a heap of black fabric wrapped around her legs.

I'd found Dr. Smoot.

CHAPTER EIGHT

"Now, now," Rose Noire was saying. "Don't let this undo all the progress you've made!"

I sighed. Rose Noire had been practicing therapy without a license on Dr. Smoot, trying to cure his claustrophobia by encouraging him to act out his related childhood terror of vampires. He was a little less claustrophobic than he had been, but the so-called therapy had sparked his new obsession with the supernatural. Not what I'd call real progress.

"It's just so small and dark," he said.

"Dr. Smoot," I called.

"I'm not going back," he wailed, clinging tighter to Rose Noire.

"You don't have to go in the shed," I said. "We can open all the doors and shine some really bright lights in there, and you can examine the body from outside."

"Oh, dear, there really is a body, then?" Rose Noire asked. "That's terrible. Such negative karma for the whole parade."

"Not to mention a real bummer for the victim," I said. Rose Noire didn't appear to notice my sarcasm.

"I'm going to do a blessing for everyone in the parade," she said, spreading her hands out as if to embrace the immediate world and then waving them around like a conductor.

"Great," I said. I meant it. I wasn't entirely convinced that having my cousin walk around burning sage and trying to beam positive thoughts at everyone would do any good — but if it didn't work, at least it did no harm, and if it did work, I wanted as much of it as possible for today's star-crossed parade. "But please don't tell anyone the reason you're blessing things," I added. "The chief wants to keep it pretty quiet for now, so he doesn't have a crowd control problem at the crime scene."

I was in favor of keeping it quiet, too. If only we could keep the news from spreading until after the parade.

"Of course," she said. "We only want good energy for a holiday parade."

"Any chance you could provide some moral support for Dr. Smoot?" I asked. "The chief would really like it if he could officially declare the victim dead."

97

"They're not sure he's dead, then? That's a relief."

"I found him, and I'm sure," I said. "But the chief has to follow the law. Dr. Smoot doesn't have to examine the body if he doesn't want to, but they can't really do anything until the body's officially pronounced dead."

Odds were if Dr. Smoot wimped out of examining the body, Chief Burke would enlist my father to perform an expert if unofficial inspection. Dad was both a semi-retired doctor and an avid mystery fan who jumped at any chance to get involved in a real life crime — especially a murder.

"Come on, Dr. Smoot," Rose Noire said, taking him by the arm and gently propelling him along. "Let's talk about this. Think what a wonderful opportunity for personal growth this offers."

I winced at hearing my cousin's new catchphrase. My broken leg this past summer, the loss of Michael's aging but still functional convertible to a falling tree this fall, last week's painful dental work — to her, they were not problems but welcome opportunities for personal growth.

If she used the same line when she heard that Michael's mother was coming for a month-long visit right after the new year . . .

Still, her approach seemed to comfort Dr. Smoot. With me leading the way, she guided him back to the pig shed. A small crowd awaited us, but fortunately it was only police and family. Including Dad, of course. I went over to stand next to Michael.

"How's it going?" I whispered.

"Werzel's going to make us all look like complete fruitcakes in his article," he whispered back.

"Good," I said. "I'm all for truth in journalism."

"On the bright side, he's lost his camera," Michael added. "It's making him quite testy, but the chief's relieved."

Dr. Smoot squared his shoulders and lifted his chin. Rose Noire nodded and patted his arm encouragingly.

"I know you can do it," she crooned.

Dr. Smoot took a step toward the shed. Then he reached inside his jacket pocket and took out something that he was careful to conceal in his hand. He lifted his hand to his mouth and slipped something in.

As if by magic, his spine straightened, his head lifted, his chest puffed out, and he began to walk calmly and confidently toward the shed. He stopped at the door and looked around to smile at us before ducking in.

"Oh, dear Lord, he's wearing the fangs," I muttered.

Michael winced, and we both looked over at Werzel, who was scribbling in his notebook, so perhaps he hadn't noticed. Bad enough that our medical examiner had to be coaxed to the crime scene, but when his grownup equivalent of a security blanket was a custom-fitted set of vampire fangs —

"Of course, the good news is that no one will believe a word Werzel writes if he puts everything in," Michael whispered.

"Thank God for the lost camera," I whispered back.

"Oh, my," we heard Dr. Smoot exclaim from inside the shed.

Rose Noire took an anxious step forward, then glanced at the chief and checked herself. Dr. Smoot popped out of the shed door. His hood was thrown back, his hair looked disheveled, his collar was askew, and if Werzel had missed the fangs before, he couldn't overlook them now, because Dr. Smoot was smiling broadly.

"You didn't tell me about the cauthe of death!" he exclaimed.

"No," the chief said. "Because technically that's what you're supposed to tell me."

"It'th all preliminary, of courthe," Dr. Smoot said, as he adjusted his collar and gathered the shreds of his professional dignity. "We can't tell until we've done the autopthy, but —"

"Can you lose those things?" the chief asked.

Dr. Smoot blinked in confusion for a second. The chief gestured slightly at his mouth.

"Oh, thorry," Dr. Smoot said. He reached into his mouth and extracted the fangs. "As I was saying, we won't know till we've done the autopsy, but my preliminary opinion is that he died from a loss of blood resulting from a wound to the heart inflicted by a sharp wooden object."

"Someone killed him by shoving a stake through his heart?" Werzel asked.

"We won't know for sure until the autopsy," Dr. Smoot said. "But essentially, yes."

Werzel glanced at Horace and then back at Dr. Smoot.

"I love this town," he murmured.

"Do you want me to —" Dr. Smoot began.

"Thank you, Dr. Smoot," the chief said, with a glance at Werzel. "And now why don't we leave Horace and Sammy alone to get on with it?"

"With what?" Werzel asked. "An exorcism, maybe?"

"Their forensic analysis of the crime scene. Horace, you carry on. Sammy, you stay with him and make sure the crime scene stays secure. Meg, do you mind if we use your old office in the barn for our incident center? We'll move operations over there."

Werzel watched as Sammy and Horace stepped inside and Sammy pulled the door firmly shut. Then he glanced around.

"You've done so well," Rose Noire said to Dr. Smoot. "I should get back to the sheep. Just come find me if you start feeling stressed again."

"And I should get back to the camels," Michael said. He went over and began untying Moe's and Curley's reins.

"Elephants for me," Dad added, turning as if to go.

Chief Burke was frowning at something in his notebook.

I studied my clipboard and turned to leave.

"Where's your barn?" Werzel asked.

I pointed. He made another reflexive grab for his camera, swore under his breath when he came up with empty air, and headed over toward the barn, pulling out his cell phone as he went.

Michael stopped untying the camels. Dad

returned to the chief's side. Sammy popped the door open again.

"Coast clear?" he asked.

"Clear," the chief said. "Round up the rest of the officers and maybe a few reliable volunteers and secure the damned perimeter of my crime scene."

"Yes, sir!" Sammy loped off.

The chief turned back to Dr. Smoot.

"So did the stake kill him, or was it done after he died?" Chief Burke asked.

"I can't tell you till I do the post mortem," Dr. Smoot said.

"I assume the time of death —"

"Impossible to say anything until after the post mortem!" Dr. Smoot exclaimed.

"Impossible for you maybe," I said. "But I can pin it down to a half-hour period."

They both looked at me.

"I was checking people in for the parade, remember?" I said. "I happened to notice that Mr. Doleson arrived almost precisely at nine. I remember thinking he was the very last person to arrive on time. And I looked at my watch immediately after I found him, and it said nine-thirty-five. I wrote it down in my notebook, just in case. So allowing a few minutes for Eric and Cal to find me —"

"Admirable precision," the chief said, with

a faint smile. "Of course, given the number of people with easy access to the crime scene during the window of opportunity, I doubt if this case will hinge entirely on the time of death, but you never know."

I nodded. No, odds were the time of death wouldn't crack the case. But it might give alibis to some of the people I didn't want to see suspected. And I realized that Spike, bless his evil little heart, had accidentally prevented Michael from being the last person to see the victim alive. Maybe I was overreacting, but I recalled that in the mystery books Dad read by the bagful, the last person to see the victim alive was always a key suspect. But between the time Mr. Doleson had kicked Spike out of the shed and slammed the door and the time I'd shown up to find the body, Michael was alibied not only by several dozen parade participants but by the chief himself. I made a mental note to give the small evil one a whole handful of treats next time I saw him.

"The time of death's not the important thing anyway," Dr. Smoot was saying. "Clearly someone thought he was a vampire!" He sounded downright happy about it.

"Halloween's over," the chief said, with an involuntary glance at Horace's gorilla suit.

104

"And while I've heard half a dozen people just today call Mr. Doleson a bloodsucker, do you really think anyone takes that literally?"

"You see a whole lot of those college students running around wearing black," Horace said. "Black clothes, black fingernails, black lipstick."

"That just means that they think they're cool, and goth," I said. "Not that they literally think they're vampires."

"Perhaps the stake's intended to be a symbolic gesture," Michael said. "Suggesting that the killer considers Mr. Doleson's business practices no better than commercial vampirism."

"That sounds more likely to me," the chief said.

"I still think you should assign someone to infiltrate the local occult community," Dr. Smoot said. He sounded as if he wanted to be recruited for the job.

"We have a local occult community?" the chief asked.

"Oh, yes," Dr. Smoot said. "You'd be amazed at some of the things that go on in a seemingly quiet town like this."

"No, I wouldn't," the chief muttered.

An idea struck me.

"Dad," I said. "What kind of wood is the

stake made of?"

"Now that's an interesting question," Dad said. He turned to the chief. "May I?"

The chief frowned slightly and tightened his lips. I had the feeling that the only reason he was putting up with what he would normally have called interference from civilians was that we'd all been moderately useful, especially in fending off the press. But this was pushing his limits. Finally he nodded.

"But don't touch anything," he snapped. "We haven't fingerprinted that thing yet."

"No, no," Dad said. "Of course not!"

He placed his hands ostentatiously behind his back, stepped into the shed, and peered at the stake, both through and over his glasses. And then he pulled out a magnifying glass to reinspect the wood. He paid particularly close attention to the areas where the bark still clung.

"Probably holly," he said, as he stood up. "Very light color, close-grained. I'd say *Ilex opaca* — the American holly. Is that significant?"

" 'Out upon merry Christmas!,' " I declaimed. " 'What's Christmas time to you but a time for paying bills without money; a time for finding yourself a year older, but not an hour richer.' "

The chief and most of the other bystanders were looking at me as if they thought I'd suddenly lost my mind, but Michael joined in on the rest of the quote.

" 'If I could work my will,' said Scrooge indignantly, 'every idiot who goes about with "Merry Christmas" upon his lips should be boiled with his own pudding, and buried with a stake of holly through his heart.' "

"*A Christmas Carol!*" Dad exclaimed. "Of course!"

"Christmas Carol?" the chief echoed. "Like 'The Holly and the Ivy'?"

"It's a quote from Dickens's book, *A Christmas Carol,*" I explained. "Something Scrooge says."

"So you think the murderer was making a statement about Christmas, not about Mr. Doleson's character?" the chief asked. He was scribbling frantically in his pocket notebook.

"No idea," I said. "Maybe it just struck the killer as appropriate. After all, Scrooge was a miser, and Mr. Doleson was no philanthropist."

"I still think you should look at the local occult community," Dr. Smoot muttered.

"Or maybe the murderer just thought he was being clever," Horace said. "Using a weapon that fit in with the theme of the Christmas parade."

"Holiday parade," I said, out of reflex. "You know what it does prove?"

Chief Burke frowned, but paused his scribbling and looked up at me warily.

"This was premeditated," I said. "The killer had to cut that stake from a holly tree and sharpen it. Or at least deliberately bring it here."

"It's not something connected with the parade?" the chief asked.

"Most of these people can't be relied on to march in the right direction," I said. "Do you think I'd trust any of them with sharp sticks? No, sharpened holly stakes are not a part of the parade."

"Didn't think so," the chief said. "But you never know. Dr. Smoot, perhaps you could —"

"Right," Dr. Smoot said. "Get on with it. You need to work the scene."

"If there's anything I can do to help," Dad said. He sounded so wistful.

"The more eyes, the merrier," Dr. Smoot said. He reinserted his fangs and ducked back into the shed.

"Excellent!" Dad said, following him.

Okay, Dr. Smoot was an absolute loon, but he'd just made Dad's day — possibly his whole year — so he was all right in my book.

The chief didn't even protest when I sidled up to stand beside him and peer through the open door of the shed. I almost wished I hadn't. Thanks to the several powerful lights that Horace had rigged up to illuminate the scene, I noticed something I hadn't seen before. A long brown feather sticking out of the pool of blood that had collected on the floor.

I pointed it out to Chief Burke.

"Is that significant?" he asked, frowning over his glasses at the feather.

"We'll collect it, in any case," Horace said. "But you'd expect to see a few feathers in a chicken coop."

"Yes, but this shed isn't a chicken coop — never was," I said. "It's a pig shed. And I cleaned it pretty thoroughly before I dragged the sleigh in here to dry. I didn't want any leaves or feathers or other stuff to land on the fresh paint. I think I'd have noticed an enormous feather like that floating around."

The others looked at the feather with new interest.

"Dr. Langslow, you're the birder," the chief said. "Any thoughts on the feather?"

"Hmm. . . ." Dad said. He whipped out

his magnifying glass again and began studying the feather. Horace turned his flashlight
so Dad would have more light, and I stuck
my head inside the door, so I could watch. I
winced when I realized what I was seeing.

"I'm afraid I can't help you too much,"
Dad said. "It's not a native species, I can
tell you that. Some kind of commercial
feather, I suspect."

"I know what it is," I said, closing my eyes
with exasperation. "It's a goose's tail
feather."

CHAPTER NINE

Horace held up the tail feather and peered at it.

"No, no," Dad said. "I don't see how this could come from a goose. It's —"

"Not a real goose," I said. "One of the six geese a-laying. The SPOOR members. They're all dressed up in Canada goose costumes, complete with tail feathers that look a lot like that."

"Oh, dear," Dad said, shaking his head. "You're right — it could be part of their costumes. But I'm sure no one in SPOOR would commit murder."

"I'm not," I said. "Some of them are total loons."

"They're very passionate about birds and the environment," Dad said. "But I can't imagine . . . oh, dear."

As president of SPOOR, he clearly wasn't happy about the fact that his fellow environmental activists had just become prime suspects.

The chief, on the other hand, brightened.

"So this tail feather belongs to one of the six people dressed up as geese?" he asked. Clearly he thought his life had just gotten a lot easier.

"Not exactly. Only six of them are marching in the parade in costume. But a few more than that showed up in costume and had to be dissuaded from joining in."

"How many more?" the chief asked, with something closer to his usual mid-case scowl.

"Thirty-seven in all," I said.

"Thirty-eight, counting Mrs. Markland," Dad put in.

"Yes, but Mrs. Markland was here in spirit only, last time I heard. She wasn't here in costume, shaking her tail feathers all over the yard."

"In other words," the chief said, "there are thirty-odd people running around in costumes that could have shed this feather."

"Odd's definitely the word for them," I said. "And they've been running around, practicing their high kicks and line dancing all morning. And shedding feathers like crazy, I imagine. So if someone wanted to cast suspicion on SPOOR . . ."

"Oh, good point!" Dad exclaimed.

The chief didn't seem as charmed by my analysis.

"So as evidence, it might be pretty darn useless," he said, scowling down as if it was the poor feather's fault.

"I'm sure many people have it in for SPOOR!" Dad proclaimed. "In our quest to preserve the natural habitat we have no doubt angered many vested interests."

The chief made a noise that sounded suspiciously like a growl and stepped back out of the shed.

Horace bagged the offending feather and whisked it out of sight.

"You don't really think one of the SPOOR members could possibly have done it, do you?" Dad asked.

He sounded so forlorn that I hesitated to say what I really thought — that yes, it was not only possible but probable that the killer was a SPOOR member — or if not, SPOOR could easily collect a quorum to elect the killer to honorary membership.

Dad must have read my answer on my face.

"Well, if it was someone from SPOOR who did it, I'm sure they meant well," he said.

"Where's Meg?" I heard someone outside

say. I reluctantly pulled my head out of the shed.

"Right here," I said.

Minerva Burke was standing beside her husband, which meant that either the chief's officers hadn't completely secured the perimeter of the crime scene yet or they weren't suicidal enough to try and keep Minerva out.

"People are starting to ask what's wrong. And quite a few of them have questions for you."

I glanced at my watch, and flinched when I saw how close to parade time we were.

"Chief?" I asked.

He looked up with a slight frown of preoccupation.

"I hate to bother you when I know you're swamped but — well, you're swamped. Would I be correct in assuming that I should start looking for another wise man to take your place in the parade?"

For a second, his face lit up with relief and utter joy. Then he quickly rearranged it into an expression of apologetic regret.

"I'm so sorry," he said. "I know it puts you in a bind, and I really was very flattered to be asked, but under the circumstances —"

"Henry!" Minerva Burke exclaimed. "You

don't mean you're going to leave her high and dry without a wise man?"

"No, I'm not going to leave her high and dry," the chief snapped back. "I'm going to give her back the costume, and she's going to recruit a new wise man from the hundreds of suspects milling around here trying to mess up my crime scene."

"She can't get just any old person to play a wise man!" Minerva exclaimed. "For one thing, ninety percent of the people here are scared witless of those fool camels. Much too scared to even get up on one," she added, which meant she'd figured out that her husband wasn't deliriously happy about climbing back in the camel saddle.

From the look on the chief's face, I could tell he thought scared witless was a sensible attitude toward dromedaries.

"And it needs to be a person of substance," she went on. "Someone with standing in the community. Someone . . ."

"Preferably someone black," I said. "Sorry if that sounds blunt, but in spite of that medieval tradition I mentioned to the reporter, I did some research and found out that Caerphilly's never had a black wise man in the parade before. And some of the Town Council members put up a surprising number of objections. Of course, they pretended it was because you've only been in town seven years, but . . .'"

I shrugged and let the sentence trail off. The chief's eyes narrowed, and he gave me a tight nod, as if to say he wasn't all that surprised and he knew exactly which council members I was talking about.

"Of course, I pointed out that I'd been in town even less time than you had," I added. "And I told them since they'd made me Mistress of the Revels in spite of being such a newcomer, I didn't see the problem in the chief being a wise man."

"I heard you'd threatened to resign if they didn't approve Henry," Minerva said. "We appreciate that."

I shrugged. I'd threatened to resign at least a dozen times, usually over far more trivial matters, and wouldn't have been all that broken up if the council had accepted any of my resignations.

"So, about that replacement wise man," the chief said. "How about Lucas Hawes?"

"No way you're going to take away our only half-decent baritone who's not down sick with the flu," Minerva countered. "What about your cousin John?"

"He's all involved in the Kwanzaa float," the chief said. "What about Reverend Pratt?"

I left the two of them to argue it out. I had no doubt that Minerva Burke would find an acceptable substitute wise man for me.

I saw a bigger problem headed my way. Eric and Cal Burke were peering around the corner of a nearby shed. I hurried over to head them off.

CHAPTER TEN

"You guys shouldn't be here," I said. "It's a crime scene. And you know how stern Cal's grandfather is about letting anyone near his crime scenes."

"Yeah, I know," Eric said.

"Eric, dear," my mother said. She appeared behind the boys, trailed by one of Chief Burke's officers. The crime scene perimeter was starting to resemble a sieve.

"Sorry, Grandma," Eric said. "I know we were supposed to wait by the float. It's just that Cal was worried. About Santa."

I glanced down to see that Cal was gazing up at me with huge brown eyes that looked perilously close to brimming over with tears. Mother put one hand on Eric's shoulder and one on Cal's. Cal just kept staring up at me.

"I heard on Deputy Shiffley's radio that someone killed Santa," Cal asked. "Is it true?"

"Well," I began. I wished Chief Burke or Minerva were in sight. I didn't know the official Burke family party line on Santa Claus. And I couldn't count on Mother for help. When kids asked the difficult questions, like where babies came from and was there really a Santa, Mother usually managed to have someone else answer.

Cal assumed my hesitation meant the worst.

"It's true, then," he said. His lip was quivering slightly, and a tear started rolling down his left cheek. "Someone killed Santa Claus!"

"No, of course not!" I exclaimed. "Someone killed Mr. Doleson. He was just pretending to be Santa, for the parade."

"Why?" Cal asked.

Was he asking, like his grandfather, why someone had killed Mr. Doleson? Or only why Santa had picked such an unpleasant deputy?

"I don't know," I said. "But I'm sure your grandfather will. You can ask him, later, when he's not so busy working on the case."

"My grandpa's helping, too," Eric put in.

"Yes, isn't it nice that Cal's grandfather is letting your grandfather help with the murder?" Mother said. "I'm sure this will be the most exciting Christmas Grandpa's

119

ever had."

"How remiss of us not to have arranged a Yuletide homicide long before now," I said.

Mother pretended not to hear.

"Now come along, both of you," she said.

Before turning to go, she gave me an approving smile, so I deduced I'd handled the Santa issue to her satisfaction. But that reminded me that I had another Santa problem.

I turned to see Chief Burke striding toward me, still dressed in his wise man's robes and turban, and with one side of his flowing headcovering pulled over his mouth, as if he were fighting his way through a desert sandstorm. All I could see was a small patch of brown skin and a pair of dark eyes.

"Very dashing, Ch— Minerva?"

Minerva Burke pulled the cloth away from her face and chuckled.

"If I fooled you at ten yards, odds are I can carry it off on top of a camel," she said.

"But aren't you needed in the choir?" I asked. "Not that I object to you being a wise man — person — but I don't want to sabotage the music."

"Lord, child, we've got four other altos in the choir as good as me, and we're a little short on menfolk with enough gumption to tackle the camel."

"The camel doesn't bother you, I take it?"

"I've survived Henry for thirty years, and raised those two mule-headed sons of his," she said. "I don't see that the camel will be that much of a problem."

With that, she headed for the camel pasture.

Moe wouldn't know what hit him. For that matter, neither would Dr. Blake.

Before I had time to savor the notion, Ainsley Werzel reappeared.

"Have you seen my camera?" he asked.

"Not recently," I said. "Where did you leave it?"

"If I knew that, I wouldn't be asking you, would I?"

I took a breath, discarded the first half dozen things I wanted to say as being too rude, and tried again.

"Sorry, what I should have said was, where do you last remember having it? Do you recall the last thing you took a picture of?"

"No! If I —"

"Meg, where's the cleanup crew?" someone called. "We need them over by the elephant pen."

"Meg, the bagpipers have been playing 'Away in a Manger' for half an hour. Can you make them play something else?"

"Meg, we need —"

"Sorry," I said to Werzel. "Things are a little chaotic right now. I'm sure your camera will turn up sooner or later. Why don't you tell me what make and model it is and —"

"But I can't cover the rest of the parade without a camera!"

"See that guy over there with the antlers on his head," I said, pointing to Jorge. Why was Jorge wearing antlers and a sweatshirt with "Blitzen" stenciled on it? Had the programmers from Mutant Wizards organized some kind of reindeer-themed float they'd forgotten to tell me about? I pushed the questions out of my mind.

"You think he's got my camera?"

"No, but if anyone can round up a digital camera for you to borrow, he can."

"But I need my own camera!"

"Fine," I said. "If I find it, I'll let you know."

"But —"

I turned away to deal with some of the other problems. Suddenly, rebel bagpipers and elephant manure didn't seem so bad.

But time was moving on, so I tried to deal as efficiently as possible with the several dozen participants who surrounded me, all shouting their questions, problems, requests, and complaints. I'd have been more sympathetic if most of them weren't asking questions I'd already answered, reporting problems someone had already solved, complaining about things I couldn't do anything about, or making requests they should have thought of six weeks ago.

"No, you can't use your loudspeakers to play 'Let It Snow' the whole time you're marching," I told the people from the Ski Club float. "The Caerphilly High School Band is marching right behind you, and you'll drown them out. But I'll ask them to go heavy on the snow-themed songs."

"Meg, can't we be closer to Santa Claus?" one of the Caerphilly Morris Dancers asked. "We've worked out this great routine to 'Santa Claus is Coming to Town.' It's so perfect — the bells make it really sound like a sleigh!"

"It's a great idea, but we really need you toward the front of the parade," I said. "We're a little weak on pizzazz up there and — would you excuse me?"

"But —"

"Bathroom," I said. "Right back!"

I turned and ran toward the house, growling, "Bathroom!" at anyone who tried to waylay me. Once I got to the house, I ran into the bathroom off the kitchen — not to use it, but because even my family don't usually follow people into the bathroom. I took a few deep breaths. Then I took out my notebook and flipped to the section on the parade. Just looking at it made me feel a little better. I crossed off a few items that I'd done or that had taken care of themselves, took a deep breath, and was just writing another item when I heard a knock on the door.

"Meg?" It was Michael. "You okay?"

I stuck the notebook and pen back in my pocket, opened the door, and walked out. He, Rob, and Dad were standing in a circle around the bathroom door, worried looks on their faces.

"I'm fine," I said. "The parade isn't. We don't have a Santa."

"We can find someone," Michael said.

"Someone who fits the costume?" Rob countered. "Not too many people around here who can fit into a costume that short — where did they get it, anyway, the kid's section of the Costume Shack?"

"Irrelevant," I said. "Since the costume has a great bloody hole in the center of the chest — no one would want to wear it even if Horace hadn't already packed it up in an evidence bag."

"Meg," Dad said. "I could do it. I already have my own Santa suit, remember?"

I remembered very well. When we were children, Rob and I had been firm believers in Santa Claus long after most kids our age had become cynical Santagnostics, in part because we had such dramatic proof of Santa's existence. I still cherished the Polaroid Cousin Alice had taken, showing a blurred figure in a red and white suit, standing in the middle of our familiar living room, placing a present beneath the tree I'd helped decorate. Later on, I'd helped to create blurred Polaroids myself, or more recently blurred digital shots, to thrill my nieces and nephews.

Between the Polaroids and Dad's practice of getting up in the middle of the night on Christmas Eve to stomp around on the roof, shaking a string of sleigh bells — wearing the suit, of course, in case any of the grandkids woke up in time to peek — Dad had a lot of practice at Santa.

He was certainly a lot closer to my idea of what the jolly old elf should look like than Mr. Doleson had been.

"Okay, Dad's Santa," I said. "But we don't have a sleigh for him to ride in — the sleigh's part of the crime scene, remember?"

"Can't we just have him ride in a car?"

Michael suggested. "We could use my convertible, so he could wave and smile at everyone."

"Yeah, but it lacks that certain something," Rob said. "No offense, Michael — love your new car, but convertibles are pretty humdrum in a parade."

For once I agreed with Rob.

"I have it," Dad said. "I have an inspiration! One that will make this Santa's most dramatic arrival in the history of the parade."

"This doesn't involve the boom lift, does it?" I asked.

"The boom lift? I hadn't thought of that," Dad said.

"Then don't start."

"If we could rig up something that looked like a chimney that would ride along beneath the boom lift," he said. "And I could tie a rope to myself and —"

"Don't even think of it," I said. "We already lost one Santa. We're not going for a double header. Can you imagine how traumatic it would be to the children of Caerphilly, seeing Santa take a forty-foot fall from a boom lift? Go back to whatever idea you were having when I made the mistake of mentioning the boom lift. What was that, anyway?"

126

"Have you seen Clarence's new motorcycle?" Dad asked.

Maybe I'd been too quick to reject the boom lift.

"It's not a bad idea," Michael said. "If we try to rig up a makeshift sleigh, it's bound to look just that — makeshift. But this — well, once they find out what happened, everyone will understand that we had to do something, and meanwhile, it's bold, it's new, it's in keeping with your goal of not having a boring, old-fashioned Christmas parade. Holiday parade," he corrected himself.

Yes, and was he forgetting how much certain members of the town council hated some of my non-traditional ideas for the parade? If I sent Santa down the road on a motorcycle, they'd freak. They'd never let me hear the end of it. They'd —

They'd never, ever put me in charge of the parade again, not if Michael and I lived here in Caerphilly for the next fifty years.

"You're on," I said. "Biker Santa it is. Rebel with a Claus."

"I'll run over to the farmhouse to get my suit," Dad said.

"I'll find Clarence," Michael said.

"I'm going to find my camera," Rob announced. "This is going to be awesome."

127

They all scattered. I pulled out my notebook and flipped it open to the page where, a few minutes before, in the bathroom, I had written "Find Santa." I pulled out my pen to cross it off, and instead of relief, I felt a wave of anger.

Someone had deliberately knocked off Santa at my parade. Someone who hadn't cared that the dead body could be — and was — found by two innocent children. Someone who hadn't cared that Ralph Doleson was about to do the one genuinely worthwhile thing he did all year. Someone who couldn't just wait until the parade was over and Mr. Doleson had gone back to his daily routine. Okay, the murderer hadn't done it to inconvenience me, but he — or she — did it on my watch. I had to do something.

Instead of crossing off "Find Santa," I changed it to "Find Santa's killer."

CHAPTER ELEVEN

As I strode outdoors again, I flinched slightly as the cold air hit me, and then forgot about it as I dived back into parade preparations. I felt more like my usual self again. Better than usual. As I stalked through the yard, I dispatched problems, answered questions, settled arguments, and calmed attacks of stage fright, almost without thinking. I was looking for a particular person. I headed toward the barn, where I'd last seen the six geese a-laying and all the surplus geese.

There were at least two dozen SPOOR members still wearing forbidden goose suits, which meant I had to keep my eye on them. It occurred to me that if they organized themselves in groups of six and each group slipped into the parade at a different point, it would take me a while before I could tell for sure that I wasn't seeing the same six geese bumbling into the wrong part of the parade by mistake.

Then I realized that Chief Burke would solve that particular problem for me. He'd undoubtedly confiscate all the goose costumes so he could figure out which one had shed the tail feather found at the crime scene. If he didn't, I'd do it myself, and tell SPOOR I was doing it on his orders.

I smiled slightly as I scanned the geese, who were happily milling around, unaware of how close they were to being plucked. From a distance, they all looked alike, but when you got a little closer, you could see subtle differences in their forms. Some were taller or shorter, fatter or thinner, neatly groomed or covered with haphazard, flyaway tufts of feathers. Slightly apart from the rest I spotted a goose that was taller and more angular than most. Its costume seemed more professional — the feathers all lying neatly and elegantly as they should. Including, I couldn't help noticing, a seemingly complete set of tail feathers.

When I got a couple of steps closer, I could see that this particular goose was reading a paperback book.

"Ms. Ellie?" I called. "Is that you?"

The goose turned, and took its head off. I was right. It was Ms. Ellie Draper, the town librarian.

"Good guess," she said, tucking the headpiece under her arm. I tilted my own head, almost instinctively, to see what she was reading. I was startled to see that the book's cover art was of a skeleton wearing a Santa suit.

"*Rest You Merry,*" she said. "Charlotte MacLeod. It's a lot of fun — I must remember to thank your father for recommending it."

I nodded. I hoped the chief wouldn't find out that Dad was recommending Christmas-themed murder mysteries. In the chief's current frame of mind, he'd find it highly suspicious, forgetting that Dad was always recommending seasonally, geographically, or professionally appropriate mysteries to anyone who would listen.

"Anything wrong?" Ms. Ellie asked.

"That depends," I said. "What can you tell me about SPOOR and Ralph Doleson?"

"Oh, dear," she said. "They're not threatening to boycott the parade again, are they?"

Again? I'd heard threats of protests, but this was the first I'd heard of a SPOOR boycott.

"Not that I've heard," I said aloud. "But it's important anyway."

"Or is Ralph Doleson complaining about

us again?"

"Not that I've heard," I repeated. "But why would he? Spill. Please."

"Why do I think someone's been making trouble?" she said. "Okay, this happened while you and Michael were in — where was it you went this summer?"

"Nice try," I said. "But Michael and I still aren't telling anyone where we went on our honeymoon. Something happened in June, then."

"We heard that a pair of bald eagles had built a nest in a large oak tree down by Caerphilly Creek. You can imagine how excited we were!"

I didn't have to imagine — when Pam, Rob, and I were children, Dad dragged us to view any number of nests belonging to rare or interesting birds. To us, of course, this usually meant spending an hour or so gazing at lumps of twigs at the top of trees, in the forlorn hope that the nest's elusive maker would put in an appearance.

"Down by Caerphilly Creek," I said. "Let me guess: the oak tree was on Ralph Doleson's property. By the Whispering Pines."

"Near there," she said. "But much closer to the Spare Attic. That off-site storage facility — did you know he owns that, too?"

"Yes," I said. "Michael and I still have a

bin there."

"Why in the world would you need off-site storage with this place?" she asked, glancing up at our three-story house.

"We don't," I said. "We needed it before we moved, though, and Doleson wouldn't rent month-to-month. Our final year-long lease doesn't run out till March."

"That man is greed personified," she said, shaking her head.

" 'Oh! But he was a tight-fisted hand at the grindstone,' " I quoted. " 'A squeezing, wrenching, grasping, scraping, clutching, covetous, old sinner!' "

"*A Christmas Carol*?" she said.

I nodded.

"I've been helping Michael rehearse."

"Very apt," she said. "I can't help but think Ralph Doleson would be better cast as Scrooge than as Santa. Can you suggest that for next year?"

"Get back to the bald eagles," I said. "They were nesting near the Spare Attic and . . ."

"We were going to put up an eagle cam," she said. "You know — a web-based camera so people could watch the parent birds incubate the eggs, and then eventually observe the hatchlings. We had the camera, and some of those nice young men at your brother's company did all the technical work to connect it to our Web site. But when we asked Ralph Doleson for permission to mount the camera on the roof of his building, he refused."

"Did he give any reason?" I asked.

"No. It was just pure meanness," she said. "It's not that it was the only possible place to put it, but it was the only place we could get it installed without special equipment."

"I can see how that would annoy SPOOR," I said. "But isn't all this talk of a boycott a little extreme?"

"If it had been just his refusal, yes," she said. "We tried to explain the importance to him, and he refused again, so we made other arrangements."

"What other arrangements?"

"It was your father's idea," she said.

I winced. I could picture Dad leading a contingent of SPOOR members on a daring midnight raid to install the webcam by stealth.

"He arranged to borrow Mr. Shiffley's boom lift," she said. "So we could put the camera in another nearby tree. But when we went out to do the installation, we found that someone had destroyed the nest."

"Oh, no."

"Including the two eggs."

"Oh, dear," I murmured. "That's a pity."

"It's also a crime," she said.

"I thought bald eagles were off the endangered species list?"

"They went from endangered to threatened in 1995, and were delisted entirely in 2007," she said. "But they're still covered by the Bald and Golden Eagle Protection Act."

"Did you report him?" I asked.

"Unfortunately, we couldn't prove it was Doleson," she said. "We all knew it had to be, but we didn't have any witnesses. So he's going to get off scot free. There's a lot of bad feeling about it among the membership. And then to hear he'd been chosen as Santa!"

"He wasn't chosen, he was a legacy," I said. "If I'd known about the eagles, I'd have vetoed him, but since no one told me anything about this before today . . ."

"I'll tell everyone," she said. "I think it will make a difference. I don't think you have to worry about a boycott — I've pointed out that *you* weren't around when the eagle slaying occurred and might not have known how unsuitable Ralph Doleson was. But next year —"

"I don't think you need to worry about next year," I said. I saw Chief Burke standing nearby, frowning at the large number of costumed geese cavorting in the area. Since Minerva had taken his costume, he was back in his usual suit.

Ms. Ellie followed my eyes.

"Oh, dear," she said. "Something's happened, hasn't it?"

I nodded.

"Was there a reason you were asking about Ralph Doleson? Is he — ?"

"Dead."

"Oh, dear," she repeated. "That's terrible."

"I thought you didn't like him," I said. I got the patented librarian stern look.

"I didn't like him, but I didn't wish him dead," she said. "Just elsewhere. Is there some reason the chief's paying particular attention to SPOOR? Apart from the fact that he knows very well how hard we tried to get Doleson arrested and how mad we were that we couldn't?"

"Yes," I said. "And he'd never forgive me if I jumped the gun and told you."

"Oh, dear," she said, shaking her head. "I do hope none of them do anything tasteless when they hear the news. Feelings have been running rather high all summer."

"I'm sure the chief will remember that," I said.

"Yes, and I hope he also remembers that the SPOOR members weren't the only ones at odds with Mr. Doleson. I think the Shiffleys were rather worked up, too."

"The Shiffleys?" I asked. "I didn't realize any of the Shiffleys had become bird-watchers."

"They're not," she said. "But they do —"

"Ladies and gentlemen!" the chief said. He had his battery-powered megaphone. "May I have your attention please!"

The crowd gradually settled down. It consisted by this time not only of the costumed SPOOR members, but also an ever-increasing number of spectators who'd figured out this was where the best pre-parade entertainment could be found.

"Ladies and gentlemen," the chief began again.

"Geese and ganders!" one goose exclaimed. A wave of laughter rolled through the crowd, and the chief waited it out.

"Ladies and gentlemen," he repeated. "I regret to inform you that we've had a crime here at the parade. And I'd like to ask your help in solving it. Will all the SPOOR members please accompany me to the barn?"

A buzz of conversation erupted, and not

all of it sounded happy.

"Oh, dear," Ms. Ellie murmured. "Some of our members don't look as if they feel like cooperating. I'll have to see if I can help."

She strolled over to where the chief was standing and said a few quiet words to him. The chief bowed slightly and gestured toward the barn. Seeing Ms. Ellie and the chief strolling along, chatting amiably, most of the SPOOR members fell into step behind them. The few would-be rebels made a big show of dragging their heels and making it clear with their body language that they were only going to the barn out of curiosity, not because anyone had the right to order them around.

Deputy Sammy came over to talk to me.

"The chief wants to know if you have any trash bags we can borrow," he asked. "We don't have any evidence bags large enough to hold the goose suits."

"There's a whole case of them right inside the barn," I said. "The Boy Scouts were going to use them in their post-parade cleanup."

"Thanks," he said.

And speaking of the Boy Scouts, if Chief Burke was going to confiscate all the goose suits and perhaps detain all the SPOOR members for questioning, perhaps I should find them and see if they really were prepared enough to fill in as the six geese a-laying.

Though why should they have to? An idea occurred to me, and I followed Sammy out to the barn.

"The trash bags are over there," I said, pointing to the corner where they were stored. Rather unnecessarily, since Sammy had already spotted the giant box with TRASH BAGS printed on it in two-inch letters.

"A school bus will be fine," the chief was saying into his cell phone. "How soon can you get it here?"

"A school bus?" I echoed.

"He's taking us to town to be interrogated," Ms. Ellie said.

"Interviewed," the chief said. "Okay, we have thirty-seven SPOOR members here. Is that all of you?"

"Thirty-eight counting Mrs. Markland," several geese chimed in. The chief scowled at his officers.

"And where is this Mrs. Markland?" he asked.

"Since I wasn't her pastor, I couldn't tell you," Ms. Ellie said. "But I can assure you she wasn't here murdering Mr. Doleson."

The chief blinked.

"That's the late Mrs. Markland," I put in.

"She's dead, then?" the chief asked.

"As a doornail," Ms. Ellie said.

" 'I might have been inclined, myself, to regard a coffin-nail as the deadest piece of ironmongery in the trade,' " I quoted.

The chief and Ms. Ellie both turned to frown at me.

"Sorry, total Dickens immersion," I said. "Just ignore it."

"We've found the trash bags, thank you," the chief said. "I'll let you know if we need anything else."

Coming from him, it was a relatively subtle dismissal.

"Great," I said. "But I need something from you."

"What?"

"Six geese," I said.

"The geese are all —"

"Only six," I said. "Look, you can't possibly talk to all thirty-seven at once. Why not take thirty-one of them to town in your school bus, and let the remaining six take themselves there by marching in the parade?"

"The costumes are evidence."

"We've got more costumes," one of the geese said.

140

"More?" The chief turned to frown at the speaker. "Where?"

"Not here," the goose said, backing off slightly. "But they're over at Dr. Langslow's farm. They don't look the same. They're left over from another event. We could send someone for them."

"You mean the white duck costumes?" a second goose asked.

"They always looked more like geese than ducks anyway," the first goose said. "They're still better than anything the Boy Scouts could whip up on this short notice."

"I've got a key to the farmhouse," I said. "I'll send someone to fetch six of the white goose costumes. If it's okay with you."

The chief frowned. He didn't like the idea, but he also knew how important the parade was to most of the town.

"And you could have some officers march right behind them to make sure they get to town," I suggested.

"My officers are rather busy."

"You could deputize someone. How about asking some of the campus police? I'm sure they'd be happy to help out."

The chief narrowed his eyes. The Camcops were probably already fuming with resentment that the crime had taken place so far off campus that there was no conceiv-

141

able reason they could use for barging into the chief's investigation. Though that didn't mean they wouldn't try.

"Oh, yes," Ms. Ellie said. "Such a good idea for promoting interdepartmental cooperation. You know how important that is to the town council."

"And the college administration," I added.

The chief had to struggle not to scowl at that. He was all for interdepartmental cooperation as long as it took the form of the Camcops accepting that their role was to give out parking tickets on campus, ride herd on fraternity parties, and stay out of his department's way when any real crime occurred. Unfortunately, the Camcops wanted to claim jurisdiction over any crime committed on campus or in which any of the victims, perpetrators, or witnesses were students, faculty, or employees of the college. Their notion of interdepartmental cooperation was that eventually they'd get around to telling the chief what they were up to.

"Of course, it's a long march," Ms. Ellie said. "Do you think the Camcops are up to it?"

A sudden smile lit the chief's face.

"Yes, that's an excellent idea," he said. Clearly he liked the notion that by asking the Camcops to guard the geese, he was dooming them to a tedious, footsore day. "Sammy, see if you can arrange that."

With that, he disappeared into my office, with Horace and Dad close behind him.

I handed Sammy my key to the farmhouse and he dispatched a deputy to fetch the spare goose suits.

"Now take off the costumes," he ordered. "All of you."

Some of the geese obeyed immediately, but others seemed strangely reluctant to shed their feathered suits. As Sammy and the other officers continued to chivvy them, the reason became clear. The suits were made of heavy polar fleece and covered with a thick layer of feathers. Despite the cold weather, the geese who emerged from their costumes were sweating profusely, and it quickly became evident that the recalcitrant geese were wearing little or nothing under their thick downy suits.

Someone should organize this, I thought. We could borrow a few garments temporarily from the bins where people had been leaving their donations for the clothing drive. Set up separate dressing rooms for the geese and ganders. Guard the exits so none of the geese would attempt to flee. Someone should —

Someone should mind her own business and get back to the parade she's already organizing, I told myself.

But the least I could do was make my suggestions to the chief.

CHAPTER TWELVE

I popped into the chief's temporary office and found that he, Dad, and Dr. Smoot were studying the murder weapon that Horace had placed on my desk — on a piece of plastic, thank goodness.

Horace was frowning.

"I've seen sticks like that before," he said.

"On *Buffy the Vampire Slayer,* they normally use something shorter and a bit more elegant," Dr. Smoot said. "And in *Dracula* —"

"I mean I've seen sticks like that in real life," Horace said. "Not being used as a stake, either," he added, quickly, as if afraid Dr. Smoot might have real-life observations of vampire-slaying stakes to share.

"Holly's a very common wood around here," Dad said. "There must be hundreds and hundreds of small holly trees in those woods." He waved his hand in a sweeping gesture at the window. The chief contemplated the woods with a frown, as if assessing an entirely new roster of suspects.

"Are you suggesting the killer went out into the woods, whittled himself a stake, and then came back to kill Mr. Doleson?" he asked.

"No, no," Dad said. "The holly stake's not fresh. It's had some time to season. A few months at least."

"So we're back to premeditation," the chief said. "Someone knew Ralph Doleson would be here, prepared a stake several months ago, and smuggled it in here today to kill him with."

"Seems like a lot of trouble when you'd have so many promising weapons already here," Dad said. "Here in the barn alone you have shovels, pitchforks, hoes, crowbars, axes —"

"And a whole bunch of other weapons that the killer turned up his nose at," the chief said. "But I don't think Meg was keeping a bunch of sharpened stakes in her barn, so unless you can show me someone who was —"

"The Boy Scouts!" Horace exclaimed. "They did it!"

We all stared at him.

"You think the Boy Scouts killed Santa Claus?" the chief asked, finally.

"No, but they made the stake! Meg and Michael let the troop camp out here last night, you know. And some of them are doing this whole project where they make their own tents from deerskin, and tent ropes from deer sinew, and so on. They've been whittling tent pegs just like this!"

We all looked down at the two-foot-long stake.

"Well, almost like this," Horace said. "Except a little shorter. But if one of them was sharpening one end of a holly stick to make another tent peg and just hadn't cut it down to the right length yet, it would look a lot like this."

The chief considered this for a few moments, with his head cocked to one side. Then he turned to me.

"You still have these Boy Scouts on the premises?"

"As far as I know," I said. "They were going to spend another night in our field and help with the post-parade cleanup."

"Show me."

I led the way to the campground. It was fairly neat and tidy. Probably a lot tidier than the same boys' rooms were at home. Some of the tents were ordinary modern tents made of faded canvas in various shades of green and khaki. But there were

147

also three teepees made of leather — presumably deerskin. They were painted in reds, blues, and greens in what I gather were supposed to be authentic Native American designs of eagles, deer, buffalo, and other animals. I couldn't help noticing that several of the buffalo looked remarkably like Homer Simpson. The Christmas wreaths over the tent flaps were a nice touch, but I wondered if I should tell their scoutmaster about the accompanying mistletoe.

"I find it hard to believe that the Boy Scouts had anything to do with this," the chief muttered.

"Me, too," I said. "I mean, I know the Boy Scouts have it in for the Easter Bunny, but as far as I know they've always been on good terms with Santa."

The chief just ignored me.

We followed Horace around as he methodically inspected all the tents. The modern ones mostly had mass-produced tent pegs, but the deerskin tents did have hand-made pegs.

"See, they're larger than the commercial tent pegs," Horace said.

"But still a good deal shorter than our murder weapon," the chief said, leaning over to inspect the peg.

"I'll get it," Horace said. He put on his

gloves and pulled one up, causing the tent with the Simpson buffalo on it to sag alarmingly.

"Hey, watch it!" came a voice from inside the tent. We all started, and turned to see the round deerskin tent-flap flip open. A scruffy shepherd began to crawl out.

"If I catch one more person messing with my stakes —" the shepherd began. Then he caught sight of us and stopped not only in mid-sentence but in mid-crawl, with one leg still inside the tent.

"See!" Dr. Smoot exclaimed. "They even call them stakes!"

"Who are you?" the chief said, training his frown on the shepherd.

"Rufus Shiffley, sir," the shepherd said.

"Wilfred's youngest?" the chief asked.

Rufus nodded, and the chief's frown faded.

"Come on out, son," he said.

Caerphilly was still the sort of small town where you carried your family tree around with you, for good or bad. All I knew from their exchange was that Rufus was part of the vast Shiffley clan who lived in the more rural parts of Caerphilly County and neighboring Clay County. Clearly the chief had pegged Rufus, and not unfavorably.

Rufus crawled out, and we could see that

he had a cast on one foot. That answered my next question — why Rufus was here sulking in his tent instead of cleaning up after the elephants like the rest of the troop.

"You said 'If I catch one more person messing with my stakes,' " the chief said. "Have other people been around here pulling up these tent stakes, or pegs, or whatever you call them?"

Rufus nodded.

"Yes, sir," he said. "All night long. It was the guys sleeping in the modern tents. They can lose a peg or two and it's not that big a problem, but with this thing, if you don't get all the stakes in the right way, it sags and leaks."

"Has anyone stolen any of your stakes?" the chief said. "Not just pulled them out but taken them away completely?"

"No, sir." Rufus shook his head. "They're all there, see? Well, they were until just now," he added, frowning at Horace.

"Sorry," Horace said.

"You don't have any spares?" the chief asked.

"No, sir," he said. "It's not something you lose that easily, unless someone's playing a joke. I don't know about the guys in the other tents."

"You mind if we borrow the rest of the

handmade stakes for a while?" the chief asked. "I realize that will inconvenience you, but we'd be glad to move your gear to one of the other tents."

"Yes, sir," Rufus said.

"Chief?" It was Sammy. "The geese are rebelling."

"Rebelling how?"

"They're all saying that if six of them are allowed to march in the parade, the rest of them are marching, too."

"Not in costumes, they aren't," I put in.

"How soon will the damned bus get here?" the chief asked, with an annoyed glance at me.

"Well, that's part of the problem, sir," Sammy said. "We're having trouble rounding up a driver, and it's going to be a bear getting it through the crowds until after the parade, so if we just let the geese march themselves to town . . ."

The chief strode off, with Sammy trailing behind him.

"Let's get Rufus moved," Horace said. "And let the chief deal with the geese."

"Right," I said. "Unless — Rufus, would you like to come inside where it's warm? You're welcome to stay in the house."

Rufus looked wistful.

"I'd appreciate that, ma'am," he said. "But

I'm sort of supposed to be guarding everyone else's stuff."

Horace and I helped him relocate not only his stuff but the stuff the other scouts had left behind in the two deerskin tents. Then we trudged back up to the house. Horace peeled off at the barn. I looked around and realized that I'd left my clipboard, the outward and visible sign of my office, in Eric's hands.

I pushed through the crowd, looking for Eric. Fragments of carols, hymns, and spirituals echoed from every corner of the yard, as the various choirs, bands, and strolling musicians rehearsed.

I walked past one of Mother's brainstorms — what I called Charity Alley. It had been my idea to invite a handful of charity and social service organizations to set up temporary stands here at the staging ground, but having them on either side of the path everyone had to take to get to the Port-A-Potties was definitely Mother's idea. From the looks of it, a fairly successful one.

Some people, though, could resist even the most heartwarming of causes. I saw Ainsley Werzel dashing down Charity Alley as if it were lined with piranhas and saber-toothed tigers instead of harmless souls like the uniformed Marine staffing the Toys for

Tots booth and the cheerful Salvation Army women with their bells. He spotted me and hurried over as if seeking protection.

"So what's with all this charity stuff?" he asked. "You've got the Salvation Army, Goodwill, Toys for Tots, America's Second Harvest, Kiva, Oxfam — what gives, anyway?"

" 'At this festive season of the year, it is more than usually desirable that we should make some slight provision for the poor and destitute, who suffer greatly at the present time,' " I quoted.

"The town doesn't look that bad off," he said. "Are you trying to tell me that you've got a lot of poor people here in Caerphilly?"

"No," I said. "I'm trying to quote Dickens. We just thought it would be nice to give people a chance to remember the true meaning of Christmas."

"Nice?" Werzel said. "Every time I turn around, someone's got their hand out. Anyway, I've been looking for someone who can answer a few questions."

"Glad to answer anything I can," I said, though I don't think I managed to feign much enthusiasm.

"So how come it's the town police chief who's doing all this investigating?" he asked. "I thought Virginia counties had sheriffs."

"We do," I said. "But Sheriff Price is getting along — I think he must be ninety by now. He can't do as much as he used to, so when the town hired Chief Burke, the sheriff appointed him assistant sheriff. The police officers and the deputies all report to him. In fact, it's really all one force, so they all get to choose whether they'd rather be called 'deputy' or 'officer.' "

"So this is just a temporary situation, then?" he asked.

"No, it's been going on for five years."

"Five years? Isn't the sheriff an elected official? You haven't had elections in five years?"

"We had them, yes," I said. "And reelected Sheriff Price."

"You reelected a guy who doesn't do anything?"

"A lot of voters do that," I said. "At least we know we're doing it. And he doesn't do anything wrong, which is more than most places can say about their elected officials."

Werzel shook his head.

"I'm guessing he ran unopposed."

"No," I said. "There were two other candidates. But everyone liked Sheriff Price's campaign platform better."

"And just what was his campaign platform?"

"That if elected he'd reappoint Chief Burke as assistant sheriff and stay out of his way," I said. "About the only people who had a problem with that were the felons the chief has put away, and they don't get a say anymore. It was a landslide."

Werzel shook his head and walked away, scribbling in his notebook. I could tell he didn't quite believe me. Clearly he'd been in the big city too long. And he wasn't just avoiding the Salvation Army kettle — he was giving it an ostentatiously wide berth.

A pity we already had someone playing Ebenezer Scrooge on the Dickens float.

Floats. I checked my watch, and realized that the time had flown faster than I realized. I only had thirty minutes until parade time.

I fought back a moment of panic. I'd spent hours rearranging the cards that represented the various floats, bands, and other participants into the optimal order and then negotiating with everyone to keep as much of that structure intact as possible. But with half an hour to go, I suddenly realized that however useful all that planning had been — if for no other reason than to keep my own sanity intact — it was time to let go of my vision of the perfect parade and let the real thing happen. As long as the Twelve

155

Days of Christmas appeared in the proper order at the beginning of the parade and Santa brought up the rear, no one else would know or care if the rest of the participants weren't all neatly arranged in the agreed-upon order.

I headed for what I'd come to think of as the starting line. My nephew, Eric, intercepted me before I'd gone more than a dozen steps.

"There you are," I said, reaching out to take the clipboard he was carrying.

"Aunt Meg," Eric said. "Can you do something about Cousin?"

I was about to say "Cousin who?" and was already looking around for a familiar Hollingsworth face when I remembered that Cousin was the name of the donkey Rose Noire had recently adopted. We'd originally named him after a particular cousin whose obstinate personality resembled a donkey's, but Mother had protested strenuously, and we'd compromised by just calling him Cousin.

I turned to see that Rob was trying to coax Cousin up the ramp onto the truck for the live nativity scene. Mary, Joseph, and assorted shepherds were standing around looking impatient, waiting for their turn to mount the ramp. What in the world . . . ?

I strolled over.

"Why don't you give it up?" I said to Rob. "Clearly Cousin isn't interested in being on the float, and I can't imagine anyone really wants to ride all the way to Caerphilly with an unhappy donkey."

"But we have to have a donkey!" Rob said, continuing to tug at Cousin's lead. "Like all the carols say. 'The friendly beasts around him stood' and 'the ox and ass kept time' and all that."

The elderly ox was already lying down and chewing his cud in a faux rustic pen atop the float, along with two of Seth Early's spare sheep.

"Don't you think you could just let him follow on behind the float?" I asked. "A century ago, Cousin would have had to pull the float, so I'm sure he'd be perfectly happy to walk behind."

"It's just not the same," Rob said.

Just then, Cousin suddenly took a couple of quick steps up the ramp. The abrupt slacking of the rope took Rob by surprise, and he fell backward. Cousin took advantage of Rob's fall to back down almost to the bottom of the ramp. By the time Rob had scrambled up and grabbed the rope again, Cousin once more had all four feet firmly braced, and two of them were back on solid ground.

"They've been at it for half an hour," said a shepherd who was cradling a live chicken in her arms.

Half an hour.

"Rob," I said. "We don't have time to fool around with Cousin. He can walk behind the float."

"But —"

"Rob, move your . . . donkey!" I snapped.

Rob blinked, then slackened the reins and allowed Cousin to back the rest of the way off the ramp. The shepherds and the Holy Family began rapidly filing up.

"Sheesh. You sounded just like Mother for a minute," Rob said. "I just wanted him on the float because I knew there's no way he'd walk all the way to town. What if he stops halfway there?"

He did have a point. Cousin was notoriously lazy — that and his foul disposition had gotten him expelled from the herd of donkeys the zoo kept for giving rides to children. He'd have been on his way to a glue factory if Rose Noire hadn't felt sorry for him.

Inspiration struck.

"Make sure there's someone around to lead him home, then," I said. "He's certainly not going on the float."

I frowned at Cousin, who laid back his ears. Since the rest of the live nativity scene had now taken their places, the ramp was unobstructed. I went to stand in front of it, and crossed my arms.

"In fact, forget it," I said. "Cousin stays behind. Take him back to his stall."

I pointed dramatically to Cousin and then toward the barn.

Cousin, his ears still laid back, walked up to me and butted me with his head. I pretended to lose my balance and stepped aside. Cousin trotted up the ramp and into the pen, where he shoved the sheep aside to attack the hay supply.

"Meg, you're a genius!" Rob said.

"Remind me later to see if Clarence does obedience training for donkeys," I said. "And in the meantime, go find the rest of the leaping lords and bring them to the starting line. And — oh, dear."

The Virgin Mary had just winced and clutched her enormous belly.

Rob followed my eyes and turned pale.

"Should I get Dad?" he said.

"No!" I said. "Dad's Santa, remember? Besides, it's her first. It could take hours."

"But shouldn't she have a doctor? And head for the hospital?"

"She will be heading for the hospital as

soon as we get the parade on the road. And Dad's not the only doctor in town. Aunt Penelope's over at the first aid tent, already on alert. She can throw on a shepherd's cloak and ride on the float, and Mary will have an actual obstetrician if she needs one."

I pulled out my cell phone, dispatched Aunt Penelope to the Nativity float, and went looking for Dad, to make sure he was in his Santa costume and not getting ready to preside over a delivery.

I finally spotted him running by with his Santa pants and boots on and the red jacket still thrown over his arm.

"Dad! Where are you going!" I shouted. "And why aren't you in costume yet?"

"Meg, you've got to come see Caroline and her Uzis!" Dad called over his shoulder as he ran past me on his way . . . somewhere.

Uzis?

I ran after him.

CHAPTER THIRTEEN

"What do you mean, Uzis?" I asked when I caught up with him. "We don't want any weapons in the parade on top of . . . everything else. Peace on earth and good will to all men, remember?"

"Not Uzis," he said. "O-O-Z-I-Es. It's what you call elephant handlers."

"Silly me," I said. "I thought you called them mahouts,"

"In India, yes," Dad said. "But these handlers are Burmese. Mahouts would have been better — the Burmese don't really celebrate Diwali. But I don't think anyone will notice. Aren't the costumes fabulous?"

We had reached the sheep pasture — now also functioning as an elephant pasture. Yes, the costumes were fabulous — both the oozies' costumes and the elaborate trappings decking the elephants were a riot of bright, contrasting colors and winking jewels. Undoubtedly fake jewels, but still, I hoped Mother didn't catch sight of the elephants and their riders until after the parade, or she'd try to desert Dickens for Diwali.

The fence was solid with tourists snapping photos continuously, like paparazzi on Oscar night, bathing the elephants with the flicker of flashes like heat lightning. Fortunately the elephants seemed oblivious to the tourists. The larger elephant was eating hay, delicately lifting small wisps with his trunk and tucking them neatly into his mouth. The other elephant was having his foot examined by two of the three oozies and an enormous white goose that I assumed was Clarence in one of the substitute costumes. Evidently the geese had won their battle to march into town.

"Caroline!" Dad called out.

The smaller of the two oozies turned, waved to us, and began slowly walking over. I recognized the woman in the jeweled turban who had brought the elephants.

"Meg, this is Caroline Willner," Dad said. "From the Willner Wildlife Sanctuary. Isn't it wonderful that she could bring both of her elephants?"

"Nice to meet you," she said.

I muttered something, but I was almost inarticulate with surprise. From the tales

162

Dad, Clarence, and Dr. Blake had told of Caroline Willner's exploits, I was expecting a strapping Amazon in the prime of life. Caroline was under five feet, plump, and probably in her eighties. She looked like someone's grandmother dressed up to go to a costume party.

"Of course," she went on, "Monty will never forgive me for upstaging his camels. He'll throw a fit when he sees us."

Monty? She meant my grandfather. I didn't recall hearing anyone call him Monty before. And she didn't look the least bit anxious about the impending fit. When Montgomery Blake lost his temper — usually over some environmental or animal welfare issue, but sometimes over people stealing the spotlight from him — most people tried to be in another time zone.

I decided I liked Caroline.

"We should talk later," I said. "Meanwhile — Dad, you need to get your costume on. I'm starting the parade in about five minutes. And tell Clarence to stop playing with the elephants and change into some other costume. We can't have a goose driving Santa into town."

"Relax." I turned and saw Clarence's towering form, now incongruously clad in a bright green Christmas elf costume, complete with green tights and a sporty feathered cap. Evidently it was another larger-than-average SPOOR member ministering to the elephant.

"Don't let Dad get lost," I said. "I know since you guys are bringing up the rear, he'll have plenty of time to get distracted and wander off somewhere —"

"I'll stick to his side and make sure he's ready to roll by the time you're down to the last few floats," Clarence said. "Don't worry."

Reassured, I headed back for the starting line. On the way, I glanced over my shoulder. Dad and Caroline were standing by the larger of the two elephants, patting his trunk and talking away. Dad had apparently put down his red, fur-trimmed hat and coat in his enthusiasm to greet the elephants, and Clarence had picked them up and was hovering nearby like an enormous elfin valet.

As I passed by the shepherds, I stopped to say a quick word to Rose Noire.

"Okay, keep your eye on the Nativity float," I said. "When that takes off —"

"Rise up, shepherds, and follow!" Rose Noire sang, in her light but beautiful soprano voice.

"Right," I said. "And while you're marching behind the float —"

"Leave your sheep and leave your lambs," she sang. "Only we won't be doing that, of course," she added, in a normal tone.

No, more likely the sheep and lambs would be leaving them, given how badly Seth Early's sheep seemed to be afflicted with wanderlust. A month or so ago we'd found one wedged into the tiny bathroom off our kitchen, drinking from the toilet like a cat. But keeping track of the sheep was Seth's problem, not mine.

"I'm afraid Mary may be starting to have labor pains," I said, getting back to the point.

"Mary?" I could tell by her expression that she was searching our family tree for a pregnant cousin.

"What's-her-name — the girl who's playing Mary on the float."

"Oh, my goodness."

"So if we have to haul her off the float and away to the hospital in the middle of the parade, can you step in as Mary?"

"Of course!" she exclaimed, and immediately threw herself into the role. She closed her eyes, crossed her hands over her heart, raised her chin, and assumed an expression of seraphic bliss.

"Great," I said. "When Rembrandt shows

up, I'll tell him you're ready for your closeup. Meanwhile, keep your eye on Mary and Aunt Penelope. And make sure Seth has enough shepherds to fill in for you if needed."

"Right," she said. "And I'll concentrate on beaming her good thoughts for a short labor."

She planted her shepherd's crook in the ground and began staring at Mary with the intensity of a Broadway understudy who has heard the show's star sneeze.

A few snowflakes floated down in front of me as I returned to the starting line.

"You're gorgeous," I muttered to the snowflakes. "But would you please stay up there in the clouds until I get this show on the road?"

As if in answer, they drifted down a little heavier. I shivered slightly, then pushed the cold aside and ceremonially uncovered the partridge.

Mother and the ladies of the Caerphilly Garden Club had done the First Day of Christmas float, building an elaborate and horticulturally improbable pear tree, festooned with both fruits and blossoms along with enough tassels, ribbon, feathers, garlands, and other gewgaws to keep a decorator's shop supplied for a year. It was done in tones of gold and yellow, with a few accent notes of green. Even the car pulling the float was color-coordinated, a butter-yellow Mercedes convertible with an evergreen-and-pear wreath on the front grill.

The partridge — a real partridge, chosen for his phlegmatic temperament from among the partridge flock at the Caerphilly Zoo after Dr. Blake had inspected the cage and pronounced it suitable — was resting under a yellow silk cage cover until his moment in the limelight began. I whisked the cover off, and the partridge blinked and looked around curiously. He looked a little incongruous in his glittering environment — had anyone bothered to warn the ladies of the Garden Club that partridges' feathers were mainly in earth tones? At least they'd had the sense not to suggest dyeing him to match his surroundings.

One of the junior zookeepers, dressed in a jeweled pear costume, was climbing onto the float.

"You've got the stuffed partridge, in case he gets stressed?" I asked.

The zookeeper nodded.

"Okay, let's get this show on the road," I said. "Wagons, ho!"

The president of the Garden Club began waving at the surrounding crowd while her husband started the convertible and eased the float into motion.

The audience lining the beginning of the parade route set up a hearty cheer.

I directed a small marching band from the middle school into place behind the float, and they launched into the first of who knows how many repetitions of "The Twelve Days of Christmas."

"Turtledoves!" I shouted.

The turtledoves followed — Miss Caerphilly County and her boyfriend, in feathered cloaks, sitting before a large heart made of chicken wire and pink Kleenex. Probably destined to become a large, damp papier mâché heart if the snow didn't hold off, but there wasn't anything I could do about that. I did scribble a quick line in my notebook suggesting that next year's Mistress or Master of the Revels insist on water- and snow-proof floats.

The three French hens rolled by, on their float from the French Cultural Alliance, followed by a fiddler playing "Un Flambeau, Jeannette, Isabelle." Four local auctioneers in blackbird costumes made rather odd calling birds, but the five gold rings were a crowd-pleaser: five local Olympic hopefuls, marching behind a set of interlocking Olympic rings made of hula hoops adorned with Christmas lights. Six Olympians, if you counted the horse one of the humans hoped to ride in the dressage event.

I was admiring the horse, who pranced and tossed his head as if he thought the whole parade had been arranged just to showcase him, when a whining voice piped up at my elbow.

"Are you people ever going to find my camera?"

Ainsley Werzel. Evidently the impending snow had inspired him to don a quilted down jacket, though I could still see the tail of the brown shepherd's robe hanging down below the jacket's hem. And he was shivering in spite of the jacket, and hunched against the cold. If I'd seen anyone else looking that miserable, I'd have felt sorry for them. In fact, to my surprise, I did feel sorry for him.

I finished shooing the Madrigal Society into place behind the Olympians and took a deep breath before answering.

"No," I said. "We haven't yet found your camera. I'm terribly sorry, but —"

"How can I cover this stupid, miserable parade without my camera?"

Stupid? Miserable? I might be biased, but I thought our parade was pretty damned wonderful. I bit back several satisfyingly withering replies. He was a guest, and what's more, a guest who had the power to make us look like idiots in the *Star-Tribune.* I looked around and spotted my nephew.

"Eric!" I called. "Can you do me a favor?"

He obediently trotted to my side.

"Can you go up to my office and find my digital camera? Mr. Werzel is going to borrow it —"

"I don't want your —" Werzel began.

"Just until we can find his camera," I continued, glowering at Werzel as I spoke, and enunciating every word with icy precision. "We understand that he needs the photos in his own camera, but at the moment we're a little too busy to look for it. I'm sure Mr. Werzel understands that we will do everything we can to find his camera . . . *after* the parade."

"Wow," Eric said. "You're getting really good at that Grandma voice."

He trotted off toward the house. I winced. Had I sounded that much like Mother?

I'd worry about that later.

"Of course, if you're not interested in taking photos of the rest of the parade . . ." I added, turning to Werzel.

"No, no," he said, backing away. "That's great. I could use your camera, sure. Just as long as everyone knows I really need my camera, too."

He backed away for about ten feet, then turned and fled in Eric's wake.

"Six geese a-laying," I called. "You're up!"

The six chosen geese stepped out in formation. I thought they looked more festive as white geese than they had as Canada geese, especially since they'd all hung garlands of holly and red ribbon around their necks.

All the rest of the SPOOR members stood around with drooping shoulders, looking ostentatiously forlorn and bereft. If they were trying to make me feel guilty, they were wasting their time.

"Seven swans a-swimming!" I called.

A tractor lurched into action, pulling the float on which seven budding prima ballerinas from Madame Vorobianinova's École de Ballet were twirling in full *Swan Lake* costume. A chorus of moos behind me announced that the eight maids a-milking were on deck. I could also hear the tambourines of the nine ladies dancing, the morris dancing bells on the shins of the ten lords a-leaping, and any second now the bagpipes would begin droning and the drummers would begin drumming.

"We might actually pull this off," I said, to no one in particular.

CHAPTER FOURTEEN

It took an hour and a half to get everyone on the road. Ainsley Werzel borrowed my camera and gave me a wide berth. I had no great confidence that I'd ever see my camera again, but if that was the price of not having Werzel underfoot for the rest of the parade, it was worth it. I could always bill the *Trib*.

About half an hour into the launch, word came back that Mary had definitely gone into labor, and one of the state troopers rushed her and Aunt Penelope to the hospital, but that I was not to worry, because Rose Noire was doing a great job as understudy.

I lost sight of the various floats and marchers immediately after they passed my post in front of the house, but farther along, the road went up a long, gentle slope. If I glanced over my shoulder, I could glimpse the floats and marchers before they disappeared over the crest of the hill toward town.

From those stolen glances, I realized that the SPOOR members, instead of marching in civilian dress, had found their backup costumes and infiltrated the parade in ones and twos, making it look as if we'd inserted white geese into the procession at random intervals as a sort of running gag.

One goose climbed into the convertible carrying the mayor of Caerphilly, who was too polite to kick him out, so the two of them sat side by side, waving to the crowd, all the way to town.

I saw several pairs of goose feet pattering along beneath the sinuous red silk Chinese dragon, and at least one pair beneath a maroon robe in the New Life Baptist choir.

By the time Seth Early's shepherds reached the hill, they were watching a mixed flock of real sheep and faux geese.

Several geese grabbed pails and joined the Boy Scout cleanup squads marching behind the large animals.

There were geese throwing Chanukah gelt from the Jewish Community Center's float, geese dancing along with the Clay County Cloggers, and geese waving and throwing confetti from the platform of the boom lift.

The Dickens float was the last straw. Since

Dr. Smoot was still at the crime scene, they'd turned to the surplus SPOOR members to find a replacement. Unfortunately, they picked someone who was much taller than Dr. Smoot, so the phantom's robe didn't come down far enough to conceal the feathered costume he was wearing underneath it.

"Oh, look," Eric said, as the float rolled away. "It's the Goose of Christmas Yet to Come."

"I give up," I said.

Clarence was as good as his word, and showed up just when I needed him, with Dad, in full costume, happily perched behind him, beaming and waving at everyone.

"Wow!" I looked down to see Cal Burke standing nearby. "Santa came after all!"

"That's Eric's grandfather, playing Santa," I said. "But he sure does look a lot more like Santa than poor Mr. Doleson, doesn't he?"

"Yeah," Cal said. And then he ran off happily to join the crowd of children tagging along in Dad's wake as devotedly as if he were the Pied Piper. I felt a sudden surge of pride — Dad really was a great Santa. For the first time in years, the children of Caerphilly would see a Santa Claus who loved his job and cared about Christmas as much as they did.

" 'He knew how to keep Christmas well, if any man alive possessed the knowledge,' " I quoted to myself. And I felt a sudden sadness that unlike Ebenezer Scrooge, Ralph Doleson never would have the chance of reforming his curmudgeonly ways.

The crowds that had lined the road were dispersing — a few to their cars, while most fell in step behind the children. Were they going to march all the way to Caerphilly?

Part of me wanted to jump in my car and follow the crowd. Or maybe race ahead on foot, hop on one of the last few floats, and enjoy the cheers and laughter of the crowds.

And part of me kept looking over toward the pig shed, where Chief Burke and his men were still doing . . . whatever they were doing. I hadn't barged in for at least an hour and a half now — hadn't even looked that way if I could help it — but I knew they were there. I also knew very well that Chief Burke wouldn't welcome my dropping in to see how the investigation was progressing.

"Nothing I can do about that," I muttered. After all the time I'd spent organizing the parade, I should at least try to enjoy it. Not to mention the fact that every single potential murder suspect I could think of had already gone to town with the parade. I headed for the house to fetch my purse from the safe room.

The kitchen looked as if a hurricane had come through. A hurricane with a bad coffee habit. I couldn't stand to leave it that way, so I made a quick pass through with a trash bag and then loaded and started the dishwasher.

Before the previous owners had added a new, larger pantry much closer to the food preparation area, the safe room had been the pantry. It was a small room opening off the mudroom, four feet wide by six feet deep, with white-painted wooden shelves lining both sides and an old-fashioned Chubb lock on the door.

I was fishing in my pocket for my copy of the key when I realized there was already one in the lock. Not good. I flung the door open.

The inside was a disaster. Had someone ransacked it? Or had whoever took over from Horace simply done a remarkably slipshod job of keeping things organized? I grabbed a few purses at random and searched them, finding plenty of money and credit cards, along with small valuable items like iPods and PDAs. So the chaos wasn't due to a thief hastily rummaging for loot.

Just bad oversight. The items neatly arranged on shelves with numbered tags on them doubtless dated from the earlier part of the day, when Horace had been in charge. But the later additions had simply been thrown in. A small pile of numbered tags that should have been attached to items lay on a shelf just inside the door.

I waded through the clutter till I could reach my purse. The SPOOR placards made up quite a large portion of the debris on the floor, so I decided to take them with me and hand them over to whichever geese I could find in town. I began dragging them out of the heap.

I suddenly realized that there was something familiar about the placards. Not the signs themselves, although I'd seen them often enough by now. About two-thirds of them were, as usual, mounted on slats — rough strips of pine one-by-two that I knew would leave horrible splinters in your hands if, like me, you were stupid enough to try carrying one without gloves. They were sharpened to a rough point to make it easier to stick your placard in the ground when you needed to take a break for splinter removal.

The remaining third were nailed to rough wooden sticks, two to two-and-a-half feet long, about an inch in diameter, and sharpened to a rough point.

Just like the stake that had killed Ralph Doleson. And like the murder weapon, they appeared to be made out of holly wood.

I stopped to put on a pair of kitchen gloves before pulling the rest of the placards out into the kitchen and sorting them into two piles. Twenty-four slat placards, all of which looked as if they'd seen quite a bit of use. Eleven somewhat newer placards mounted on holly sticks.

And one placard by itself, with no stick of any kind — though it had a few staples still clinging to the top and bottom center, showing where it had once been attached to something.

I pulled out my cell phone and dialed the chief.

"I'm busy," he said. "Is this important?"

"I think I found out where the killer got the murder weapon," I said.

He didn't say anything immediately.

"Well?" he said, finally. "I'm listening."

CHAPTER FIFTEEN

After hearing what I'd found, the chief showed up on the back porch in under five minutes and shook an impressive amount of snow off his coat and boots before stepping inside.

"Did you touch these before you put on those gloves?" the chief asked, nodding at the placard collection.

"Yes," I said. "Not only just now, but earlier, when I confiscated them from the SPOORs. And then I gave them to Rob to lock up in the safe room, so his fingerprints will be on them, too. For that matter, since I found the key in the safe room lock when I got here, anyone could have been in there."

While waiting for the chief, I'd laid the placards out neatly on the kitchen floor. The ones on slats were in two rows where our kitchen table would have been if we hadn't taken it to the barn to serve as a prop table, while the placards on holly sticks were lined up on the other side, in front of the sink and refrigerator. The stickless placard lay in the center of the room in lonely splendor.

The chief pulled out his cell phone and punched a couple of buttons.

"Horace?" he said. "I'm in Meg's kitchen. Can you come over here? Bring your kit."

He flipped his phone closed and continued to stare at the orphaned cardboard.

"We'll need your prints and Rob's for elimination purposes," he said.

"Okay," I said. "And Jorge Soto was helping Rob. And Horace might have touched them when he took them into the safe room. And —"

"We'll follow their history, thank you," he said. "It didn't occur to you to wonder why one of the signs was missing a stick?"

"I didn't notice the missing stick till just now," I said. "I didn't take them away one by one. I picked up the whole pile and carried them off."

"And you put them in here?"

"I gave them to Rob to put in here. Which, wonder of wonders, he actually did. He and Jorge. But you'll have to ask them whether they did it immediately or whether they left them lying around somewhere in plain sight for a while. You know Rob."

The chief nodded.

Horace came in with a blast of frigid air, shook himself like a dog to get rid of the snow, and looked questioningly from me to the chief. Then he took a look at the placards and went pale.

"Oh, my God," he said. "Those look just like —"

"Check that one," the chief said, pointing to the stickless placard.

Horace pulled on a pair of gloves and examined the cardboard.

"You think that thing used to be attached to our murder weapon?" the chief asked.

"I can't tell for sure till I measure these staples against the holes in the stake," Horace said.

"I know that," the chief said. "But if you had to guess?"

"Yeah," Horace said. "The sticks are exactly the same, and these staples should match the tiny holes on the murder weapon."

The chief took out his notebook and began scribbling in it.

"And look!" Horace said, pointing to something on the cardboard. "A couple of these staples have bits broken off. It's possible that the broken-off bits are still in the stake — which means I might be able to prove that the two were once part of the same staple."

He looked so triumphant and excited that I didn't have the heart to ask what good that would do. Even if he could authoritatively match the two sundered bits of staple, and even if that led us to figure out who had stapled the cardboard on the stake, I didn't see that his forensic staple analysis would get us one inch closer to figuring out who had used the stake to kill Ralph Doleson.

"That's nice," the chief said, in a rather mechanical tone. Clearly he shared my skepticism.

"I know it's a small bit of evidence, and there's no guarantee it will be useful, but you never know," Horace said. "Don't you remember that case in Canada where a few cat hairs proved to be the critical piece of evidence?"

"I do," the chief said, forcing a more cheerful demeanor. "And I completely agree. For all we know, the staple could be the key to the case, and I'm extraordinarily grateful that you're available to analyze it. I'm sorry if I seem a little distracted. It's been a long, hard day."

Horace seemed mollified.

"I should take all of these signs in for possible comparison analysis," Horace said.

"Meg, can I borrow some more big trash bags?"

I saw the chief open his mouth to veto the mass sign confiscation — the police station didn't have a very large evidence room, and the overflow usually ended up in the chief's office. Then he closed his mouth again, nodded, and looked back at his notebook. I handed Horace our box of trash bags.

"If you don't need me for anything, I'm going to catch up with the parade and see a little of the festival in town," I said.

"Good idea," the chief said.

Just then the power went out, as it nearly always did when we had heavy rain, high wind, or even a moderate amount of snow. Horace groaned. The chief made an impatient noise.

"We've got flashlights in the pantry," I said. I heard shuffling noises as Horace headed that way. "And there's a spare house key on the key rack. Horace, could you lock up when you leave?"

"Roger," Horace said.

I left them to it.

Outside, the air was bitter and snow was falling down in earnest — little tiny flakes, but so dense that they seriously reduced visibility. Maybe going to town wasn't such a great idea after all.

Of course, if I didn't go to town, Michael would have no way of getting home. And if I was going to be snowbound someplace — which looked increasingly more probable — I wanted it to be with Michael.

I took the truck.

CHAPTER SIXTEEN

Luckily the Shiffleys' snowplows and the parade traffic had kept the road to town relatively clear — so far. But I wasn't used to driving on snow, and my heart raced every time I hit the slightest patch of ice. Not seeing more than a few feet beyond the windshield was unnerving. I was relieved to think that Michael would insist on driving home.

I caught up with the parade just as Dad made his triumphant entry into the town square. They'd set up a massive throne on the portico of the town hall, and the crowds cheered hysterically as Dad raced up the two flights of marble steps and then jogged back and forth through the snow along the edge of the portico, fists upraised, looking like a Yuletide Rocky Balboa.

Then several volunteers dressed as elves emerged from the courthouse dragging fake sleds full of real presents, announcing the next part of the festivities. More elves began marshalling the assembled children into orderly lines and marching them up the courthouse steps for their moment with Dad.

I could see volunteers leading the last of the sheep off in the direction of the college barn. Everyone without children or animals in tow headed for the food. I didn't think any of the kids in line were likely suspects or witnesses, so I followed the rest of the crowd.

Every church and civic group in Caerphilly and Clay counties was selling some kind of food or drink. The New Life Baptists and the Clayville Congregationalists had rival barbecue pits. Caerphilly Presbyterian was roasting turkeys, Trinity Episcopal had baked hams, and St. Byblig's Catholic Church was dishing out its justly famous potato-leek soup. In the interests of ecumenicism, I abandoned my diet for the day.

I ended up in the Garden Club's dessert tent, sampling half a dozen kinds of cakes and cookies, accompanied by a mug of hot chocolate. Everywhere I went I'd been congratulated repeatedly on the success of the parade. The few people willing to talk about the murder were more interested in picking my brain than giving me useful information. Most people seemed to think I was weird, wanting to talk about murder this close to the holidays.

So once I'd filled my dessert plate, I found a place in a back corner of the tent where I could analyze the day's events in relative peace and quiet. And keep an eye on Dad — if I craned my neck just right, I could look past the trash barrels behind the tent to the snow-filled town square beyond. I couldn't quite see him, but from the length of the line leading up to his throne — not to mention the happy faces of the children and parents as they left the square for the refreshment tents — I could tell he was a success.

Just then a figure blocked my view — someone putting something in one of the trash cans. He lifted the lid, dislodging an inch or two of snow. Then he stuffed a pale blue paper bag into the trash. He looked around anxiously to see if anyone had noticed and I recognized him. Jorge Soto. Then he hurried off.

How odd. What was Jorge so eager to get rid of? If he'd just walked up and lobbed the bag into the trash in a matter-of-fact way, I'd never have thought twice about it, but his conspicuously furtive manner caught my attention immediately.

So I'm nosy. I finished my hot chocolate and went out to raid the trash can.

I could ignore the cans whose lids had more than a slight layer of snow, but four of them had been recently opened. The first two I inspected held only plastic bags full of discarded paper plates and cups, but in the third I found the blue bag. Inside was a gray sweatshirt with "Blitzen" stenciled on it. I remembered seeing Jorge wearing it before the parade. It seemed in perfectly good condition — almost brand new. Why had Jorge discarded it?

Could it have anything to do with the dark stains on the front, near the hem? Only a few small spots, but still —

"What's wrong, Meg?"

I jumped, even though I realized it was only Deputy Sammy. On impulse, I showed him the sweatshirt.

"Is that blood?" I asked, pointing to the spots.

He peered at it.

"I'm no expert," he said, finally. "Could be. Or it could just be chocolate. Does this have anything to do with the murder?"

"I don't know," I said. "Here, take it." I stuffed the sweatshirt back into the blue bag and shoved it at him. "Have Horace test those stains, will you?"

He took the bag, holding it as far from his body as possible, as if he thought it might explode.

"If the stains turn out to be blood, the chief will want to know where you got this," he said.

"If the stains turn out to be blood, I'll gladly tell him," I said. "Thanks, Sammy."

I went back to the town square. The snow was still falling, though not as heavily. Most of the kids had gotten through the line by now and the crowds were thinning. I strolled around the perimeter, looking at the Christmas decorations. Here in the heart of town, where the newest buildings dated from the 1920s, the town had gone in for Victorian, heavy on the evergreens with a lot of gold-sprayed pine cones, velvet ribbons, and the occasional cluster of fruit, real or fake. Mother thoroughly approved of the town square. And with the gently falling snow frosting everything, it looked particularly magical. I passed a photographer with a Nikon in his hands and a press ID hanging from his neck — presumably Ainsley Werzel's much-delayed photographer. I was pleased to see him busily photographing one of the more picturesque stores — the toy store, whose window was filled with a model train set running through a magical landscape of cotton snow, cellophane ice, and battery-lit porcelain buildings.

If I'd found Michael, I'd have suggested inspecting the decorations in other parts of town. The street where at least a dozen homeowners were locked in a fierce annual competition to see who could mount the most impressive light display. The dorms, with their funky, non-traditional Christmas displays. And the upscale glamour of the ritzy neighborhood where all the senior faculty lived.

But I was tired and my feet were getting colder by the second, so I decided to climb the courthouse steps. I could watch Dad at close range and scan the thinning crowds for Michael. Or, better yet, I could wait inside the courthouse. I found a bench just inside the door, worn smooth by the derrieres of countless witnesses waiting outside the nearby courtroom. I could sit there to think.

Come to think of it, it might be even easier to think lying down.

I was just closing my eyes when I heard a door open.

"I can't keep covering this up indefinitely," a woman's voice said. "Either you come clean and go to the police or I will."

Whoever she was talking to said something that I didn't catch, though I could tell it was a man's voice.

I lifted my head and peered down the hallway toward the voices. I couldn't see anything, but I heard the door to the back parking lot open and close.

"Idiot," the woman's voice muttered. I recognized it now. Caroline Willner.

I put my head back down and feigned sleep as she strode past me and out the front door, slamming it behind her.

Interesting. Who and what was Caroline threatening to go to the police about? And did it have anything to do with the murder? And if it did, was threatening a very smart thing to do?

Before I could figure out who Caroline was protecting, pretending to be asleep gave way to the real thing.

CHAPTER SEVENTEEN

I awoke, as I had for weeks, to the sound of Michael declaiming Dickens. Though normally he did it at the other end of our house, not in my ear when I was fast asleep.

" 'It was cold, bleak, biting weather,' " he declaimed. " 'Foggy withal: and he could hear the people in the court outside go wheezing up and down, beating their hands upon their breasts, and stamping their feet upon the pavement stones to warm them.' "

"That bad, is it?" I sat up and shoved my hair out of my eyes. I had a crick in my neck. However inviting it had seemed when I lay down on it, the courthouse bench wasn't a particularly comfortable mattress.

" 'The city clocks had only just gone three, but it was quite dark already,' " he said, more conversationally, as he sat down beside me.

"Actually, it's nearly six," I said, glancing at my watch. "I slept a whole hour."

"You needed it," he said, abandoning Dickens for the time being. "What do you say we go home and start broiling those steaks?"

"The power went out just before I left."

"Okay, grilling the steaks on the back porch."

"Perfect."

We headed back for the truck. The snow had stopped, but the temperature had plummeted into the teens after sunset and the only people left on the square were a couple of church groups packing up their kitchens and striking their tents. Luckily all the Christmas lights and the glowing shop windows made it easy to find our way back to where I'd parked the truck.

"So why did Chief Burke round up the whole SPOOR membership and haul them down to the police station?" Michael asked as we were dusting the accumulated snow off the truck.

I sighed, and as he eased the truck carefully onto the road and drove slowly home, I gave him a rundown on the goosefeather found at the scene and Ralph Doleson's reputation as a despoiler of eagles' nests.

"That explains it," Michael said. "Though if I were the chief, I'd take a close look at Doleson's tenants, too."

"Yes," I said. "I'm sure they have all kinds of motives for killing him. Of course, that only shifts the investigation from Dad's friends to Rob's. Doesn't anyone we don't know or don't like look the least bit suspicious?"

"There were hundreds of parade participants, and thousands of spectators, all milling around today," he said. "I imagine when the police start sifting through his papers and checking his background, they could come up with a few more suspects."

"Like maybe a posse of parents who thought Doleson's surly behavior was ruining their kids' Christmases?" I asked. "Just how did Ralph Doleson get the role of Santa to begin with? He's not my idea of a proper Santa."

"Nor mine," Michael said. "But at least he was an improvement on the last two Santas."

"What was wrong with them?"

"That's right, it was all before you came to town. My first Christmas here, Wilmer Pruitt had the role."

"Wilmer? Isn't he —"

"Serving time down in Richmond for shoplifting, yes," Michael said. "They fired him as Santa a couple of years before. The police department got tired of stationing a burly armed elf on either side to keep him from pilfering the present bag or picking the children's pockets. After they fired Wilmer, the Shiffleys got one of their clan chosen."

"Figures," I said. The Pruitts and the Shiffleys were the two oldest families in town. The Pruitts were rich and treated the town and the college as their personal fiefdom. The Shiffleys had cornered the Caerphilly market in plumbing, carpentry, and every other skilled or unskilled angle of the building trade. The two families weren't exactly Montagues and Capulets, but there was no love lost between them.

"Orville Shiffley was a very popular Santa until the year he showed up completely blotto ten minutes before parade time."

"Shades of *Miracle on 34th Street.*"

"Not the first time he'd appeared less than completely sober," Michael said. "That alone wouldn't have disqualified him. A very cheerful drunk, Orville. But they had to find a replacement Santa in a hurry when Orville fell off the 4H Club float and broke his leg."

"Bet Orville wishes he'd stayed in the sleigh," I said. "What was he doing on the 4H Club float?"

"The can-can, apparently. Anyway, Doleson filled in at the last moment, and after that we were stuck with him."

"Doesn't sound as if either previous Santa's a viable suspect, then," I said. "Even knocking Doleson off wouldn't get back their jobs."

"No," Michael said. "After today, I think your father has a lock on the job for next year, if he wants it."

"He'd love it," I said. "I hope someone got a few pictures of him."

"Werzel's photographer did. Which reminds me — I've got your camera in my pocket. Had to find someone to burn Werzel's pictures on a CD before he'd give it up, but I figured if we let him go back to D.C. with it we'd never see it again."

"Has he gone back to D.C.?" In front of Michael, I didn't have to disguise my eagerness.

"No idea," he said. "Let's hope so."

As we pulled in, I saw almost no cars around the house. The few left belonged to relatives who were over at Mother and Dad's farm having an enormous potluck supper. Even the police had gone, though they'd left a padlock on the pig shed door and several miles of yellow crime scene tape wound around it. Given the snow drifts and the arctic cold, I didn't think too many people would drive by to see the crime scene tape, but doubtless it made the chief happy to know it was there.

We went in through the kitchen, to avoid tracking too much snow and mud into the front hall, and I noted with delight that someone — probably Horace — had tidied the kitchen back to normal. Possibly cleaner than normal, if Horace had been involved. Ever since he'd become a crime scene technician, he didn't consider a room clean if he could find any trace evidence in it.

"Nice," Michael said. "Let's see what your mother's minions have accomplished in the rest of the house."

Mother had volunteered to decorate the interior as well as the exterior. She'd had her crew doing the decorations all morning, and we'd both been too busy to check the results. Mother's taste and mine didn't always agree, so I braced myself as we stepped out into the front hall.

"Oh, my," Michael said. "She's done a fabulous job."

I had to agree. Mother had continued the evergreen and red velvet bow motif from outside into the hall. Garlands ran up and down the banisters and around the door and window frames, with sparkly gold bells here and there as accents. Nests of candles surrounded by sprigs of holly decorated every horizontal surface, and an intricately woven ivy globe with a sprig of mistletoe inside hung from the central light fixture.

Evidently she'd rejected our eight-foot artificial tree as highly unsuitable, and substituted a twelve-foot real spruce. She'd probably raided every chic Christmas boutique in the state to find enough glittering baubles to cover it, but I was touched to see a few familiar favorite ornaments that usually graced the family tree tucked in between the sparkly glass balls, gilded cherubs, feathered birds, and other brand-new finery.

The evergreen boughs draping the living room walls were festooned with the holiday cards we'd received from friends and family. I tried not to think how many. I was using the parade as my excuse to send out holiday cards after Christmas. After all, that's why I called them holiday cards. New Year's was also a holiday. So was Valentine's Day. Maybe even St. Patrick's Day.

Michael flipped our stockings up onto the mantel and lit the fire before we checked the dining room. Mother had done it up in a food motif, accessorizing the ubiquitous evergreen boughs with gold-painted carved apples, pineapples, pomegranates, grapes, strawberries, and bananas. More gilded fruit formed a centerpiece on the table, surrounded the candles in the windows, and nested between the dishes and glasses in the built-in china cupboard. King Midas would feel right at home.

She had also dug out all our wedding present silver and arranged the serving pieces in a nest of holly and ivy on the sideboard, giving the impression that if you lifted the covers you'd find an elegant feast.

My stomach growled at the thought.

"It's fabulous," Michael said. "We'll thank her tomorrow. Let's grill."

He went out to the kitchen to find the steaks. I started to set the table — with the good china. Mother's décor deserved it. I was opening the silverware drawer when I heard an odd sound, and went to the living room to look outside.

"Is that what I think it is?" Michael asked, sticking his head out of the kitchen.

"If you think it's sirens, then yes."

A police car raced by with its lights flashing. As they passed our house, they cut the sirens. How odd.

"Where do you suppose it's going?" Michael mused.

A second police car passed, followed by a car that could have been the chief's. It was hard to tell through the tall hedge that separated us from the road, not to mention the fact that they were all going so fast. Dangerously fast, considering the condition of the roads.

"They're going down to the Pines," I said.

"You don't know for sure."

"Where else?" I asked. The road meandered past half a dozen farms, then deadended at Caerphilly Creek, where Ralph Doleson had transformed an abandoned textile factory into the Spare Attic and a run-down motel into the Whispering Pines. "And I bet it's something about the murder."

"I suppose we'll find out in the morning," Michael said, looking wistfully at the fire.

"Or we can follow them, and find out now," I said, heading for the hall closet.

"That's crazy," he said. "What if we get stuck in the snow?"

"It would take a lot to stop the truck. And it's only a few miles. We could walk home if worse came to worst. 'Walking in a Winter Wonderland,' like in the carol."

Michael didn't argue that hard for staying in, which meant his curiosity was as bad as mine. We threw on all our warm clothes, climbed into the truck, and set off down the road at a considerably slower pace than the police cars had gone.

CHAPTER EIGHTEEN

We had to pull over twice on the way to let faster-moving vehicles pass. One was another police car, and the other was a car with D.C. license plates.

"Could that be what's-his-name?" Michael asked. "The reporter?"

"Werzel," I said. "More than likely. I bet he's got a police scanner and overheard whatever's going on."

When we reached the end of the road, we found that the police cars were all clustered in the parking lot of the Spare Attic. All the Pines residents were out in force, watching — some of them with coats thrown hastily over pajamas.

"Maybe you should park the truck by Rob's unit," I said. "We can always say we came to visit him."

"Not that we'll fool anyone," Michael said. "Like, say, the chief, if he asks us what the blazes we're doing here."

But the chief wasn't visible. I assumed that he and most of his officers were inside. The only one I could see was Sammy, who was outside arguing with Ainsley Werzel.

Sammy wasn't really doing much arguing — just standing in front of the entrance with his arms crossed, shaking his head, and saying a few words now and again. Werzel was yelling and gesturing histrionically, like a coach disputing an umpire's bad call in the World Series.

I spotted Jorge Soto in the crowd. Had Horace tested the sweatshirt yet? I wondered. Surely the stains would only turn out to be chocolate. Or maybe barbecue sauce. Or —

Jorge saw me looking his way, left the group he was standing with, and came over. I moved a little closer to Michael.

"What's going on?" I asked.

"Burglary, we think," he said. "We heard sirens, and then all the cops in the county showed up. There's a humongous truck parked on the other side of the Spare Attic — you can't see it from here. We figured someone must have tried to break in. Stupid thing to do. Like there's any doubt that it's related to Doleson's murder."

"Related how?" Michael asked.

"If they catch the burglar, isn't it almost

certain they'll have the killer?"

"Maybe someone just tried to take advantage of Doleson's death to burgle the place for some reason unrelated to the murder?"

Jorge shrugged.

"Maybe," he said. "I guess there could be more than one person wanting to break in there. After all, that's obviously where he keeps the dirt."

"Dirt?" I echoed.

"Stuff he was blackmailing people with."

"Doleson was a blackmailer?" I asked. "Are you sure? How do you know?"

"He was a blackmailer, yeah," Jorge said. "And I'm very sure, because he tried to blackmail me."

"About what?" I asked. "Sorry — maybe I shouldn't ask, but —"

"He threatened to turn me over to Immigration if I didn't pay up."

Oh, dear. Was Jorge illegal? Not only did I like him, but he was a key employee at Mutant Wizards. Could the company get in trouble for having him on staff? Even though he'd passed a background check before hiring? Would the police scrutiny surrounding the murder cause a problem for him? Could Rob somehow arrange to sponsor him legally? It would be a small disaster if the company lost him. Then again, if he'd lied about his immigration status . . . and there was that damned sweatshirt.

He must have guessed from my face some of what was going through my mind.

"Oh, don't worry, I'm legal," he said. "Got my green card, working toward naturalization."

"That's a relief," I said.

"But I figure Doleson snooped around in my room — we all know he does it — and found some of the papers I had there. In my spare time, I do volunteer work at the Latino Community Center, helping people cope with the ice."

"The ice?" I repeated, looking down at the snow, slush, and ice at our feet. Surely immigrants had bigger problems to cope with than adjusting to the normally mild Virginia winters.

"Immigration and Customs Enforcement — ICE," he explained. "We don't get many illegals at the center, but even people who are legal need help dealing with the bureaucracy — it's hard enough to do if English is your first language. People who need help getting their working permits renewed. People who are legal but want to apply for citizenship. People in danger of losing their green cards over some minor brush with the law, like a traffic offense. My English is good enough to decipher the forms. And I'm no lawyer, but I know when to call one in."

"That's great," I said. And I meant it; particularly since, given how busy the programmers at Mutant Wizards were, he didn't have all that much spare time to begin with. I hoped I was suspecting him unjustly.

"You pay it forward," he said, with a shrug. "Anyway, I guess when he saw all the immigration information I had, he jumped to the conclusion I was illegal, and thought he'd try to squeeze me."

"Did you report him?"

"I thought of it," he said. "But he was a real vindictive guy. Might try to do something to get back at me."

"What could he possibly do?"

Jorge looked uncomfortable. I saw him glance over to where Werzel was still pacing back and forth like a caged tiger in front of Sammy's guard post. Yeah, smart to make sure the press was out of earshot before talking about blackmailable secrets.

"Before I found out he was spying on his tenants, I sometimes invited the people I was helping over to my apartment," he said. "I don't always know their status when they first come to see me. If they're illegal, I tell them that there's not much I can do and refer them to an immigration lawyer I know. But what if Doleson spotted someone who turned out to be illegal? He could report me and I'd lose my green card like that!"

He snapped his fingers and shook his head sadly.

"It'd be your word against his," I said.

"Yeah, but he'd have his digital photos," Jorge said. "Hard to explain those away."

"Digital photos?"

"He's always taking pictures of people coming and going," Jorge said. "He's been doing it for years — no idea why."

"I can guess," Michael said. "Up until five or six years ago, the Pines was the sort of motel couples went to if they didn't want to be seen together."

"Yeah, it always was a dive," Jorge said, wrinkling his nose as if remembering a bad smell. We all glanced back at the ramshackle building. With several inches of snow softening its contours and hiding some of the shabbiness, it looked almost habitable.

"And it was the only motel like that in Caerphilly County," Michael went on. "So everyone knew where to look for their cheating spouses."

"You mean people were still stupid enough

to go there?" Jorge asked.

"You'd be surprised," Michael said. "Not everyone was smart enough to take their infidelities out of the county. But what really did Mr. Doleson's business in was when people found out he used his digital camera to take pictures of everyone who came there. And sold the evidence for a hefty fee."

"You're kidding!" I exclaimed.

Michael shook his head.

"He'd been doing it for years. Of course, until the last few years he used Polaroids. When people learned that he'd supplied evidence in a few bitterly contested divorces, his business disappeared completely. That's why he converted the place to apartments."

"Lucky he did," Jorge said. "Or I'd still be sleeping on someone's couch." Caerphilly's chronic housing shortage was legendary. "Anyway, even if he didn't have anything to blackmail me with, just reporting me would cause a major hassle. I know people who have spent years trying to clear up completely bogus accusations."

"But you think he was blackmailing other people?" I asked.

Jorge nodded.

"Everyone assumed his blackmail business folded when he converted the Pines to an apartment building," Michael said. "I guess everyone underestimated him."

"You know," I said, "this could explain why they kept Doleson on as Santa. Maybe he was blackmailing someone on the town council."

"I wouldn't put it past him," Michael said.

"When they seize his blackmail files, they'll find out," Jorge said. "I'm sure that's what the burglary is all about."

"You think he kept his files at the Spare Attic?" I asked.

"Yeah," Jorge said. "Most of the bins have walls made of chain link."

"I know," I said. "We still have a bin there."

"But Doleson's own storage place is a room with reinforced walls and a huge, fancy padlock on the outside."

"You've seen it?"

"Not myself, but I've talked to guys who have," he said. "And it stands to reason he wouldn't keep anything really valuable in his unit here at the Pines. The walls are like cardboard."

"Like?" I said. "The walls are cardboard, period. One night, when his neighbors were making a racket, Rob tried to pound on the wall and ended up putting his fist through it."

"So the killer is someone Doleson was

blackmailing," Jorge went on. "And then the killer came to steal the incriminating evidence before the police have a chance to find it. This could break the case wide open!"

"Or confuse it," Michael said. "After all, if Doleson was blackmailing a lot of people, the killer would be only one of multiple people desperate to remove incriminating evidence."

Maybe Jorge believed his theory that the burglar had to be the killer, or maybe he wanted us to believe it because it diverted suspicion from anyone who wasn't the burglar. Telling us about Doleson's attempt to blackmail him could be another very clever way to divert suspicion. I was suddenly glad I'd turned over the Blitzen sweatshirt to the police.

Michael and Jorge were so caught up in their discussion that they didn't notice the sudden flurry of activity at the door of the Spare Attic.

The police were leading out their suspects: Clarence Rutledge and Caroline Willner.

Chapter Nineteen

Caroline waved cheerfully at us, as if her midnight arrest for burglary were merely a continuation of the day's festivities. Clarence looked a little more serious, which meant that the grim reality of their situation had begun to sink in with him. Then again, perhaps Caroline, like Dr. Blake, had become accustomed to the occasional brush with the law in her years of rescuing and defending animals. Clarence would get used to being in hot water if he kept hanging around with Caroline and Dr. Blake.

Curiosity got the better of me, and I began to inch a little closer to the action.

Clarence and Caroline were both dressed entirely in black — black coats, pants, hats, shoes, and gloves — though the foot-and-a-half difference in their heights made the effect more comical than threatening. As I moved closer, I could see that Clarence's black garb was largely wool and leather, while Caroline had donned a quilted black velvet coat with faceted jet buttons and a fuzzy black crocheted scarf and hat set. What the well-dressed felon wears to an evening crime. Caroline had also smeared eyeblack under her eyes, the way football players do on sunny days, though presumably it was intended to reduce her visibility rather than to protect against glare. Apparently Clarence had decided that his beard made the black paint unnecessary.

"I'm afraid we'll have to take you down to the station for questioning," the chief was saying.

"Oh, dear," Caroline said. "In this weather?"

The chief scowled at her, but said nothing. I couldn't help myself.

"If you'd wanted better weather for your arrest, you should have picked better weather for your burglary," I said. "Do you need anything? Like the name of a good criminal defense attorney?"

I had pulled out my notebook-that-tells-me-when-to-breathe and flipped to the back, where I keep a list of useful phone numbers — including two local lawyers who had represented wayward friends and family members in the past. I ripped out a clean sheet and began copying the names.

"Thank you, dearie," Caroline said. "But I'm sure we can work this out amicably."

Clarence gave her a startled glance and stuck out his hand. I gave him the numbers. The chief looked annoyed, and Caroline shook her head as if sorrowful over his lack of confidence, but Clarence tucked the paper away in his pocket and seemed a little less stunned.

"Thanks," he said. "Say, could I leave my motorcycle at your house for the time being? I don't think the chief can spare anyone to ride it into town, and there's no place here to lock it up."

"Fine with me," I said. "Maybe Michael would be willing to try riding it back to our house."

"Absolutely," Michael said, stepping forward. "Happy to oblige."

The chief nodded.

"Sammy," he said. "It's getting colder by the minute. Why don't you check out that motorbike so Meg and Michael can be on their way?"

Sammy went over and removed the saddlebags from Clarence's motorcycle. We watched as he gave the bike itself a cursory once-over, then nodded. Clarence pulled his keys out of his pocket, held them up so the chief could see them, and then, after the chief nodded his permission, tossed them over to Michael.

"I should get going," Michael said. "In case the snow starts up again earlier than predicted. And while there are still some people coming along behind me to dig me out if this thing gets stuck."

"We'll have someone here for another hour or so," the chief said.

Michael nodded. He climbed aboard the motorcycle, started it, and began riding it slowly across the snow-covered parking lot toward the only slightly less snow-covered road.

I watched while the officers guided Clarence and Caroline into the back seat of one of the cruisers. The cruiser followed in Michael's wake, with the chief's car bringing up the rear.

There were still two police cars in the parking lot, though, along with an enormous truck that I recognized as Caroline's — the one she'd brought the elephants in.

Had she driven the truck out here in this weather? Or did they have another partner in their scheme, whatever it was?

Where was the animal angle in all this? With both Clarence and Caroline involved, there had to be a bird or animal welfare issue behind the burglary. In the several years we'd had a storage unit at the Spare Attic, before moving to our enormous house, I'd never seen any wildlife other than mice in the walls and birds nesting in the rafters. There were probably whole colonies of birds and mice there still — while Doleson might not cherish them and want to protect them, he would never have bothered spending money on extermination. No wonder the Spare Attic was rapidly emptying.

If the place had been a cosmetics testing lab, a fly-by-night puppy mill, or a dog-fighting ring, I could understand their interest in burgling it. In fact, if that had been the case, I'd have been surprised that they'd left Dad and Dr. Blake behind. But the Spare Attic?

Was the burglary related to the murder or just a distraction?

I wasn't going to get any answers here, and I wasn't getting any warmer, either. The inhabitants of the Pines were starting to drift back indoors, and I saw that Ainsley Werzel had taken refuge in his car and was talking to someone on his cell phone.

Make that trying to talk to someone on his cell phone. As I watched, he threw the phone violently onto the floor and I could see him mouthing what I suspected were curses. Cell phone reception in the remoter parts of Caerphilly County was unreliable at the best of times, and tended to shut down entirely in bad weather.

I got back in the truck and headed slowly for home.

Michael was just wheeling the motorcycle into our barn when I pulled into the driveway. I spotted a cluster of vehicles farther toward town, where the road wound through a small stand of trees. I went out to the middle of the road to get a better view.

Michael strolled up beside me.

"Motorcycles are definitely a lot more fun in the summer," he said. "I'm chilled to the bone. What's going on down there?"

"No idea," I said. "Should we go and see?"

"Not me," he said. "My teeth are chattering. I'm going to go in and build up the fire. You should join me."

"In a minute," I said. "There's someone heading this way."

Apparently Michael's curiosity was as strong as mine. Even though his teeth really were audibly chattering, he stayed with me until we recognized Deputy Sammy trudging toward us through the snow.

"Are your phones working?" he called.

"Went out with the power hours ago," Michael said. "And I haven't tried my cell phone recently, but I wouldn't count on it."

"Darn," Sammy said. "Ours aren't working either. And a big old tree fell across the road while we were out at the Spare Attic. No way to get over or around. Do you have a chain saw?"

"Sorry, no," Michael said. "We've got a couple of bow saws."

"Thanks," Sammy said. "But the trunk is two feet in diameter. I don't think a bow saw's going to be much use."

"I'm really sorry," Michael said. "I've been meaning to get a chain saw, but I just haven't gotten around to it."

News to me. I wasn't even sure Michael had ever used a chain saw in his life, and I couldn't think of anything he ever did that seemed to require one. Then again, chain saw cravings were definitely Y-chromosome linked. Michael and Sammy were shaking their heads solemnly, as if Michael were confessing and Sammy graciously absolving him of a serious moral failure. If only I'd known, I'd have given him a chain saw for Christmas instead of the llama.

"Maybe we can borrow one from a neighbor," I said. "Seth Early's only a mile away."

Sammy and Michael looked at each other, then shook their heads, as if admitting that even a chain saw wasn't worth floundering another mile through the snow with temperatures in the teens.

"Meanwhile, invite whoever's trapped on our side of the tree to come in and warm up," I added.

"You're got heat?"

"We've got a fire in the fireplace," I said. "And blankets. And we can make instant coffee on the camping stove. If you're hungry, we could even grill something."

"I'll go tell the chief," he said. He trudged back toward the cluster of vehicles.

While Michael stirred up the fire and started the water for coffee, I readied beds for the overnight guests we'd probably be having. I changed the sheets in Rob's room and the guest room, added extra blankets, and dragged the rest of the available bedding to the living room. Anyone who valued privacy more than heat could drag his bedroll into one of the empty bedrooms, and the rest could have the two sofas or bivouac at the foot of the Christmas tree on our camping mattresses.

"Do you think we've got enough blankets?" Michael asked.

"Probably not, but this is all we have," I said. "And it's not as if we can go out in the middle of the night in a snowstorm and buy more."

"We could borrow some gear from the Boy Scouts — I doubt if they made it back out to their campsite tonight."

"Great idea," I said.

Just then the door opened, and our guests stumbled in. Caroline, Clarence, Chief Burke, Sammy, two other Caerphilly officers, and Cousin Horace. The officers were all carrying plastic garbage bags and powerful flashlights.

"Meg, do you mind if we take the truck and the van into your barn?" the chief asked. "We can't leave the evidence unguarded, and I can't ask anyone to stay outside with it. The temperature must be in the teens by now."

"Fine with me," I said.

"And I'd like a private room where I can talk to Mrs. Willner," he said.

"How about the dining room?" I suggested.

He thought about it for a moment.

"Fine," he said.

I followed him to the dining room. He flicked the flashlight around, inspecting the room, while I tidied some of the gilded fruit and greenery off the table so he'd have room to work, and lit a few of the oil lamps we kept handy for our frequent power outages. Caroline came in and sat down.

Clarence followed her and hovered nearby.

"We don't want to talk to you," Clarence said. "Do we, Caroline?"

"I'm sure we can clear this up," she said. She looked ashen, and I wanted to order her to bed.

"But we don't want to —" Clarence began.

"Fine," the chief said. "You're not talking. You can not talk to me some more later, but right now it's Mrs. Willner's turn not to talk."

"Coffee?" Michael said, appearing with a trio of cups. Clarence grabbed one and fled to the living room after one last pleading look that was wasted, since Caroline was sitting back with her eyes closed. She smiled faintly as Michael handed her the second cup. He handed the third to the chief and left.

"Anything else you need?" I asked.

The chief walked over to open a small door in our dining room wall, pulled the rope until the dumbwaiter was level with the opening, and then ostentatiously propped the door open. Clearly he hadn't forgotten the time last summer when I'd used the dumbwaiter to eavesdrop while he was questioning suspects in another case.

"This will do fine," he said. "Thank you."

I walked out and closed the door.

"I'm going to do some laundry," I called to Michael. Which wouldn't sound implausible to him or anyone who knew me. I clean under stress.

"With no power?" he called back.

Rats. There was that small flaw in my cover story.

"I can still sort the dirty stuff and fold the clean," I called back. And I did go down and throw a load of sheets in the washer, so it was ready to run when the power returned. Then I waited until I heard Michael and Sammy going out the back door.

"We're off to burgle the Boy Scouts!" Michael called downstairs.

As soon as the door closed, I crept up out of the basement and dashed into the powder room off the kitchen. The powder room had originally been a short servants' hallway between the kitchen and the dining room. When indoor bathrooms became popular and servants too expensive, the owners had put a door at the kitchen end of the corridor, installed a sink and toilet, and blocked off the dining room end with built-in china shelves. But since only the back of the shelves separated the powder room from the dining room, sound traveled rather well. And given how much the boards at the back

220

of the shelves had warped over the years, I easily found a chink to peek through.

CHAPTER TWENTY

Caroline Willner sat at one end of our dining table. The coffee had revived her. She had clasped her hands over her stomach and was smiling benignly at the chief, as if this were a social visit rather than an interrogation.

"So of course, when Dr. Langslow asked me to bring the elephants, I thought it was a wonderful idea," she was saying.

"Yes, I understand that," the chief said. "I mean what were you doing at the Spare Attic this evening?"

"Loading our truck," she said.

"Yes, we noticed that," the chief said. "But according to the records in Mr. Doleson's office, the storage bin where we found you belongs to Mr. Norris Pruitt. You want to tell me why you were burgling Norris's bin?"

"We weren't burgling," Caroline said. "We were helping Norris empty it."

"At 10 P.M. in the middle of a

snowstorm?" the chief said. "What's so all-fired important that it couldn't wait till morning? He got snowshoes and a generator stowed away there?"

"We were rather busy earlier," she said. "With the parade and all. And I have to go back to the sanctuary tomorrow with the truck, so this was the only time we could do it."

She sat back, folded her hands in her lap, and smiled innocently at him.

"And Mr. Pruitt will confirm this if I call him?"

"Oh, yes," she said, but her voice sounded a little anxious.

"And you never considered that maybe this wasn't the right time to help Norris with his bin? Right after the building's owner had been murdered?"

Caroline shrugged.

"I'm not from around here," she said. "How could I even have known Mr. Doleson owned the facility without you telling me? I just knew it was Norris's bin."

"And the reason you brought this with you?"

The chief held up a pair of bolt cutters.

"Norris had lost his key," she said. "So careless of him. That was one of the reasons he needed our help."

She sat back and smiled calmly at him. The chief asked her the same questions several times over, in slightly different ways. Caroline remained steadfast and showed no further signs of anxiety. She even smothered the occasional yawn, which meant she was either a consummate actress or not too worried.

Or maybe just exhausted. I was yawning myself.

I heard noises on the back porch — stamping noises, as if several people were shaking the snow off their boots. I tiptoed out of the powder room and set another pan of water over the camping stove to heat as Michael and Horace came in, laden with sleeping bags.

A minute or two later, Caroline Willner strolled into the kitchen.

"Would you like some more coffee?" I asked.

"I don't suppose you have the makings for a martini?" she asked. "I would kill for a martini. That wasn't a confession, by the way, just a cliché."

Michael grinned.

"I could throw one together," he said.

"Make it two," I said.

"Three," he corrected.

"Extra dry, with an olive," Caroline said.

"In fact, under the circumstances, I wouldn't say no to an extra olive. Thank you, dear."

Michael went into the pantry to rummage for ingredients. Caroline sat down, leaned back in her chair, and closed her eyes. For a few seconds, she looked every minute of her age, and I wondered if we shouldn't be urging her to go to bed instead of plying her with alcohol. Then her eyes opened and I felt reassured by the slight twinkle in them.

"Your phones really are out?" she asked.

"Afraid so," I said.

"Pity," she said. "I really would like to get word to Norris. He'll be a nervous wreck."

I already suspected that it was Norris she'd been berating back at the courthouse. I deduced from her mentioning Norris that she either thought I knew what she and Clarence had been up to or was too tired to remember that I wasn't supposed to know.

"Just why were you . . . helping Norris Pruitt empty his storage bin in the middle of the night? Why didn't he come himself?"

"Too terrified," she said. "Nerves of butter, that's Norris. Of course, he's wonderful with wounded animals. I've seen him stay up all night nursing an injured falcon or feeding orphaned wolf cubs. But to come out here by himself in the middle of the

225

night? Never happen."

"Why would it have to happen?" I asked. "It's his storage bin. Why couldn't he just come out in broad daylight to clear it out?"

"Your martinis, madams," Michael said, handing us each an elegant stemmed glass. I took a sip and decided we should have inaugurated this particular wedding present a lot sooner.

"Excellent," Caroline proclaimed. "This one's a keeper, dear. To your first Christmas together."

We all drank to her toast. Technically it wasn't the first time Michael and I had spent Christmas together, but I'd stopped fighting the world's tendency to start the clock on our relationship with the day we'd eloped, forgetting all the interesting times that preceded it.

"Getting back to Norris," I said. "Why couldn't he just clean out his storage bin himself?"

"Didn't have the key," Caroline said.

"He couldn't have just asked Ralph Doleson for another key?"

"Doleson's the reason he doesn't have a key in the first place," she said. So much for not even knowing Doleson had owned the Spare Attic. "Changed the locks on poor Norris, and wouldn't give him a new key."

"Was he behind on the bin rental?" Michael asked.

"No, he was paid up a year in advance, the way Doleson always made people do," Caroline said. I nodded.

"Then what happened?"

Caroline took a long sip of her martini, savored it for a moment with closed eyes, and then swallowed.

"Norris has a little problem," she began. And then she left the sentence hanging, as if she'd said enough for us to deduce her meaning.

"When Mother says someone has a little problem, she usually means the person she's gossiping about is a galloping dipsomaniac," I said. "Is that Norris's problem?"

"Good heavens, no!" she exclaimed. "He's as sober as a judge."

Clearly she hadn't met some of Caerphilly County's justices.

"Then what's his little problem?" I asked.

"He . . . tends to borrow things."

"Oh, that little problem," I said, nodding. "Another kleptomaniac." We had a few of those in the family, too.

Caroline winced.

"Oh, I'm sure that's not it," she said. "He's just curious — always picking things up to look at them. And so easily distracted.

He . . . wanders off with things. I suppose the police would call it kleptomania."

"The police would call it larceny," Michael said. "Grand or petit, depending on what kind of things catch his eye."

"Let me guess," I said. "The bin was where Norris stashed the stuff he'd wandered off with while distracted."

"Exactly, dear," she said. "Every few months, we help him empty out the bin and return everything."

"Every few months?" I echoed.

"We have to do it fairly often," she said. "Before he forgets where he's found everything. I suggested labeling everything, but he really isn't very methodical about it. Sometimes, we have a fair number of things we can't identify well enough to return."

"So what do you do with that stuff?" I asked.

"Donate it to Purple Heart," she said. "We used to do the Salvation Army, but Purple Heart picks up — so convenient."

"I should go see if the rest of our guests have everything they need for the night," Michael said.

I suspected what he really wanted to do was find a quiet corner to howl with laughter without hurting Caroline's feelings. I wondered what Purple Heart and the Salvation Army would think when they learned they'd been obliviously receiving stolen goods.

"Ralph Doleson found out about Norris's little problem," Caroline went on. "And he changed the lock on Norris's storage bin and has been forcing the poor man to pay him money not to tell the police."

"He was blackmailing Norris."

"Oh, dear," she said. "That's such a nasty word."

"It's a nasty crime," I said. "So you decided to take advantage of Ralph Doleson's death to steal back the incriminating evidence."

"No, we planned to take advantage of Ralph Doleson's absence during the parade to steal back the evidence," she said. "Since I would be down here with the truck, and Doleson would be stuck for several hours in town, giving out presents. It seemed like the perfect opportunity."

"Until Ralph Doleson was murdered."

"Yes," she said. "That came as a horrible shock to us, and we almost gave up our plan. But Norris was afraid the police would start combing through all the bins in the Spare Attic and become suspicious, so we went ahead, a little later in the day than we planned. I suppose that wasn't such a good idea."

I didn't argue with her.

"Does Norris have an alibi for the murder?" I asked.

"He was helping me with the elephants."

"Doing what?"

"Helping put on their trappings," she said. "And fetching hay and —"

She fell silent.

"Running errands?" I suggested.

She nodded.

"And he was wearing the goose costume?"

Caroline nodded. She probably realized the goose costume was too multicolored to show blood spatter and heavy enough to protect the clothes beneath. She sipped the last bit of her martini and sighed.

"Would you like another?" I asked. "I'm sure Michael would be happy to bartend again."

"No, thanks," she said. "One's my limit after midnight, or should be. Is that offer of a bed still open?"

I showed Caroline to our guest room and made sure she had more than enough blankets. When I came back down, Michael and one of the police officers were unrolling the Boy Scouts' sleeping bags in the living room, as near the fireplace as possible.

They'd doused the oil lanterns, but the fire reflected off all the tinsel and lit the room with a flickering golden glow. Someone's battery radio was playing Christmas carols.

It would have been such a peaceful heartwarming scene if our uninvited guests had been relatives instead of cops, and if the back yard wasn't still festooned, under the snow, with crime scene tape. And if we didn't still have an unsolved murder in town.

At least I assumed it was still unsolved. I decided to risk seeing what I could learn from the chief.

CHAPTER TWENTY-ONE

I knocked on the dining room door.

"Yes?"

The chief sounded tired and cranky. I didn't blame him. I peeked in.

"They haven't found a chain saw," I said. "So we're making up beds for everyone."

He nodded.

"I'm putting you in Rob's room," I said. "It's the most comfy, aside from the official guest room, which we thought Caroline should have."

A faint smile.

"Can I talk to you for a minute?" I asked.

He nodded again and leaned back, looking more tired than wary. I came in and closed the door.

"I can tell you what you're going to find when you finish inventorying the contents of Norris Pruitt's storage bin," I said.

"Not another body, I hope." He sat upright again and suddenly looked much more awake.

"No, of course not," I exclaimed. "Only a whole bunch of bright baubles that don't belong to Norris, and would have been returned to their rightful owners if Caroline and Clarence had gotten away with their burglary. Norris is a magpie."

"A chronic shoplifter, you mean?"

"A kleptomaniac, I imagine. And one of Ralph Doleson's blackmail victims. You did know he was a blackmailer, right?"

"Well, I do now," he said. "I don't suppose you know any more of his victims?"

"Not yet," I said. "I mean, I heard rumors, but —"

I decided to shut up and hope he hadn't noticed the "not yet." He sighed, but didn't give me his usual lecture about not interfering with police business. That alone proved he was exhausted.

I thought of steering him toward Jorge, but decided against it. After all, the chief was investigating all the residents of the Whispering Pines. He'd have talked to Jorge already. And if Jorge turned out to be innocent, he wouldn't appreciate my singling him out. He seemed paranoid — perhaps justifiably so — about coming to the attention of law enforcement. Maybe I'd have a word with Jorge privately, urging him to tell what he knew about Doleson's blackmailing operations.

Then again — Jorge was looking more like a suspect all the time. Maybe I didn't want to have too private a word with him. Not until Horace had had time to test that discarded sweatshirt.

I'd worry about all that later.

"You'll probably find the photos or documents or whatever he uses to blackmail people with when you finish searching the Pines and the Spare Attic," I said aloud.

"Pretty broad area to search," the chief said. "You got any more specific suggestions?"

"They say Doleson has a large and very private bin at the Attic," I said.

"With a big old padlock on it. We'll be looking into that. Of course, we have to deal with Mrs. Willner and Mr. Rutledge first. At least now I understand why they both tried to confess to the murder."

"They didn't," I said, with a wince.

"Separately."

"I thought Clarence wasn't talking."

"This was in the heat of the moment, when we apprehended them. Now, he's keeping his mouth shut, except to say that as soon as his lawyer is available, he'll confess everything he knows about today's events, and not to listen to a thing Caroline says, because she'll just try to cover for him."

"If you ever arrest me, that won't be my definition of not talking."

"And Caroline keeps saying it was all her idea, and we shouldn't blame poor Clarence. Not that either one of them makes that plausible a suspect. Caroline's too short, and Clarence too well alibied. Thanks to those fool amateur videographers, we can prove he was giving the tourists elephant rides during the whole window of opportunity. But this puts a new light on it."

"It does?" My stomach tightened. I'd thought I was helping get Caroline and Clarence out of trouble. Was my attempt going to backfire?

"They could both be covering for Norris Pruitt," the chief said. "Which could make them accessories after the fact."

"*If* Norris is guilty," I said. "You haven't even talked to him yet — he could have an ironclad alibi."

"We've already talked to him," the chief said. "He was one of your blasted parade geese. One of the ones who's tall enough — I suppose your father told you what he and Horace figured out from the stake's angle of entry."

Dad hadn't, but only because I hadn't talked to him since the parade began.

"Exactly how tall did they decide the killer has to be, anyway?" I asked.

"At least six feet two. That narrows our suspect list down a bit."

"Still a lot of people who qualify."

"Yes, but the list of tall folks with a motive is considerably shorter," the chief said. "And Norris Pruitt has the same blasted lack of an alibi as most of the geese, and what's more, his costume has a noticeable shortage of tailfeathers."

"Oh, dear." Perhaps I shouldn't have repeated what Caroline told me.

Then again, if she and Clarence were helping Norris . . .

"Just one thing," the chief asked. "Were you the ones who reported the burglary?"

"No," I said. "We didn't know about it until we saw the police cars going by. And our phones have been out for hours. Didn't someone out at the Pines report it?"

"No," the chief said. "Their phones probably went out about the same time yours did. And you know what cell phone reception is like out here at the best of times."

"Don't you have some kind of caller ID on your 911 line?" I asked.

"It shows the burglary was reported from Geraldine's Tea Room."

"That's only two blocks from the police station. And Geraldine closes at six."

"Someone jimmied the lock on her back door and used the phone in her office to call in the report."

"Debbie Anne didn't recognize the voice?"

"Debbie Anne said the caller was deliberately disguising his voice," the chief said. "Or her voice. She couldn't rule out a female caller."

"And you thought it was me? No way. Do you really think I'm that shy and self-effacing?"

The chief sighed, took off his glasses, and rubbed his eyes.

"I thought maybe you were snooping around there, saw something suspicious, came into town to report it, and got cold feet at the last minute. Afraid I'd chew you out for interfering. And finagled the lock at Geraldine's so you could report it without being identified."

"Sorry," I said. "But it wasn't me, and I have no idea who it was. Must have been some other bashful good Samaritan."

Someone knocked on the dining room door.

"Chief?" Sammy Wendell opened the door

far enough to stick his head in.

"What now?" the chief asked. He sounded more tired than grumpy.

"We've finished inventorying the contents of Mr. Pruitt's bin," Sammy said. He looked as if about to say more, then glanced over at me and fell silent.

"Well?" the chief said. "Read it."

Sammy glanced over at me again, then shook his head and held up a sheaf of papers.

"It's a long list," he said. "Do you want the details or the summary?"

"Start with the summary."

"Okay," Sammy said. "Electronics: seventeen assorted cameras, six iPods, nine cell phones, three portable DVD players . . ."

I closed my eyes in dismay as Sammy droned on. The list also included jewelry, silverware, purses and wallets — many with the identification still in place — small bits of decorative china and glassware, items of clothing.

Norris Pruitt had been busy. If he'd accumulated this much stuff in just a few months, Caroline and Clarence must have been rather busy, too, after their previous visits to the bin.

Busy covering up for him. Were they still

covering up, this time for murder?

I slipped out of the dining room. Sammy was still reading as I closed the door behind me.

"Seven dog collars. Three squeaky toys. Two rawhide bones, partially chewed . . ."

Even without murder charges, Norris Pruitt was in a lot of trouble.

I heard the front door open and turned around to see who it was.

Ainsley Werzel.

"No way back to town tonight," he said. "Haven't you people out here in the sticks heard about snowplows yet?"

"We've heard about them, yes," I said. "But considering how few big snows we get here in Virginia, the county wisely doesn't buy a lot of expensive equipment that would spend most of its time rusting in a garage. And it's not the snow blocking the road; it's a giant tree that —"

"Whatever," he said. "Mind if I sleep in your barn?"

Chapter Twenty-Two

Better the barn than the house, I supposed, and I was about to give permission when I remembered what else was currently in the barn.

"You'd better bunk here in the living room," I said. "The barn's unheated and —"

"It's okay," he said. "I don't mind. I'm sure you've got a full house. Don't want to be a bother. No room at the inn and all that."

"Yes, but as I was about to say, the police are using the barn right now," I went on. "And I don't think they'd be too happy about civilians being in it."

"Well, if it's no trouble," he said. "I'll take you up on that living room spot."

I had the feeling he could be all kinds of trouble if he tried. His small, restless eyes barely met mine before taking off to examine every detail of the hall, and his fingers twitched slightly, as if he were already mentally composing some kind of sordid exposé. I hoped he knew nothing of Michael's long-ago career as a soap opera heartthrob and his more recent stint as an evil but sexy wizard on a cult hit TV show. Not that there was anything wrong with the fact that, unlike many actors, he'd earned a living during his New York years, but the college was more easily embarrassed. For that matter, any number of my family members had colorful pasts — or presents — that I would rather not see turning up in the *Star-Tribune.* Why couldn't the man have been stranded on the other side of that blasted fallen tree?

I waved him into the living room and was reaching to bolt the door when I heard a timid knock and opened it again.

Horace.

"Hey, Meg," he said. "The chief still up?"

"In the dining room."

Horace nodded and trudged toward the dining room. What was he so glum about?

A few moments later, Sammy came out and went into the living room. I tagged along. Clarence sat staring into the fire.

"Clarence?" Sammy said. "Chief wants to know if he can see you for a moment."

"I'm not talking without my attorney,"

Clarence said.

"He just wants to show you something."

Clarence thought for a moment, then heaved himself to his feet and followed Sammy. I tagged along again, but hung back just inside the dining room door.

Horace and the chief were staring down at something on the table. I couldn't see what without getting so close that the chief would notice me and kick me out.

"I'm not talking without my attorney," Clarence repeated.

"You don't have to talk," the chief said. "I'm going to talk to you. Do you recognize those?"

He pointed to Horace, who picked up a set of keys in one latex-gloved hand.

Clarence peered, then shook his head, clearly puzzled.

"You don't recognize them? Never seen them before in your life?"

Clarence tilted his head, perhaps sensing that there was a trap behind the words.

"Yeah, I know you're not talking now," the chief said. "But when we can finally get you and your attorney together, we're going to do some talking together. And you can explain to me how Ralph Doleson's keys ended up in your motorcycle saddlebags."

"What?" Clarence jumped to his feet.

"That can't be! I've —"

Then he remembered that he wasn't talking and clamped his mouth shut. Clearly he was tempted, though. Points to Clarence, not only for smarts, but for self-control.

"How do you know they're Doleson's keys?" he asked finally.

"We suspected they might be, from this," Horace said. With one gloved finger he singled out and held up a small metal disk with "RAD" engraved on it. "And several of them fit his apartment, his office, and the Spare Attic's front door."

"Someone could have put those in my saddlebags anytime," Clarence pointed out. "The motorcycle was just sitting around parked at Meg and Michael's house for hours before the parade, and then again for hours in town after the parade. And if I'd had his keys, why would we have broken into the Spare Attic? And — sorry. I'm not supposed to be talking."

"You're not forbidden to talk," the chief said. "You're just not required to. Of course, if you want to clear this up tonight . . ."

"I'll wait for my lawyer," Clarence said.

"Tomorrow, then," the chief went on. "Once you've talked to that blasted attorney of yours. In the meantime, I think we could all use some rest."

Clarence, Horace, and Sammy shuffled out. I lingered and watched for a few moments as the chief gathered up his papers.

"Of course, now Clarence has all night to invent an innocent explanation for the keys being in his saddlebags," I said.

He stood up.

"I prefer to think that he has all night to come to his senses and tell the truth," he said. "You still have a room left for me?"

"Room at the inn? Of course."

I led him up to Rob's room, on the third floor. I could see Deputy Shiffley laying out a sleeping bag outside the door of a bedroom at the other end of the hall, so I deduced that Clarence had opted for privacy over warmth and taken refuge there. I wished them all a good night and went down to see what Michael was up to.

I found him sipping the last of his martini and putting the steaks back in the freezer.

" 'Scrooge took his melancholy dinner,' " he quoted. "And so forth."

"Does that mean you've already eaten?" I asked. I'd grown used to Michael's habit of speaking in scraps of dialogue when he was directing or acting in plays, but tonight I was too tired to puzzle out his meaning.

He cocked his head for a moment, as if hunting for a bit of Dickens that fit the occasion, and then shrugged.

"Sorry," he said. "I know it's an annoying habit, all this quoting."

"It's interesting," I said. "And this is much nicer than when you were quoting *Who's Afraid of Virginia Woolf?*"

"I'm also too tired to eat now, and I'm even too tired to think of a Dickens quote to say so."

" 'And being much in need of repose,' " I quoted — though not, I suspect, with complete accuracy — " 'Scrooge went straight to bed, without undressing, and fell asleep upon the instant.' "

"Oh, well done!" he said. "Though I think I can manage the undressing part. And since I expect to be in much more congenial company than Scrooge was, maybe we should rethink that falling asleep upon the instant part, too."

"You're on," I said. "We'll see if you're too tired to remember anything from *Romeo and Juliet.*"

I peered into the living room on the way upstairs. The fire was dying down. Everyone was asleep, or at least huddled motionless in a sleeping bag, except for Ainsley Werzel. He was standing in a corner, muttering curses as he waved his cell phone around in what I could have told him was a fruitless quest for a signal.

CHAPTER TWENTY-THREE

December 24, 7:50 A.M.

Ding-dong merrily on high
In heaven the bells are ringing
Ding-dong verily the sky
Is riv'n with angels singing.
Glo-o-o-o-o-o-o-o-o-o-o-o-o-o-o-o-o-oria
Hosannah in excelsis!
Glo-o-o-o-o —

"Arg," I muttered, from under the covers. "Don't those angels know what time it is?"

"It's almost eight," Michael said, with a yawn. "I expect most angels get up at dawn for choir practice, and think we're pretty lazy, not being already awake to hear them carol."

I stuck my nose out from under the covers and realized that if I kept it out I'd risk frostbite. The odd gray color of the light peeping in through the break in the curtains meant we had not only plenty of snow covering the ground, but also more snow lurking in the clouds overhead, waiting to fall.

"Inconsiderate angels," I said. "You'd think there might be at least one seraph thoughtful enough to say, 'Hey, between the parade and the murder and having a dozen houseguests dumped on them in the middle of the night, they had a hard day yesterday. Let's let them sleep in.' Are there no night owls in heaven?"

"In heaven, certainly." Michael slid out of bed and went over to peer out one of the front windows. "But not, apparently, in the Baptist section. It's Minerva with the New Life choir."

"Someone must have found a chainsaw and cleared the road, then."

"Thank goodness," Michael said. "I was beginning to worry about my show tonight."

I opened my mouth to point out that the predicted second round of snow was a much bigger threat to Michael's one-man Dickens show than even the most enormous fallen tree. But I thought better of it. For all I knew, the meteorologists might have changed their forecasts again. And Michael was already showing subtle signs of pre-performance jitters. Why remind him that he might be getting worked up over a show destined to be snowed out?

I put a pillow over my face. The choir boomed one final, glorious, five-part "Hosannah in excelsis!" into the skies and then, after a brief pause, launched into "We Wish You a Merry Christmas."

"You don't suppose they're really expecting figgy pudding and a cup of good cheer?" I muttered. "I thought your history professor friend said that historically accurate wassail would be mulled beer."

"I'll put on the coffee," Michael said, heading downstairs. "I rather think that would be the suitable Southern Baptist equivalent. Especially before noon."

"Before noon? Try before dawn."

I pulled on my robe and stumbled over to the window. The singers were standing in a circle around our doorstep, their maroon robes brilliant against the snowy yard. Every syllable they sang came out as a separate little white puff, so when the whole choir got going, it looked as if they were sending up smoke signals. It was easy to tell that a couple of the choir members were just mouthing the words.

I could see my own breath, too, which meant that either the power was still off or it hadn't been on long. I flicked a light switch back and forth a few times. Nothing.

The idea of a cold shower in a cold house didn't appeal to me, so I threw on several layers of clothes and followed Michael downstairs.

He had pulled out our camping stove and was heating two enormous pots of water.

"We'll have to give them instant coffee," he said.

"I imagine they won't care as long as it's hot."

Roused by the carolers, our guests were waking up and either gathering at the front windows to appreciate the music or stumbling into the kitchen in search of caffeine. Except, of course, for Clarence, who went outside leading Spike — probably to take his mind off his legal problems with another canine behavioral therapy session.

Just as the water came to a boil, "We Wish You a Merry Christmas" gave way to a solo rendition of "Rise Up, Shepherds, and Follow." I selfishly grabbed one of the first cups of hot water, stirred in the instant coffee, and inhaled the steam as I blew on the top of the cup.

Okay, it was still too early, but the alto voice doing this solo was worth waking up for. I closed my eyes to enjoy both the music and the steam, and jumped when someone spoke at my elbow.

"Is Henry up yet?"

Minerva Burke, resplendent in her maroon robe, billowed into the kitchen.

"Not yet," Michael said, handing her a cup. "I'll start working on breakfast for our guests," he added to me.

"He cooks?" Minerva said. "No wonder you married him. Henry burns toast. Speaking of Henry . . ."

"He's up in Rob's room," I said. "Third floor. Want me to show you the way?"

Minerva nodded, Michael handed her a second mug for the chief and I led the way. But when we reached the second floor landing, she stopped.

"Can I have a word with you?" she asked.

"Sure," I said. I leaned against the banister. "What's wrong?"

"It's this murder investigation."

Had the chief asked her to warn me off?

"Don't worry," I said. "If I think of anything else important, I'll call the chief, and I won't interfere with his investigation by trying to dig up information myself."

"Well, I wish you would." She took a quick sip of her coffee. "I'd like him to spend at least part of the Christmas holiday with his grandchildren, and the way things are going, that's looking less and less likely."

251

"The investigation's not going well?"

"I have no idea if it's going well or badly," she said. "Not having seen the man since last night. But from the number of messages coming in, clearly it's still going. Someone has to keep working on it, and he's not going to ask anyone to do what he won't do himself. The more he works on it, the higher his blood pressure will rise. As it is, I can't in good conscience give him a piece of my sweet potato pie, and you can't imagine how much Henry loves that pie."

I made a sympathetic noise.

"I picked up tickets to that show of Michael's tonight," she continued. "But the way things are going, I'll be by myself. Again. I was used to doing without him on holidays back in Baltimore. Big city like that, you're bound to have a few people mean enough to shoot each other on Christmas or New Year's. But here — well, I expected better."

She shook her head as if sadly disappointed by the inconsiderate behavior of the local criminal classes.

"I'm not asking you to interfere," she went on. "But in a small town, people talk to each other more than to the police. Henry should learn to work with that. If you hear something he needs to know, please tell him."

I nodded.

"And if he won't listen, tell *me*. He in the room at the end of the hall?" she asked.

I nodded again and left her to wake the chief. I strolled downstairs and followed the intoxicating smell of cooking bacon into the kitchen.

I heard the chief and Minerva coming back downstairs again. Outside, Horace was handing out steaming cups of coffee, and I could hear cheerful voices chattering and car doors slamming. The New Life choir was moving on in search of new audiences. In the kitchen, I found Rob sitting at the table, wolfing down a plate of scrambled eggs and bacon. Michael had both burners of our camping stove going and was frying up more eggs and bacon.

"I made it!" Rob announced, as if reporting a major triumph.

"Are the roads bad, then?" I asked.

"Horrible," he said, through a mouthful of egg. "They're pretty full up over at Mother and Dad's. I had to sleep on the couch. By the way — look at this."

He held up his iPhone, which showed a rather nice picture of Michael on the camel.

"That's great," I said.

"Here, look through them," he said, handing me the phone.

I paged through his photos. Rob was getting to be a half-decent iPhone photographer. Quite apart from the good shots of Michael, I wondered if any of his photos might help with the murder investigation. If I could see them full size, that is.

"Can you give me copies of those?" I asked. "Not just the ones of Michael, all of them."

"Sure," he said. "Let me have that for a second." He took the iPhone back and began tapping on the screen. "There. I e-mailed them to you."

"You're getting signal?" Michael said, his hand reaching to the pocket where he kept his own cell phone.

"For now," Rob said. "Out here in the boondocks, it'll vanish again when the new storm gets going."

"That's right — you have Internet access on that thing," I said. "Can I borrow it back for a few minutes? I really want to see what the papers are saying about the murder."

"You just want to see if anyone said anything nasty about your parade," he said, but he handed over the iPhone. "Use it all you like. Snow makes me want to hibernate.

I'm going upstairs to take a long nap."

He slouched out of the room.

"So, if the roads are open, will the chief and his troops be leaving soon?" I asked.

"No idea," Michael said. "Sammy thought they'd want to use our barn for a while. At least I assume that's what he meant when he said they were still maintaining their incident command center."

"The chief must have sent him to some kind of training class," I said, as I fumbled my way to the Internet. "Horace always talks that way for a week or two when he's had some new kind of training."

I wasn't as deft at iPhone navigation as Rob — probably because I hadn't spent every waking minute of the last year playing with the thing. But I opened a browser and navigated to the *Trib*'s Web site.

I winced to see that the story about our parade was the third one down on their home page. Did that mean it was on the front page of the print edition? With the headline SANTA SLAIN IN RURAL VIRGINIA PARADE?

"That's awful," I said aloud.

"What's awful?" Michael asked. He slid a plate of bacon and eggs in front of me and leaned over my shoulder.

"What if some kid sees this?" I said, pointing to the headline. "Couldn't they at least say 'Santa Impersonator'?"

"Too long for a headline," he said, peering at the tiny screen. "And I guess they figure anyone old enough to read it doesn't have to be protected."

"That's true," I said. He returned to his cooking and I figured out how to scroll down the article with one hand while eating with the other.

"Just our luck to have a *Trib* reporter here for the murder," I grumbled, through a mouthful of eggs.

"Is it bad?" he asked.

"Could be worse," I said. "And maybe I misjudged Werzel — this is certainly not the slash job I expected from him."

"Probably because it's not his byline."

I scrolled up to the top of the article again.

"You're right," I said. "Good eyes; I didn't even notice that. Who's this Keating person?"

Michael shrugged.

"He must have shown up after Werzel called about the murder. Or maybe wrote it from the facts Werzel phoned in."

"Good grief," I said. "You should see what it says at the bottom of the article: 'Staff writer Ainsley Werzel contributed to this report.' I feel sorry for him. He hung around

256

all day, had to rough it in our unheated living room overnight, and all he gets is 'contributed to this report.' That's not fair!"

"Maybe that's why he's still hanging around again today," Michael said.

"Werzel? Damn," I said. "Sorry for him doesn't mean I want him around. Maybe he just doesn't know the road is open."

"I think four or five people have already made a point of telling him," Michael said. "He says he's looking for his camera, but I suspect he's on the prowl for dirt."

"Has he reported the camera?" I asked. "Maybe he didn't lose it after all — maybe Norris Pruitt lifted it."

"Not sure he's officially reported it, but I'm sure the chief knows it's missing," Michael said. "Maybe when they catch Norris Pruitt, they'll find the camera."

"True," I said. "It wouldn't be in the stuff they seized from Norris's bin; Doleson was holding that hostage for several months. But unless Norris has undergone a miraculous transformation, he's probably filching things and stashing them somewhere."

Michael nodded. He slid the last of the bacon into a covered dish and turned the camping stove off.

"That should do it," he said. "Werzel just went outside — maybe I should keep an eye on him."

"Or maybe just tell him now that the road's open he should hit it?" I suggested.

"Never wise to antagonize the press," he said. He topped off his coffee cup, put on his heavy jacket, and went outside.

The idea that Norris might have filched Werzel's camera cheered me no end. Odds were that by the time Werzel got his camera back, the parade, if not the murder, would be old news and whatever embarrassing or unflattering photos the camera contained would never see the light of day, much less the Style section of the *Trib.* Still — perhaps I should ask Clarence and Caroline, if they found it first, to give me a few minutes alone with its delete button.

If Clarence was still outside, maybe I could have a private word with him. I threw on my own wraps and went outside myself. I was still standing on the back porch, adjusting to the cold and looking around for Clarence, when I heard Michael's voice.

"This is Ernest," Michael was saying. "Our first llama."

First llama? I'd been referring to him as "the" llama. And while I had to admit he wasn't much trouble — far less than most human visitors — I wasn't ready for an entire herd of Ernests and Ernestinas grazing in our tiny pasture. Though I feared Michael was.

I started to say so and stopped. Not a discussion I wanted to have in public, and especially not in front of a reporter. But I made a mental note that we needed to have that discussion soon. Meanwhile, I crunched through the snow to the pasture. Michael was leaning against the fence, gazing proudly at Ernest. Werzel looked grumpy, so I assumed he'd seen the "contributed to" credit. And he obviously wasn't enjoying Michael's discourse on the joys of llama ownership.

"Right, right," he said. "So what can you tell me about this Doleson guy?"

Michael and I both immediately put on appropriately somber, regretful expressions. Michael, of course, was the better actor, but I'd had plenty of experience behaving properly at funerals of relatives I'd hardly met — and a few I'd met and heartily wished I hadn't.

"A terribly sad business," Michael said, shaking his head. I shook mine too, in solidarity.

"Sad?" Werzel said. "Who are you kidding? From what I hear, he was the biggest louse in town. If you liked him, you must be the only two who did."

"I didn't know him very well," I said.

"But any man's death diminishes me," Michael intoned.

"Dickens?" I asked. "Not *A Christmas Carol,* I know that."

"Donne," Michael said.

"Oh, right."

"Done what?" Werzel asked.

"John Donne," Michael said. "Seventeenth-century poet. 'No man is an island'?"

"Oh, I get it," Werzel said, though from his expression I didn't think he did. "Getting back to Doleson —"

"Look, if you're trying to get us to say something snarky about the dead guy, forget it," I said. "We didn't know him very well, but we can still feel sad about someone dying in such a horrible way at a season when people are thinking about holiday celebrations, not funerals."

Michael nodded solemnly. Werzel looked back and forth between us for a few seconds.

"Right," he said. "I'm going to see what the chief is up to."

CHAPTER TWENTY-FOUR

Michael and I both breathed a sigh of relief.

"I'm going to rehearse," he said. "I can't do it in the barn with Chief Burke and his men, so I guess I'll stay out here."

"Don't be silly," I said. "The cold air's not good for your voice. Rehearse in the house. I'm used to it, and our house guests will just have to deal."

"I'll probably drive them all out again," he said.

"You make that sound like a bad thing."

Michael did go to the other end of the house, where he could really cut loose and declaim at full volume. Very soon everyone else found it important to be out in the barn or back in town. I never got the chance to ask Clarence or Caroline about the camera.

Our land line wasn't working yet, but I checked in with a few people while my cell phone still had signal. Our Virgin Mary had given birth to a nine-pound baby girl, to be named Noel Grace. Dad got rave reviews on all sides for his performance as Santa. All the parade participants had made it safely home, except for the animals, who were warm and snug at the college barn. But I failed miserably in my subtle attempts to gather information about Doleson. Did people really know that little about him? Or were they just unwilling to share what they knew? I finally abandoned all subtlety and called several of the worst gossips in town, with no luck. Either no one had any dirt on him or they weren't going to share it within the remaining useful life of my cell phone battery. The signal was getting fuzzy anyway, so I gave up.

Around ten, the snow began again. At first only a few scattered flakes came down at apparently random intervals, like advance scouts. Then, all of a sudden, as if the scouts had sent back particularly good reports, the flakes began coming down more heavily. And not big, damp flakes that promised a wet, sloppy, but short-lived snow. These were tiny, earnest little flakes that meant real accumulation if they kept it up for a while. Which, according to the weather reports I could get on my battery-operated radio, they would.

I didn't tell Michael. He could look out

the window for himself, and if he hadn't, no need for me to upset him.

As the snow arrived, the remaining police officers departed, although before they left, they wrapped a few more rounds of crime scene tape around the pig shed, the barn, and several unidentifiable snow-covered lumps in other parts of the back yard.

I wrapped presents, muttering along as Michael rehearsed. Then I packed the borrowed Boy Scout equipment, still muttering.

About noon, I heard the noise of heavy machinery outside — probably the Shiffleys' snow plow going by at close range.

Michael strolled into the kitchen and put the tea-kettle on the camp stove.

"Maybe we'll make that show after all," he said. So he had been peeking.

A few moments later, I heard the strains of "Good King Wenceslas" out in the yard.

"More carolers?" Michael asked.

"No," I said peering out. "It's the Boy Scouts. Come to fetch their camping gear, I assume. And looks as if they're starting their cleanup, even though the litter's buried under the snow. They're caroling while they work."

"Excellent," Michael said. "I'd go and

help them if I didn't have to rehearse some more."

"Will they bother you?" I asked, suddenly anxious. "I can tell them to keep it down if you need to concentrate."

"What more perfect background music could I have for rehearsing *A Christmas Carol*?" he said. He took his coffee cup and his script and headed back toward his office. I put on my coat, hat, boots, and mittens, picked up my coffee, and went outside.

I had to admire the Boy Scouts' dedication. It was still well below freezing and as in the carol, the snow was deep and crisp and even — three inches of it and counting. It covered everything, including the trash they'd come to pick up. I'd have been tempted to postpone the cleanup until warmer weather. But the Scouts were rummaging all through the yard and up and down the road, excavating even the smallest lump under the snow to fill the huge black plastic trash bags they were dragging behind them.

Randall Shiffley, who owned the construction company and served as one of the scoutmasters, had apparently used his tractor not only to plow snow but also to drag over a Dempster Dumpster, which stood at the end of our yard closest to town. Some

264

of the older Scouts were dusting off the temporary trash barrels we'd scattered throughout the yard, gathering them up, emptying them into the Dumpster, and finally loading the trash barrels onto a big Shiffley Construction Company truck. I was relieved to see that the Scouts gave the various objects festooned with yellow crime scene tape as wide a berth as if they were radioactive.

Randall was sipping coffee from an insulated mug and observing the action with an approving look on his face.

"I had to come out anyhow, to pick up the camping gear, so I thought we might as well make a start," he said. "Get the trash cans out of your way, do what we can. We'll need to come back after the snow melts for the final policing, of course."

"That's great," I said. "You think they'd like some hot chocolate, or maybe some cider?"

"I'm sure they'd appreciate either one," he said. "It's a cold day, and this is thirsty work."

"I'll go make some if you'll help me carry it out," I said. "And I've got a lot of their gear inside — we borrowed it for our unexpected houseguests."

"That's fine," he said. He followed me

back to the kitchen and sat at our kitchen table, sipping his coffee, as I heated the milk and cider over the camping stove.

"By the way," I said, "I heard you might be one of the people who isn't entirely broken up by Mr. Doleson's death."

"You heard right," he said. "You probably also heard about when I tried to punch his lights out."

"Over the eagle's nest thing?"

Randall nodded.

"I didn't realize you were that much of a bird lover," I said.

"Well, I guess I like birds as well as the next guy. But this wasn't just any bird. It was a bald eagle. Our national bird."

"Oh, I see," I said, feigning ignorance. "I just heard it was an eagle. Michael and I were out of town then."

"Yes, a bald eagle. Only eagle we usually get in Virginia. And everyone knew Doleson had smashed that eagle's nest, but he was too sneaky to leave any evidence. Not that Chief Burke didn't do his best."

"No wonder all the SPOOR people were so upset," I said. "I'm surprised Dad didn't tell me about it."

"I think your father felt that what happened was his fault," Randall said. "Since he was president of SPOOR when Doleson

266

did it. Which is nonsense — no one blames your father at all. Not much you can do when you've got a sneaky, mean bas— er, scoundrel like Doleson."

Randall still seemed quite worked up about the eagle, even four or five months after the event. Worked up enough to take revenge? I had a hard time believing it. But then, I had a hard time believing Clarence could be involved, either. And I remembered what the chief had said about the killer's height — at least six foot two. Like Clarence, Randall was tall enough to have staked Doleson.

"So yes, I was mad at him," Randall was saying. "And since he was still trying to cause me trouble over punching him, I guess you could say I had a double motive. That what you're asking — whether I could have killed him?"

"Or whether you know anyone who might have?"

"Lot of high words down at the American Legion hall after the bald eagle incident. But not a lot of people mad enough — or stupid enough — to actually do anything."

"Of course, if you're thinking of killing someone, you wouldn't necessarily run around making threats first," I said. "Makes it so much easier for the police."

"True," he said, with a slight nod, as if conceding a point. "Still — there was some talk of boycotting Doleson's businesses, but hardly anyone rents storage units from him anymore, and it's not as if the poor souls living at the Pines have anywhere else to go, so that died down. Most anyone did was get up a petition to get him kicked out of the Santa job, and you can see how much notice the Town Council paid to that."

"It still seems incredible that the Town Council made him Santa," I said. "Do you think he had something on one of them?"

"You mean, was he blackmailing them?" Randall tilted his head as he considered the idea. "It's a thought. If the chief ever finds Doleson's files, maybe we'll find out."

"Ever finds the files — you mean they weren't at the Spare Attic?"

Randall shook his head.

"One of my cousins is a deputy," he said. "He's back out there tonight, searching the Attic and the Pines, top to bottom. And no luck. So either Doleson didn't have files or he kept them someplace they haven't found yet, or someone got out to the Attic before the police did."

"And before Caroline and Clarence did," I added.

He nodded.

"So who do *you* think killed Doleson?" I asked.

Randall tipped his chair back and folded his arms behind his head as he considered the question.

"Plenty of people mad enough," he said. "But it's hard to think of anyone mean enough to do it at Christmas, and risk spoiling the parade like that. Still — the Lord moves in mysterious ways, and if He was moved to call Ralph Doleson home at what might seem to us an odd and inconvenient moment — well, I'm not going to complain."

In other words, good riddance to bad rubbish. I wondered what he meant by Doleson still trying to cause him trouble. Legal trouble, perhaps? I was searching for a tactful way to ask when Randall spoke up again.

"I don't know who killed him," he said. "But I'll tell you who didn't do it."

"Who's that?"

"Norris Pruitt, that's who. There's no love lost between me and any of the Pruitts, you understand. But Norris? He has the height, yes, and the strength, but he sure as hell doesn't have the gumption. Or the cunning to cover it up even as well as the killer did. And you can tell Chief Burke I said so."

"It's not as if he listens to me," I said.

"And after all, the chief knows Ralph Doleson wasn't exactly well liked in Caerphilly."

" 'Oh! But he was a tight-fisted hand at the grindstone!' " Randall and I both started as Michael stepped into the kitchen, declaiming from memory, but carrying the script behind his back.

" 'A squeezing, wrenching, grasping, scraping, clutching, covetous, old sinner!' " Michael went on. " 'Hard and sharp as flint, from which no steel had ever struck out generous fire; secret, and self-contained, and solitary as an oyster.' "

"Yeah, that was Doleson all right," Randall said.

"Actually, that was Scrooge," I said. "Michael's rehearsing. Don't you say his name in there, somewhere?"

Michael consulted his text.

"You're right," he said. " 'Oh! But he was a tight-fisted hand at the grindstone, Scrooge!' " he repeated. "For the show tonight," he added, for Randall's sake.

"A one-man show of Dickens's *Christmas Carol,*" I said.

"I heard," Randall said. "I've got tickets. It's still on, then?"

"Far as I know," I said. "Assuming the power's still on at the theater, and anyone can get there."

"Power's fine in town," Randall said. "So far, anyway. And plenty of people can walk to the college theater. But if I were you, I'd head in there now, before the second storm gets going."

I looked at Michael.

"We'd probably get snowed in there rather than here," Michael said. "And that would spoil our plans for a quiet Christmas alone together."

"I could try to bring you back afterwards on the plough," Randall said. "Of course, I can't do anything about the power in the house — odds are that's out till after the second storm. But if I can get through, I'll bring you back."

"But you can't guarantee that even you can get through," Michael said. "How many inches were they predicting? Six to twelve?"

"Ten to fifteen, last I heard," Randall said, looking out the window and nodding. "You don't see many snows like that around these parts."

He sounded as if he approved of the weather's rare burst of industry.

Michael looked wistful.

"You want to do the show," I said. "And I want to see it. Let's get packing."

"You're on," Michael said.

I handed Randall the tray of ciders and

hot chocolates and turned to go upstairs.

"Take the truck," Randall said. "No offense, Meg, but that Toyota of yours can't handle what's on the roads now. And as for that little windup convertible of Michael's —"

"No way I'm taking the convertible out in this," Michael said. "The truck it is."

"And if you can be ready in half an hour, you can follow me back to town," Randall said.

CHAPTER TWENTY-FIVE

Half an hour later, we were on the road, sandwiched between the tractor Randall Shiffley was using to pull the Dumpster and the truck carrying the Boy Scouts and their gear. We'd packed enough clothes for several days. We didn't know if the rest of the family would come to town to ride out the storm or hole up at Mother and Dad's farmhouse, but just in case, we brought all the Christmas presents and a cooler containing our contribution to tomorrow's potluck dinner. We also brought our camping gear, in case we ended up sleeping on the floor of Michael's office in the drama department building. First Llama Ernest was with us, in an old horse trailer we'd bought in case of just such an emergency, and Spike was in his dog carrier on the seat between us. We didn't even have children yet, and already our days of traveling footloose and fancy free were clearly behind us.

And what were we going to do with Ernest if there wasn't room for him in the barns of the college Agricultural Sciences Department?

I'd worry about that later. First things first: get Michael to the theater, so he could start all his pre-performance rituals. Then I could get Ernest settled — wherever — and look for someplace better than Michael's office for the two of us.

I reached back to pat the pocket where I'd put my notebook.

There was one silver lining to being snowbound in town — at least we wouldn't be completely cut off from hearing any news about the murder investigation. And maybe even helping with it, assuming I could find a way of helping that wouldn't look like interference.

Behind us, in the other truck, I heard the Boy Scouts strike up another chorus of "Jingle Bells."

"This must be how our pioneer ancestors felt, heading west in covered wagons with all their worldly belongings," Michael said.

"Maybe your pioneer ancestors," I said. "Mine stumbled off the ship from England, still seasick, got down and kissed the ground, and refused to stir a step from the Virginia coast. Caerphilly is as far inland as I've ever lived."

He chuckled, and began singing along with the Boy Scouts. I filed away my worries for the time being and joined in.

Caerphilly looked magical, with all the Christmas lights ablaze and the snow frosting the evergreen wreaths and garlands and the red bows trimming them. Even the police station looked welcoming, with candles in all the windows, including the narrow barred windows in the attached jail. Seeing Caroline's truck in the parking lot dimmed my enjoyment a bit, though.

"They'll be fine," Michael said, noticing the direction of my gaze. "As soon as Norris hears they're in trouble, he'll show up and face the music."

I smiled, and nodded, but I wasn't so sure. Norris had been letting Caroline and Clarence clean up after him for years. I wouldn't want to bet that he'd stop now.

Our caravan stopped in front of Dunsany Hall, where Michael's office was, and paused while we dragged our luggage into the lobby. Then I climbed back in the truck.

"You're all right driving in this?" Michael asked, looking around rather dubiously.

"I'll see she gets safe to the college barns,"

Randall called back.

"And I'll walk back over once I get the llama settled," I said.

The truck peeled off at the courthouse, where I could see a lot of idling cars — presumably the Boy Scouts' parents, come to collect them. I kept following the tractor. The going got rougher as we neared the Ag Sciences barn on the edge of the campus. I slipped and slid into what I hoped was a parking space and not a part of the surrounding organic farmland — it was hard to be sure with all the flat bits uniformly coated in snow. I waved good-bye to Randall and went to lead Ernest inside the barn.

I worried briefly about taking him out in the biting cold and driving snow, but I reminded myself that with his unsheared coat, Ernest was more warmly dressed than I was. After all, llamas routinely braved the cold of the Andes. He could handle a Virginia snowstorm.

He stepped out of the horse trailer, sniffed the frigid air appreciatively, and looked around with interest as I led him to the barn.

Of course, the barn was still occupied by the animals that had been in the parade. Everyone had probably spent the brief interval between storms shoveling out their own houses, and even if anyone had had time to consider taking the animals home, it wouldn't have been safe to try.

So Ernest might not get a stall by himself. I hoped he wouldn't mind.

If Clarence and Caroline were still busy down at the police station and Dr. Blake presumably snowbound somewhere, I should check on the animals.

To my relief, the barn was heated, and I stopped just inside the door to shed my wraps.

The friendly beasts around me stood — Cousin, the donkey, was stretching his neck over the top of a stall, as if begging for rescue. I gave him a wide berth, in case he was feeling crankier than usual. Several sheep were inside the next stall, and the ox and cow beyond them. The various fowl cooed, clucked, or fluttered in a series of coops nearby. The coops all had full food and water compartments, and I could hear the sound of crunching hay from somewhere in the barn, so I relaxed a little. Someone had been looking after the animals.

I led Ernest into the stall with the sheep — since they were Seth Early's sheep, they had probably spent as much time in our yard with Ernest as they had in their own pasture. Ernest seemed happy to see the sheep, and they didn't seem to mind him, so I shut the stall door and breathed a sigh of relief.

I leaned on the door and watched Ernest and the sheep for a few moments. I found it strangely soothing. Maybe a few more llamas wouldn't be such a bad idea. But no more than we could fit in the horse trailer.

I saw a bin of fresh carrots just inside the barn, and I fed a few to Ernest. And then one to Cousin, being careful to pull my fingers back as soon as he reached out for it, since no one had quite convinced Cousin that donkeys were not carnivores.

I could see the camels, Larry, Curley, and Moe, a little farther down, just beyond the cows, and realized that I had never gotten around to asking Clarence what kind of treats camels liked. Well, no time like the present to satisfy my curiosity.

All three camels accepted carrots — Larry and Moe eagerly, and Curley with an ill-tempered grumble, as though he were only doing it to avoid hurting my feelings.

Strange, but like llamas, camels had a curious calming effect on me. I stood watching their slow, meditative chewing. Almost instinctively, I began doing the breathing exercises Rose Noire was always nagging me to try when I was feeling stressed.

Everything would be fine, I told myself. Sooner or later, the chief would figure out who'd killed Doleson, and if I had the chance, I'd do what I could to make it sooner. The audience might be smaller, but Michael's show would go well; and if we couldn't get home, we had a place to sleep.

Suddenly I spotted a flicker of movement at the other end of the stable, behind some hay bales.

"Who's there?" I called, and reached into my pocket to finger my probably useless cell phone.

CHAPTER TWENTY-SIX

"Don't mind me," a quavery tenor voice said.

A large, disheveled shape swaddled in a voluminous khaki overcoat appeared from behind the hay bales. After a moment, I realized I knew him.

"Norris?" I said. "Is that you?"

He took a step or two closer. Norris Pruitt was tall — taller than Michael's six feet four — and about as pale as a human being could be without actually qualifying as albino. A few tufts of his straw blond hair stuck out from under his tan watch cap. The only spots of color on him were the bright red patches of chapped skin on his cheeks and nose, and the red rims around his pale gray eyes.

"What are you doing here?" I asked, taking an involuntary step back.

"Don't mind me," he said. "I only came to see to the animals. Normally Clarence would be seeing to them, but . . ."

He shrugged.

"But Clarence is down at the police station, answering questions about the burglary he and Caroline committed to help you," I said. I decided mentioning the murder would be a tactical mistake.

"They didn't have to," he said. "I never asked them to."

"You didn't have to. They've been helping you out of jams for years, haven't they? What did you expect them to do when they found out Ralph Doleson was blackmailing you?"

He hunched his shoulders tighter and shook his head. He looked like a wounded bear.

"I'm sorry," he said. He sat down heavily on a hay bale and buried his face in his hands. "I didn't mean to cause trouble." His shoulders heaved as if he were sobbing convulsively.

Was he talking about his thefts or the murder? For some reason I found it hard to think of Norris as a killer. I inched closer, and had to resist the temptation to pat him on the shoulder and say "There, there."

One of the cows stuck her head over her stall door and snuffled at Norris's hair briefly, as if considering whether its resemblance to hay went as far as the taste. Norris reached up and stroked her face absently.

I knew I should call Chief Burke and report that I'd found his missing suspect, but I gave in to curiosity.

"How did you get Ralph Doleson's keys, anyway?" I asked.

Norris stiffened.

"Ralph Doleson's keys?" he whispered. "Did I have them? I don't even recall seeing him yesterday. I don't see how I could possibly have . . . borrowed his keys."

"Are you sure?" I said. "Just having the keys doesn't mean you killed him. Since he was blackmailing you, no one would blame you if you went into the shed, found him already dead and —"

"No!" Norris exclaimed. "I could never have done that, even if I had found him. And I didn't. I didn't."

He was rocking back and forth now, and looked so miserable that now I really couldn't help going over to pat his shoulder. I did refrain from saying "There, there."

"You have to tell the chief," I said, as gently as I could. "You can see how bad your hiding from the police looks. Turn yourself in, and tell the chief the truth, and I'm sure Clarence and Caroline will do everything they can to help you."

He nodded.

"I can call the chief now, if you like," I said.

"No," he said. "I'll call them."

He reached in his pocket, took out a cell phone, and looked at it as if he'd forgotten how to use it.

"I guess I should dial 911," he said, frowning at the cell phone.

"If you like," I said. "Though I'd just use the non-emergency number. Here, let me do it."

He nodded and put the cell phone in my outstretched hand. I punched in the familiar digits — all the more familiar because Norris's cell phone was the same make and model as my own.

"Debbie Anne?" I said, when the dispatcher answered. "Can you tell the chief that Norris Pruitt's over here in the college barn, and he's ready to turn himself in?"

"My gosh," she said.

I said good-bye, cut the connection, and held the phone out to Norris.

"No, you keep it," he said. "It's yours anyway. Sorry."

I did a double take. No wonder the phone had felt so familiar. I took a step away from him as I tucked it back into my pocket.

"Here," he said, handing me something else. "I'm really sorry."

It was my notebook-that-tells-me-when-to-breathe. I stuck it back in my other pocket and put a good ten feet between me and Norris. I could hear sirens in the distance already, so I whiled away the time until the chief and his officers arrived by patting myself down to see if I was missing anything else.

A stray sheep came up and thrust its head at Norris to be scratched. He was still sitting on the hay bale, disconsolately petting the sheep, when Sammy and Horace burst in.

"Hands up!" Sammy shouted. He was aiming his gun at Norris. I backed away and Norris froze with both hands tightly clenched in the sheep's thick fleece.

"Mr. Pruitt?" Horace said.

Norris was staring fixedly at Sammy's gun with his mouth hanging open.

"Mr. Pruitt!" Horace said, more loudly.

Norris flinched, but didn't answer. I suspected he was about to curl up and faint, like a startled possum.

"Norris?" I said gently. He shifted his gaze to me. "Remember we agreed you were going to talk to the police?"

He nodded.

"Sammy and Horace are just here to talk to you," I said. "You don't have any weapons, do you?"

He shook his head.

"Then why don't you hold your hands up so they can see that?" I said.

Norris nodded, and began lifting his hands. Since he hadn't relaxed his death grip on the sheep's wool, the poor animal began struggling and baaing in protest as it felt itself being hoisted up by the fleece.

"Put down the sheep, Norris," I said.

"Put down the what?" I looked over to see that Chief Burke had just arrived.

"The sheep," I said. "That's right," I added, as Norris set the sheep down and patted it apologetically. I breathed a sigh of relief. It was a little unsettling to see how easily Norris could lift a two-hundred-pound sheep. He lifted his hands high over his head and then looked to me for approval.

"That's great, isn't it, Chief?" I said, smiling and nodding at Norris.

"Fine," the chief said. "Sammy, put that fool thing away before you shoot one of the sheep. Mr. Norris isn't going to hurt anyone, is he?"

Norris shook his head vigorously.

"Thank you," the chief said to me. "We'll

take it from here."

"Look, Norris was here looking after the animals," I said. "He and Clarence. If —"

I paused. Norris was still very skittish.

"If Norris has to leave," I said, "and Clarence is still down at the station —"

"Don't worry," the chief said. "If we find it necessary to detain both Mr. Rutledge and Mr. Pruitt overnight, I'll have someone look in on the animals."

"You can always call me if you need help," I said. "Or my dad, if you can find him. If Rose Noire's in town, I'm sure she'll be dropping by to check on them, but I don't know for sure she is."

"I'll keep an eye on the animals, Chief," Sammy said. Yes, if there was even a chance Rose Noire might show up, Sammy's crush on her would ensure that he'd take every opportunity to visit the barn.

"I'll help," Horace said.

The chief nodded. His eyes were on Norris, and his body language clearly said that he couldn't wait for me to leave so he could talk to his suspect in privacy.

I fed Ernest another carrot in passing, by way of farewell, and left them to it.

It was slow going outside — not that I minded. I had on enough layers to keep me warm, and I had plenty of time to fill before

Michael's show started. Before I had even gone two blocks, the chief and his forces left the barn, bundled themselves and Norris Pruitt into the three police cars they'd come in, and began slipping and sliding slowly in the other direction, toward the station.

As I hiked along, I tried to push Norris and the murder and all the unanswered questions about it out of my mind and occasionally I succeeded for whole minutes at a time.

I exchanged jovial Christmas greetings with various people I passed, all of them so completely bundled up against the biting cold that I had no idea who they were. I wondered if they recognized me or were simply greeting with enthusiasm anyone else brave enough to be out in the storm.

Foot traffic increased as I passed through Caerphilly's small commercial area, and the stores were doing brisk business. Last-minute Christmas shoppers streamed out of the toy and department stores onto snowy sidewalks already crammed with shoppers whose grocery bags overflowed with milk, bread, and toilet paper — Nature's White Sale, Michael called it.

Cars had almost completely disappeared, though, and even trucks and SUVs were getting scarce. Every so often a snowplow would cruise by, with one of the Shiffleys at the wheel, working to keep the roads clear. Of course, they were handicapped by not having the kind of full-sized snowplows you'd find in larger cities farther north, and this particular snow would have challenged the largest snowplow on the planet. The Shiffleys were losing ground. Though knowing the Shiffleys, they'd keep trying until they cleared the snow or until it melted or until they all got themselves stuck in various ditches and snowdrifts. Shiffleys were notoriously mule-headed.

And notoriously good at holding grudges. Was Ralph Doleson's murderer chugging along on one of those snowplows? If one of the Shiffleys was the killer, Randall might know, or at least suspect. Was that why he was so convinced of Norris's innocence?

Randall had said that Norris didn't have the gumption to kill. I wasn't sure murder necessarily required gumption. At least not Ralph Doleson's murder. The killer could just as easily be someone who was scared and angry and cornered and had the strength to kill just by lashing out. If Norris had been carrying the holly stick when he encountered Doleson, and if Doleson had threatened him . . . I could see Norris lashing out. The shock of what he'd done could well account for Norris's dazed state.

Of course, I couldn't imagine Norris managing even the most rudimentary escape and cover-up. But had the killer been clever, or just lucky?

Still . . . I had a hard time seeing Norris as the killer. And if it wasn't Norris, who was it?

Randall Shiffley himself was on the list, unfortunately. I liked Randall, but he could be pretty inexorable when he got an idea into his head. Did he consider slaying a bald eagle a sin punishable by death? I couldn't quite rule it out. And if Randall decided Doleson needed killing, he'd carry out the project efficiently. He had the gumption and the brains. And the anger. Was he really operating the boom lift during the whole window of opportunity?

And Jorge, who claimed not to be black-mailable, but still seemed very worried about Doleson. And who just might own a bloodstained sweatshirt.

Of course, Doleson had other blackmail victims. I knew of two now — surely there were more? And the chief would find them as he continued investigating. Just because he'd found Norris Pruitt didn't mean he was going to ignore other suspects. I should leave the case to him, and stop worrying.

Of course, I've never been very good at leaving anything to other people.

CHAPTER TWENTY-SEVEN

Back at Dunsany Hall, things were quiet. I passed by the counter that served as the theater's box office, where two people were buying tickets. That was encouraging. I went upstairs to Michael's office. To my relief, he'd left the door unlocked for me.

Spike was there, asleep in his carrier. I let him out and gave him an early supper and a bowl of water. He bolted the food, sniffed dismissively at the water, and began exploring all the exciting new smells that permeated the unfamiliar room.

I sat down at Michael's desk, turned on his computer, and used my illicit knowledge of his user name and password to log into the college's computer system. I wanted Internet access so I could see what else the media were saying about Doleson's murder.

And specifically what line Ainsley Werzel was feeding the *Star-Tribune*. Call me paranoid, but I had the nagging fear that if he didn't get a sexy angle or inside scoop, Werzel would slant the facts or even make stuff up if he thought it would help his story.

This time there were two articles about us listed on the *Trib*'s homepage. Both carried Werzel's by-line, so perhaps his persistence had paid off. They were evidently filed this morning after Werzel had found a working phone or computer. The headline read SANTA MURDER SUSPECTS ARRESTED FOR BURGLARY. It made the failed break-in at the Spare Attic sound like a twenty-first-century Watergate. The accompanying pictures didn't help. No shots from the scene, of course, since Michael had reclaimed my camera from Werzel before the break-in, but they'd found an old shot of Clarence, in his biker's leathers, looking like a thug. Caroline's picture wasn't brand new either — I'd guess it had been taken a good ten to fifteen years earlier, and showed her with what I first thought was a leopard-fur stole around her shoulders. Then I realized that the stole was actually a pair of half-grown leopard cubs, one of which was licking her face while the other appeared to be teething on her hand.

The accompanying text completely left out Clarence's professional identity as a well-respected holistic veterinarian and animal behavior therapist, and merely referred to him as a suspect in "the brutal slaying of Caerphilly County businessman Ralph Doleson." It didn't really explain Caroline at all, but left the impression that she was a rich dilettante who kept exotic animals as pets, rather than a committed animal welfare activist who'd taken in hundreds of abused or abandoned birds and animals, nursed them back to health, and when necessary had given them a comfortable, permanent home at the Willner Wildlife Sanctuary.

Werzel had also written a sidebar on the history of the Caerphilly County Christmas parade. Some indiscreet soul had spilled the beans about Wilmer Pruitt's shoplifting conviction and Orville Shiffley's bacchanalian exploits. In fact, those weren't the only black marks on the parade's history. In the seventies, a group of students from rival Clay County had kidnapped Caerphilly's Santa Claus and paraded him in triumph down the main street of Clayville. They'd returned Santa after a few hours, but not the bag of presents. And one unseasonably warm Christmas in the fifties, Miss Caerphilly County had tried to shed her fur coat and experienced a costume malfunction that was still remembered fondly by the old-timers who'd seen it.

But no previous Master or Mistress of the Revels had had to cope with a murder during the course of the festivities. I sighed. I wasn't sure this was a distinction I wanted.

I jumped as a loud sneeze suddenly resounded through the office. I whirled around to see who had come in, but the door was still closed.

I heard another sneeze, and realized it was coming from near the floor. I peered down and saw Spike standing with all four feet braced against the force of a third enormous sneeze. Then he sniffed slightly and looked up at me as if registering a complaint.

"Sorry," I said. "I'll tell Michael he needs to dust more often."

Spike sighed, trotted over to a chair that stood against the wall, and curled up underneath it.

I turned back to the computer, though I kept glancing over my shoulder. Maybe, along with the dust, I should speak to Michael about having Rose Noire feng shui his office. I recalled her saying that it was very bad to put your desk so you had your back to the door of the room. I could see why. I kept nervously looking over my shoulder to see if someone had snuck in. I'd have locked the door, but it was the old-fashioned kind that could only be locked with a key. If I kept feeling so jumpy, perhaps I'd hunt Michael down and get the key.

The last half of Werzel's sidebar about the parade pretended to give some of the highlights of this year's parade. As I expected, Werzel had gone out of his way to make us seem ridiculous. He didn't feature any of the beautiful or ingenious floats — only the few really peculiar ones I hadn't been able to keep out, like the boom lift and the canine carillon. I was already annoyed by the time I got to the next-to-last paragraph. Werzel had cornered Caerphilly's mayor and asked if he or the town council had considered canceling the parade out of respect for the murder victim.

"Well, no," the mayor was quoted as saying. "I guess that would have been up to Ms. Langslow."

Gee, thanks, Your Honor. See how fast you can pass that buck. I could hear him saying it — not that he'd ever said anything that brief, but I could imagine Werzel plucking that one quotable sound bite out of ten or fifteen minutes of blather.

Then I read the last paragraph and exploded.

"Ms. Langslow was not available for comment."

I snarled a few words I didn't normally say aloud. Spike lifted his head and watched with interest as I pounded the desk a few times. Not available for comment? The man had slept by our fire, eaten our bacon and eggs for breakfast, and been introduced to our llama. I'd answered countless questions from him throughout the course of the day, and if he'd asked me that one, I'd have answered it, too. I was perfectly capable of spinning out a decent answer to Werzel's question — something suitably sentimental about knowing that Mr. Doleson wouldn't want to upset and disappoint the children who had loved him in his Santa role for so many years.

I searched the *Trib*'s Web site until I found a page about how to make complaints and submit corrections. With a phone number. I picked up the receiver and then made myself put it down.

Bad idea. Not complaining to the *Trib* — that was a very good idea. But a bad idea to call now, when I was still hopping mad and would come off like a crank or an idiot. I realized I should give myself a few hours to calm down and then decide what to do — write a brilliant and incisive letter of complaint, citing all the facts and all Werzel's omissions and misstatements? Or call to confront his editor in person, once I'd regained my cool and could adopt the icy precision Mother used to such devastating effect in such situations?

Then I smiled. "What would Mother do?" had never exactly been my mantra. But in this case, I realized, I should do exactly what Mother would do.

I consulted the address section of my notebook, picked up the phone, and called one of my cousins.

Cousin Heather had been knocking around the journalistic scene in Washington for a decade or so, and was currently doing her crusading reporter thing at one of the city's alternative papers, writing exposés of political and financial scandals. She claimed that she was blissfully content with her current job and wouldn't even consider a move to the cold, corporate world of the *Trib.* Of course, as far as I knew, the *Trib* hadn't done anything rash, like offering her a job, that would force her to prove her dedication to alternative journalism.

But however scornful she was of corporate journalism, what she didn't know about the *Trib* and every other media organization in Washington, large or small, wasn't worth knowing.

"Mur Cromuf!" she said, on picking up

the phone. Maybe I was imagining the sound of crumbs hitting the mouthpiece.

"And a Mur Cromuf to you, too," I said. "Eating a late lunch?"

"Sorry," she said. "Yeah, trying to finish up an article before I go home to eat my solitary supper. I was going to take your mother up on her invitation to see Michael's show and stay at your house tonight and have Christmas dinner with y'all tomorrow, but it looks as if Mother Nature is going to interfere. The roads are impossible. I meant to call you so you wouldn't worry."

"No problem," I said. I wondered, briefly, how many other people Mother had invited to stay with Michael and me, and whether any of them had four-wheel drive and would turn up on our doorstep in our absence. "Good call, not trying to make the trip. We don't have power, and however bad the roads are there, trust me, they're worse here. Look, while I've got you on the line — what do you know about a *Trib* reporter named Ainsley Werzel?"

"He's a total jerk," she said.

"I already know that."

"And with any luck, he won't be a *Trib* reporter much longer. No idea why they hired him in the first place, or why he's stayed there as long as he has."

"And how long is that?"

"About four months. Of course, you can't just fire people these days, you know. Not in a litigious town like D.C. You have to prove they're completely incompetent. Takes time, even when it's true. Any day now, they'll decide they've got enough ammo and they'll kick him curbside. Meanwhile, they're trying to minimize the damage he can do by assigning him to spin his wheels on nothing stories. How'd you run into him?"

"Apparently one of the nothing stories they assigned him to was the Caerphilly Christmas parade."

"Ouch!" she said. "Sorry. *Trib*'s perception, not mine. So I guess he lucked out, stumbling on your murder."

"It's not my murder," I said. Snapped, really, and then thought better of it. "Sorry. Touchy subject. And what's the best way to complain to the *Trib* about him?"

"You sure you want to complain?" she said. "Some editors like it when their reporters hit close to home. Makes them feel they're pulling no punches and being a thorn in the side of the establishment and all that. And they'll never hang their reporters out to dry in public. They may read Werzel the riot act back at the newsroom, but they'll defend him to you."

"Even if he's lying?" I explained about Werzel's "unavailable for comment" line with a few acerbic comments about the character assassination he was trying to pull on Clarence and Caroline.

Heather thought for a moment.

"Okay, the no comment thing's not fair," she said. "But technically, it might be accurate. Maybe he was phoning in the story, and his editor asked him if he'd gotten a reaction from you. And he couldn't reach you in the five- or ten-minute window left to get your comment. Me, I wouldn't say someone was unavailable for comment unless I'd tried pretty damned hard over a reasonable period of time and thought they were deliberately unavailable, but Werzel's a sleaze."

"So your advice is to just ignore it?"

"No, my advice is to keep your eye on him. Sounds like he's starting to flail. His editor's probably pushing him. Asking for better quotes, more damning evidence. Werzel's going to try to deliver, whether there's anything to deliver or not."

"Like making things up?"

"Maybe. Or at least making much more glaring omissions and misquotes. If he's already starting to slant things and weasel, there's always the chance that before too long he'll be out without you doing anything. And if you do complain, be very business-like and make sure you've got at least three real howlers he's pulled. Clear, provable errors. Until then, if you need to vent, don't call the *Trib* — call me."

"Thanks," I said. "I feel better, knowing that the *Trib* already knows he's an idiot. Wish I knew what inspired them to hire him in the first place."

"I heard he started with them as a stringer. They wanted to expand their coverage of Virginia state politics. And they probably remembered his one big story — the Emerson Drood case."

"Emerson Drood?" The name sounded vaguely familiar.

"It was about ten years ago. That politician from somewhere near Charlottesville — was it Fluvanna County? Anyway, you remember — the one who pulled out of the House of Delegates race when they found out he'd spent time in a mental institution."

"I remember," I said. "I never could understand what the fuss was. I can think of any number of politicians who belong in the nuthouse."

"Yeah, but getting committed tends to put off the voters," Heather said. "Especially if you lie about it and some reporter outs you."

"Werzel outed him?"

"Yeah, and then he was the one who tracked Drood down and got that big final interview just before the guy hanged himself in a sleazy motel room. You remember that part, right?"

"Vaguely," I said.

"Anyway, it was good detective work on Werzel's part, tracking Drood down. I'll give him that. And he did get that incredible final interview. But to me there was always something not quite right about it."

"You think he made up the interview?"

Silence for a few moments on the other end of the phone. Then she sighed.

"The guy's such a louse I could almost believe it," she said. "But no, the interview was too solid — had too many new revelations that turned out to be absolutely true. I meant not quite right about the way he got the interview. No way I believe Drood would have talked that much in his right mind. Who knows what kind of tricks or pressure Werzel used? And two hours later, Drood offs himself. Don't tell me the two weren't related."

"Drood committed suicide when he realized how indiscreet he'd been?"

"Maybe. Then again, according to the coroner's report, Drood had a high blood alcohol content — .02 something. Here it is — I've got one of the articles online — .025. Blotto. So maybe Werzel got him drunk and tricked him into giving such a candid interview. Or maybe Drood got drunk after Werzel left, when he realized what he'd done. Either way, don't tell me that remorse and embarrassment over what he'd said didn't contribute to his suicide. Though the more I think about it — maybe Werzel didn't make up the interview, but I wouldn't put it past him to tinker with what Drood said to make it a better story. I mean, the guy wasn't around to contradict anyone, was he? I guess the *Trib* didn't share my skepticism, though."

"But if that was his one big article, and that was ten years ago . . ."

"Yeah, go figure. I guess maybe the *Trib* made allowances for the fact that even the best reporters on a small-town weekly have limited opportunities for big exposés. After his big story, he stayed with the same newspaper — the *Fluvanna Gazette* — until it folded last year. He did a few stories for the *Trib* as a stringer, and somehow he wangled a staff job — maybe he had something on someone in the *Trib*'s HR department. Or maybe someone liked his style — he can be pretty funny, in a mean, snarky way. But the grapevine says he's on thin ice, and the *Trib*'s had him doing way beyond the Beltway stuff, human interest stuff — not hard news. Maybe he figures your murder — sorry, *this* murder — is his last chance to make it big. No wonder he's trying so hard."

"Thanks," I said. "It all makes more sense. I'll keep my eyes open for those provable errors, and hope the *Trib* cans him before he commits any more errors at all."

"Good," she said. "Hey, if the roads get better tomorrow, I could maybe come down for Boxing Day. Will there be turkey left?"

"Probably," I said. "Since right now neither Michael and I nor Mother and Dad have power, I doubt if anyone has even started thawing the turkey. You might get to help us cook it on Boxing Day."

"I'll check with you before I head out, then," she said. "Call me if you need any more scoop on Werzel. Or if you get any scoop I can use."

"Will do," I said, and we hung up.

I sat back and thought about what I'd learned from Heather. I decided finding out Werzel was in the doghouse instead of being the *Trib*'s golden boy didn't make me like him any better. But maybe it would make it easier to put up with him in the short term. He'd get his comeuppance.

"Meg?"

I nearly jumped out of the chair.

CHAPTER TWENTY-EIGHT

Jorge Soto had opened the door very quietly and was peering in.

"Sorry," he said. "I didn't mean to startle you."

"Not your fault," I said. I glared at Spike, who could at least have barked or something when he heard someone approaching.

What was Jorge doing here?

"Enough to make anyone jumpy," Jorge said, as he stepped into the room. "Knowing that the murderer's still running around loose."

"Is he?" I said. "Chief Burke has arrested Norris Pruitt. So if you think he did it . . ."

"Do you?" he asked.

"Not really," I said.

"You have someone else you think did it?"

"Not really," I repeated.

He nodded.

I was suddenly acutely conscious of how tall Jorge was. Not quite as tall as Michael, but definitely well over six feet. Even across the room, leaning against the wall, he seemed to loom over me. Having people loom over me didn't usually bother me — in fact, at five feet ten, I didn't often get loomed over at all. But right now, anyone tall enough to loom over me was tall enough to be the killer, and that made me nervous. Even worse, this was someone who might have been trying to hide evidence. I eyed the room for possible weapons. I settled on a wrought-iron fireplace set I'd made for Cousin Horace and had yet to wrap. The poker would make a lovely club. I had to fight the temptation to stand up and grab it.

Or was that a good instinct?

"You didn't tell the chief about Doleson trying to blackmail me, did you?" Jorge asked.

Would that question have made me quite as nervous under other circumstances? If we'd been in a public place instead of a small office on a deserted floor of a building that would not begin to fill up with theatergoers for another hour or two?

"No, I didn't," I said. "But I think you should."

He looked relieved.

"Michael and I both think so," I added.

He frowned slightly in annoyance. Was he annoyed because I was nagging him to talk to the chief? Or because I had just reminded him that I wasn't the only person to know about Doleson's blackmail attempt?

"I know you think I'm being paranoid," he said. "But you don't get it. I'm not worried about Chief Burke. He'll find the real killer."

"Even if people don't tell him what could be vital information?"

"If he goes through Doleson's papers, the chief will find whatever stuff Doleson's got that he could use to blackmail people," Jorge said. "And if he's got stuff on me, I'm sure the chief will see it's bogus. Or he'll talk to me and I'll tell him."

"But you're hoping Doleson threw away whatever he'd been collecting on you when he found out you weren't blackmailable," I said. "Okay. Can't you just tell the chief that you suspect Doleson of blackmail?"

"And say what — that there are guys living at the Pines who shouldn't be as broke as they are? Guys who looked nervous every time Doleson came around? And that Doleson lived pretty well, for someone whose sole source of income was a mostly empty storage building and a run-down apartment building? You really think that would help?"

"I don't know," I said. "But as you said yourself, there's a killer out there."

"And the chief would only think I was trying to divert suspicion away from myself."

I stood up, and pretended to stretch my back, as if I'd been hunched over the computer too long. Maybe I could work my way over to the poker.

"Why would he suspect you?" I asked.

"Maybe because they're going to find my fingerprints inside the shed where Doleson was killed."

I couldn't keep my mouth from falling open in shock.

"What are your fingerprints doing there?" I asked.

"From when I was helping clean it up — the night before the parade. Don't tell me you don't remember."

He looked stricken. I shook my head slightly.

"There were a lot of people helping out the night before the parade," I said. "I don't specifically remember seeing you."

"I was helping Rob — remember?"

I remembered that Rob had made a half-hearted effort at cleaning the shed out in the morning, and that when I'd inspected it, I'd immediately rolled up my sleeves and done it right. But if Rob had had anyone helping him, I hadn't noticed.

"Not really," I said.

Jorge groaned, and buried his face in his hands.

"But I was pretty busy, you know," I said. "I'm sure some of the other people there will remember you. Rob, for example."

"It'd be so much better if you remembered it," he said. Was that a plea to lie for him? Or maybe a threat? Or just an accurate assessment of Rob's potential value as an alibi?

"I'll think about it," I said. "Maybe something will jog my memory. But don't you have something else that's going to need explaining?"

He looked puzzled.

"The sweatshirt you threw away after the parade? The one the police now have?" I decided it would be better not to mention the part I'd played in getting it to the police.

"Oh, damn," he said. He closed his eyes and slumped against the wall.

"Are they going to find bloodstains on it?"

"Maybe," he said. "I don't know. And if those are bloodstains, I don't know whose blood. Could be Doleson's. I helped Rob put Spike in his crate after he bit Doleson, remember? I figured maybe he had some blood on his muzzle and it rubbed off on my shirt. I can't think of any other way I could have gotten blood on it. But do you really think the chief's going to believe that? Especially if —"

"Aunt Meg?"

I jumped, even though I recognized the voice. Jorge jumped too. My nephew, Eric, was standing in the doorway.

"Sorry," Eric said. "I didn't mean to interrupt."

"It's okay," Jorge said. "I was just going. Look," he added, to me, "we need to talk later. Think about it."

About what? Whether I'd seen Jorge helping out with the shed and with Spike? The bloodstained sweatshirt? Or the fact that Jorge had just become a really serious suspect?

"I hear you," I said.

Jorge gave me one more pleading look, then nodded and left.

"Sorry," Eric said again. "I didn't mean to chase him off."

"He really was about to leave," I said. I didn't think Eric needed to hear about my suspicions of Jorge, or how overjoyed I was that my conversation with Jorge was interrupted by a twelve-year-old who, in spite of his recent growth spurt, was still not nearly big enough to be the murderer.

Eric looked anxious. He seemed so young and vulnerable.

Not just vulnerable — upset.

"Did you get through to your parents?" My sister, Pam, her Australian-born husband, and Eric's five siblings were spending the holiday in Melbourne, with the other side of their family. Eric, thanks to severe and persistent airsickness, was staying with my parents, as he usually did when the rest of the McReady clan made one of their frequent trips down under.

He nodded.

"They're fine," he said. "They all send their love."

"So what's wrong?"

"Why do grownups always assume there's something wrong?" he said. He tried to assume a look of bored exasperation that he'd copied from his older siblings during the worst of their teen years, but he hadn't quite mastered it yet, thank goodness.

"Why do teenagers always lump grownups together in that stereotypical us and them way?" I countered. "You're starting it a few months early."

He grinned at that, and looked about six again. But the grin vanished too quickly.

"Besides," I went on. "After everything else that's gone wrong in the last day or so,

I've gotten out of the habit of expecting anything but bad news. If you've got good news, my apologies, and bring it on."

He nodded, but didn't blurt out any glad tidings.

"Kind of a weird Christmas," he said.

Okay, we'd go the indirect route.

"Weird, yeah," I said. "Which makes it normal for our family, right? Remember the Christmas when your grandfather fell off the roof?"

He grinned at that.

"How about the Christmas when Natasha gave everyone live goldfish?" he said.

"The Christmas your Uncle Rob set the house on fire?"

"How about —" he began. Then he took a deep breath. "How about the Christmas when I thought we'd all really blown it? When Santa didn't bring anybody anything?"

"I remember," I said. Eric had been six or seven, and absolutely obsessed with some toy he'd asked Santa for. So obsessed, in fact, that when he woke up at four A.M., he'd crept down to the living room to see if Santa had come through. Our family tradition was to put all the wrapped presents between family members under the tree in the days leading up to Christmas, while

Santa deposited his bounty, unwrapped, after we'd gone to bed on Christmas Eve. And we maintained a strict rule that no one was allowed to go into the living room until the whole family was up. Then Dad would fling open the French doors and everyone would exclaim with delight and surprise at all the wonderful things Santa had brought.

"No one could figure out what was wrong that Christmas morning," I said. "Here you were, the youngest — the only one we were absolutely sure still believed in Santa — and no one could find you."

"When I saw that there was nothing under the tree, I knew I must have blown it, big time," he said. "And not just me, but all of us. I figured whatever it was, Mom and Dad hadn't guessed, but Santa knew. And as soon as Mom and Dad saw the empty stockings and all, they'd start asking some pretty tough questions, till they found out whatever it was we did."

"I told everyone it was a bad idea to wait until morning to put the presents out," I said. "I knew, as late as we'd all been up, that we'd be dragging if we had to get up early, and I suggested it was better just to stay up a little longer. But no one listened to me. And even I didn't expect the power to go out and knock out all the alarm clocks so we'd all oversleep."

"And you knew just where to find me," he said.

"The tree house wasn't such a tough guess."

"I always thought it was really nice the way you convinced me that you'd peeked too, just after dawn, and you guessed York-town must be toward the end of Santa's run."

"I remember explaining that if we'd all really been wicked, we wouldn't just have empty stockings but lumps of coal," I said, wondering if there was a point to this trip down memory lane. Not that there had to be, but most people looked a little more cheerful when reminiscing about Christmases Past.

"And you never told anyone what I did," he said.

"You told them yourself, a year or two later."

"Yeah, but I was really glad you let me tell them," he said.

I quelled a momentary burst of impatience. Yes, I wanted to get back to my online sleuthing, but something was bother-ing Eric. He stared down at the floor for a few long seconds, and then looked up to meet my eyes. "I think I might be in trouble."

"How?" I asked.

"You know that reporter?"

"Ainsley Werzel? All too well by now."

"I sort of borrowed his camera."

"Sort of borrowed? You mean you took his camera?"

"Well, when I first picked it up, I thought it was yours," he said. "You have almost the same model. And when I realized whose it was, I remembered that he'd been taking all these nasty pictures of people. Like trying to get them doing something silly or not looking very good. I thought it was really rude."

"I agree," I said. "And I admit, it crossed my mind how much I'd like to steal his camera and erase all his photos."

"But I didn't steal it," Eric protested. "He left it lying around, and I picked it up to give it to him — well, to you, till I realized it wasn't yours — and then I thought if I could just keep it for a few minutes and go someplace where no one would see me, I could look through the pictures and delete any that would embarrass people, and then just put the camera back where I found it. So I stuck it under my coat. And before I got a chance to look at the photos, he started making that big fuss about losing it, and I was embarrassed to give it back."

"I'd just have left it lying around someplace," I said. "Let him think he'd forgotten where he'd left it."

"Yeah, I thought of that," he said. "But Mr. Pruitt was around — Mr. Norris Pruitt. And you know how he is."

"I do now," I said. "Okay, good call not leaving it around for Norris to pilfer. But you could have told the truth. At least the part about finding it lying around. You could have said you picked it up for safekeeping and forgot."

"Yeah, I realize that now," he said. "But Mr. Werzel was so mad, and it all happened so fast and I didn't think what to do till later. And once he made that report to the chief, I was scared to. Mr. Werzel would have had me arrested."

I shook my head, but he was right — Werzel probably would have tried. Probably still would, if he found out now. And stressed as the chief was by the murder, he might well have been in the mood to teach Eric a lesson.

"What can I do?" Eric asked. "I can't just give it back."

"Maybe you can't, but I can," I said. "Have you got it here?"

He nodded and reached into his pocket to

317

pull out the tiny silver camera. He handed it to me and then sighed as if I'd taken a ton of rocks off his shoulders instead of a few ounces of metal and plastic from his hand.

"You can tell them what happened," he said. "I know I should have brought it back sooner, but I was too scared to do it myself. You can make them understand."

I was going to miss that when he got a little older — that childish confidence that Auntie Meg could fix anything.

Then again, Rob still turned to me regularly to bail him out of scrapes with that same absolute trust that I could and would rescue him.

"You really should have turned it over as soon as Mr. Werzel made that fuss," I said. "You know that."

"Yeah," he said, looking down at the floor. "And if you think I should take it back myself, I will. I just don't want to do it all by myself."

"No, I'll take care of Mr. Werzel," I said. "I'll tell him about you thinking it was mine and giving it to me. Which is the truth — I'll just let him think I was the one who identified it as his camera."

"Thanks," he said. "I promise I won't ever do anything like this again."

"One thing," I said. "Did you mess with his pictures?"

He shook his head.

"I didn't even look at more than the first one or two," he said. "I could tell it wasn't yours."

"Good," I said. "I want to be telling the absolute truth when I say that you had nothing to do with the missing pictures."

"But how do you even know there are any missing?" he asked.

"There may not be now, but before I give this back to him, I plan to look through all of them and delete any that I'd cringe to see published in the *Trib.* For instance, I remember him taking a picture of my rear end when I was bending over to see if Spike was bleeding to death."

Eric grinned.

"So you're going to do the same thing I was going to do."

"You bet. Now run along and sin no more. Leave that to me."

"Thanks, Aunt Meg." He hesitated, then reached over to give me a quick hug before turning to go.

"Oh, Eric — can you do something for me?"

"Sure." He paused in the doorway.

"If you see Michael, could you get him to

send someone up with the key to the office?"

Eric grinned.

"So you can keep people like me from bothering you," he said.

"So I can lock it up when I leave," I said. "We've got all the presents here — including yours."

"Oh, in that case — yeah, I'll find him," Eric said. He closed the door behind him.

I stood up to look over the desk at Spike. He was still under the chair, curled up so tightly he looked like a black and white fur hat.

"You're a lot of help," I said. "Next time, bark, will you?"

He ignored me.

I sat back down to examine the camera.

Chapter Twenty-Nine

Luckily, since Werzel's camera was the same make and practically the same model as my own, I didn't have much trouble turning it on. Not exactly a professional photographer's camera. No wonder Werzel had been so desperate for his lost photographer to show up.

Though it was odd that even after the real photographer arrived, Werzel continued looking so insistently for his camera. Especially since he wasn't much better a photographer than I was. His photos didn't have as many of what Michael called "unidentified flying pink sausages" — pictures in which I'd accidentally put part of my thumb or forefinger in front of the lens — but just as many of his shots were ever so slightly out of focus. Or noticeably askew. Or awkwardly framed. The occasional shot good enough to print looked more like an accident than anything else.

I deleted half a dozen embarrassing or unflattering shots of myself and others — shots sufficiently in focus that some editor at the *Trib,* in an evil moment, might have considered using them. Of course, by the time the news about the murder had broken, the photographer had arrived, so odds were the *Trib* wouldn't need any of Werzel's shots at all.

Except, of course, for the shots of Ralph Doleson while he was still alive. Those might have a news value that outweighed their poor quality. My temper flared all over again when I saw the shots of Doleson booting poor Spike out of the pig shed.

Perhaps it was a pity I'd decided to wait until after the parade to report Doleson for animal abuse. If I'd dragged one of the several nearby police officers over to have him arrested on the spot, maybe he'd still be alive.

No use second-guessing things like that, and it wasn't as if it was my fault the killer had found Doleson alone. Like Ebenezer Scrooge, he'd helped seal his own fate by the way he'd lived.

Werzel had snapped a couple of shots of Spike lying in wait outside the pig shed, and then a rather nice shot of Clarence ministering tenderly to the small evil one. And another predictable but amusing shot of Spike sinking his teeth deep into the heavy leather gloves Clarence had taken to wearing when treating his more savage patients, like Spike and the zoo's wolverines.

I reached over and plugged the card reader into Michael's computer. The shots of Spike and Clarence were too good to let go. Before I gave the camera back, I was going to keep copies of them for myself.

I turned back to the camera and clicked ahead. Another couple of photos of Spike, none of them as good as the first few. A distant shot of Michael, Dr. Blake, and the chief on their camels.

Followed by a candid shot of Ralph Doleson, sitting on the seat of the sleigh. He was looking up at the camera as if surprised, and he was holding a boot in his hand.

"What's that?"

I jumped a foot. I'd been staring so intently at the camera's tiny LCD screen that I hadn't even heard Rob open the door and walk in.

"You scared me to death," I said. "I'm definitely going to get Michael to rearrange his office furniture before one of his students sneaks up and gives him a heart attack."

"I bet he doesn't spend much time on the

computer with his back to the door like that," he said. "I wouldn't, if I were him. You're the one who gets so wrapped up in the computer that you don't notice what goes on around you."

"Did you at least bring the key?" I asked.

"Key?"

Okay, so Michael hadn't sent him.

"Never mind," I said looking back at the camera.

"What's so interesting?"

"It's a picture of Ralph Doleson," I said, handing him the little camera.

Rob peered at the screen and frowned.

"He's sitting in the sleigh where he was killed," he said. "With one boot on and one off. I only got a quick glimpse through the door, but doesn't this look a lot like . . . ?"

"Like a picture of Santa taken just before the killer staked him," I said. "I got a lot more than a quick glimpse, and that's exactly what it looks like to me, too."

"What's it doing in your camera?" Rob asked.

"This is Werzel's camera," I said. "It only looks like my camera."

"You switched cameras by mistake?"

"That's what it looks like," I said. Which wasn't precisely a lie, but it kept Eric's secret. "Let me see that again."

"No wonder he was so frantic to find this," Rob said.

He handed the camera back. I studied the picture of Ralph Doleson for a few more seconds, and then clicked the button to see what was next.

Yet another of Werzel's badly shot mistakes. A blurry brown shape on the right, a blurry red blob on the left. I squinted, to see if I could figure it out. Rob leaned over my shoulder.

"Closeup of Rudolph's nose?" he suggested.

"No," I said, as my stomach turned over with a wrenching twist. "Blood spatter on the lens."

"Are you serious?"

I turned the camera over and peered at the lens.

"Maybe it's my imagination," I said. "But there is something crusted around the edge of the lens. See?"

I held it out for his inspection. He stared for a few seconds, then turned pale and sat down in one of Michael's guest chairs.

"That's really blood?" he asked, in a slightly choked voice.

"Put your head between your legs and breathe slowly," I said, mentally kicking myself for having forgotten Rob's notorious squeamishness at the very thought of blood.

"Maybe we both just have overactive imaginations," he said.

"I doubt it. No wonder Werzel was so frantic to get it back. He's the killer — and this camera proves it!"

"Wait a minute," Rob said, sounding stronger. "That can't be blood. How could there be blood spatter on the camera, when there wasn't any on his clothes? I think someone would have noticed if he was running around looking like Sweeney Todd."

"I bet there was blood on his clothes," I said. "That's why he suddenly showed up in one of the county-issue shepherd's robes."

"I just thought he was trying to blend in and get into the spirit of things," Rob said. He shook his head, which looked rather odd, since he was still hanging upside down in fainting prevention mode.

"Maybe you thought that," I said. "I knew he had a sneaky reason for doing it, but I just assumed he was trying to make us forget he was a reporter so he could catch people doing embarrassing things."

"We have to tell —"

"I know, I know." I automatically reached into my pocket and took out my cell phone.

And got absolutely no signal, of course.

"You'll never get a signal in this weather,"

Rob said, peering up at me. "I'm even having trouble on the iPhone. This whole county might as well be back in the twentieth century. Use the land line."

I nodded, and used Michael's phone to dial the police station's non-emergency number.

Debbie Anne, the dispatcher, answered. She'd have answered 911, too, but she'd be less apt to gossip about my calling if I used the non-emergency line.

"Meg!" she exclaimed. "You made it into town! Does this mean Michael's show is on?"

"With or without an audience," I said. "Look, could I talk to the chief for a moment?"

"I'm sorry," she said. "He's not here. He's out at — out of the station."

I had to smile. The chief had probably told her off again for talking too much and telling too much police business to civilians.

"I don't suppose you know where he is," I said.

"I'm sorry," she said. "I can take a message."

"Could you tell him to call me as soon as he can?"

"Can I tell him what it's about?"

Debbie Anne and I fenced back and forth

327

for a few more rounds, with me trying to find out where the chief was and her trying to find out why I was calling, before we settled for a draw. I gave her Michael's office number, told her I'd be there for the time being, and signed off.

"He'll call back," I said.

"Why didn't you just tell her why you called?" Rob said.

"I'm not sure," I said. "Maybe because Werzel showed up at the burglary scene almost as soon as we did. What if he has a police radio? A lot of reporters do. Or what if Debbie Anne says something to the wrong person? I hear a lot of stuff leaks out of the police station, and I suspect Debbie Anne's part of the problem."

"So what do we do now?"

"I don't know," I said. I looked at the phone as I thought it over.

"A watched phone never rings, you know," Rob said. "We should think of something else."

"Such as?"

"If Werzel's the killer, why did he do it?"

"How should I know?" I said. "Unless — hang on."

I turned back to the computer and Googled Emerson Drood.

"What's that?" Rob asked. He came and

perched on the desk so he could look over my shoulder. I felt less stupid about not recognizing Drood's name when Heather first mentioned it.

"A state politician," I said. "From somewhere near Charlottesville. He killed himself about ten years ago. If I'm right . . ."

But nothing on the first couple of pages looked promising. Most were pages that mentioned both Ralph Waldo Emerson and Dickens's *The Mystery of Edwin Drood.* A couple of the articles mentioned Emerson Drood's death, but nothing about the circumstances.

"So far this is not keeping me awake," Rob said. "Are you sure what you're looking for is even available online? Not a lot of newspapers were ten years ago, you know."

"Yeah, and the one I'd really like to see is defunct anyway," I said. "Let me try something else."

This time I typed in "Emerson Drood" and "Whispering Pines" and clicked on the most promising of the resulting links.

"What does the Pines have to do with this Drood guy?" Rob asked.

"Maybe everything," I said, as I scanned down the article. "Aha!"

"Aha what?"

"Fifth paragraph. 'Drood's body was

found at 1:14 A.M. on the morning of August 5 by the night desk clerk of the Whispering Pines Motel in nearby Caerphilly County.' ”

“Someone was murdered at the Pines?” Rob said, looking pale again. “What room number?”

“It doesn't say,” I said. “And the death was ruled a suicide, if that makes you feel any better.”

“Not appreciably, but thanks.”

“I wonder what the clerk was doing, snooping in the rooms in the middle of the night?”

“Looking for small portable valuables, I imagine,” Rob said. “That was one of Doleson's hobbies. So what does Werzel have to do with this?”

“I'm not sure,” I said. “But whatever it was, I think Doleson was blackmailing Werzel about it. You heard about the way Doleson was always photographing people who came to the Pines. I bet he had some kind of dirt on Werzel.”

“Like maybe that Werzel killed Drood?”

“Maybe,” I said. “No idea why he would, though. Werzel supposedly got a dramatic last interview with Drood just before the suicide. Seems more plausible that Doleson knew there was something fishy about that

330

interview."

"What do you mean, fishy?" Rob asked.

"What if Doleson knew that Werzel wasn't there with Drood long enough to get such a long interview? Maybe Doleson eavesdropped and knew Werzel had faked some of the interview."

Rob shook his head as if it all sounded rather weak. I agreed with him. Then I had another idea.

"Doleson was always snooping, right?"

Rob nodded.

"What if Doleson found the body and didn't report it?"

"Why would he do that?"

"Maybe he wanted to loot the dead guy's luggage before calling the police. Or dump the hassle of dealing with the cops on his poor night clerk. Or maybe he was on the way back to his office to report it. Whatever it was, before he could do it, Werzel drives up. What does Doleson do?"

"Grabs his digital camera and starts snapping shots."

"Bingo!" I said, so loudly that Spike woke up and growled at me. "Doleson gets some lovely shots of Werzel entering the room. Then Werzel fleeing the room. And then the dead body Werzel apparently left behind. Werzel's the prime suspect if the police are thinking murder. And Doleson could have made it look even worse — like claiming he'd heard what sounded like a struggle. He's got the perfect ammo for blackmailing Werzel."

Rob whistled.

"Sounds plausible to me," he said. "Why doesn't the chief call back?"

"It's Christmas Eve, he's got a big murder case, and he doesn't know I've got a key piece of evidence."

We both looked at the phone again. It stubbornly refused to ring.

"So are we just going to stay here till it rings?" Rob asked. "No offense to Michael, but it's kind of creepy up here with no one else around."

"Very creepy," I said. "And no, we're leaving. Minerva and the chief are coming to the show — she said so this morning. Let's go downstairs and wait for them, and I can tell the chief in person."

"What if he skips the show to keep working on the case?"

"Then we'll tell Minerva, and she'll help us reach him. Debbie Anne might not put me through to the chief, but she wouldn't stonewall Minerva."

"Great idea," he said.

I shut down the browser and began turning Michael's computer off. Rob went over, opened the door, and stood fidgeting in the doorway.

"The small evil one should go back in the crate," I said, over my shoulder.

"Okay, I'll — damn!"

I glanced up to see Rob clutching his hand, as the tip of Spike's tail disappeared out the door.

"I think we're going to have to start spelling in front of him," I said, as I picked up my coat and purse.

"Won't work," Rob said, over his shoulder. "He's psychic. I'll get him."

He took off down the corridor. I stuck the camera in my pocket and went over to prop the carrier door open. I heard a clatter outside in the corridor.

"Rob?" I called. I stepped out into the corridor and looked in both directions. Only a few scattered bulbs on the night system lit the corridor, but I could easily see that it was empty. No Rob. No Spike. Nothing at all, except for a cleaner's mop and an overturned bucket at the far end of the corridor on the right, where it turned a corner. The noise had probably been Rob tripping over them.

I started down the corridor in that direction. Strange that I didn't hear them, but maybe Spike was traveling even faster than usual. If he'd taken to a stairwell, they could be on another floor by now.

I rounded the corner and almost ran into a cleaner's cart. Then I realized there was a shape lying on the floor beyond it.

"Rob! Are you all right?"

He didn't answer. I knelt down beside him. He was breathing, but his eyes were closed. I reached to check his pulse.

"He's not dead," said a familiar voice.

I looked up to see Ainsley Werzel standing a few feet away. He was pointing a gun at me.

"Now give me the camera," he said.

CHAPTER THIRTY

"Mr. Werzel? Is that you?" I said. I pretended to be peering through the gloom as I said it, and I talked as loudly as I could, hoping that someone would hear and come to rescue me. Then I realized that no one but Rob and I knew that Werzel was the killer. If anyone else was close enough to hear Werzel's name, they'd make tracks in the opposite direction.

"Shut up," Werzel growled.

"What's wrong?" I asked.

"Don't pretend to be stupid," he said. "I know you're not stupid. Nosy, but not stupid. Give me the camera."

"You don't have to act as if I was stealing it." I pulled the camera out of my pocket and held it out. "I was going to bring it back to you. My nephew thought it was mine and brought it to me — I have one just like it."

I tried to sound matter-of-fact and calm, as if I hadn't quite noticed he was pointing a gun at me. He didn't seem to be buying it. He leaned forward carefully, snatched the camera out of my hand, and then retreated to a safe distance.

He turned the camera on and began pressing buttons. His eyes kept flicking down to the camera's display screen and then back to me. I deduced that he was scanning the photos.

Then he stopped.

"Yeah," he said. "Pretty incriminating shot, this one. But the great thing about digital cameras is that you can delete anything you like, and no one the wiser."

He pressed more buttons. Deleting his way through the rest of the shots, no doubt. Then he nodded, turned the camera off, and stuck it into his pocket.

"Now pick him up," he said.

"Rob?" I said. "He shouldn't be moved. He could have a concussion."

"Yeah," he said, hefting a long Maglite in his left hand. "I was aiming for a concussion. If you don't want to pick him up, I could whack him on the head another couple of times and we'll just leave him there."

I decided picking Rob up was the better option. I bent down and found Spike there, licking Rob's head.

"Damn," Werzel said. "If the circum-stances were different, I could do one of those great tearjerker stories. Faithful hound licking the blood off his fallen master's wound."

Blood? Yes, I could see it now. Just a trickle, that Spike was licking up eagerly. I decided not to explain that it wasn't either devotion or savagery on Spike's part — he just liked the salty taste. He'd have licked the wounds of a mortal enemy — or Rob's face after a sweaty tennis match — with equal fervor. Werzel would find that all too hilarious.

Spike growled a little when I picked Rob up.

"Chill, Spike," I said.

"Put him on the cart," Werzel said.

I draped Rob carefully over the cleaner's cart. He groaned slightly.

"Okay, roll him that way," Werzel said.

I thought of saying something melodramatic like "You'll never get away with this," but I didn't like the twitchy sound of his voice. I concentrated on going as slowly as I could without ticking him off. Slowly was better for Rob's head, and also maximized our chances of running into someone who might help.

But the corridors we rolled through

remained disappointingly empty. I realized that we were heading for the service elevator. Spike was trailing behind us.

"Why are you kidnapping us?" I asked. I didn't shout, but I tried to project from the diaphragm, the way Michael was always trying to teach his theater students.

"Shut up and keep pushing," Werzel said. "There's room for two on that damned cart."

I shut up. Not talking to Werzel made it easier for me to concentrate on coming up with an escape plan. Unfortunately, while I could come up with several different ways I could escape, I hadn't yet thought of any way for *us* to escape. And much as I tried to convince myself that if I escaped and ran for help, Werzel wouldn't dare hurt Rob, I didn't believe it. Werzel had already killed at least once — what did he have to lose?

Dunsany Hall was utterly and depressingly empty. The students had long since gone home for the holidays, of course, but you'd think at least one of Michael's colleagues would be dropping by to check on his e-mail or something. We rolled through empty corridors until we reached the freight elevator. No one stumbled on us during the long wait for the ancient machinery to crank its way up to our floor.

"Roll him in," Werzel said, gesturing with the gun. "And kick the mutt out," he added, as Spike tried to follow me.

"And here I thought you were shocked when Ralph Doleson kicked Spike," I said, as I reached down to pick Spike up. "You weren't shocked by what he did — you were shocked to see him. And — ouch!"

Predictably, Spike bit me, and then scampered off the way we'd come.

"Good riddance," Werzel said.

"You're not afraid he'll run downstairs and warn people that there's something wrong?" I said.

Werzel seemed to find that funny. He'd seen Spike in action enough to know that a Lassie-style rescue wasn't too probable. Ah, well. Surely we'd see someone once we got outside.

But when the elevator doors opened and we rolled out onto the loading dock, I realized that between the gathering darkness and the steady snowfall, I could hardly see ten feet. And that no sane person would be lurking in the alley behind the Drama Department on a night like this. And more immediately, that my coat was still lying beside my purse on the floor of the corridor upstairs, where I'd dropped them when I'd found Rob.

"Over there," Werzel said. He gestured with the Maglite. "The blue Subaru." Yeah, I could have guessed that — it was the only vehicle in sight.

I looked from the cleaners' cart to the Subaru. No way I could roll Rob there through a foot of snow, so I carefully picked him up and staggered over to the car.

"In the luggage compartment."

I settled Rob in the back of the Subaru. It already contained several cardboard boxes filled, as far as I could tell, with paper. To fit Rob in, I had to move one box out completely and put it in the back seat. Werzel stood about fifteen feet away, probably to make sure he had time to shoot me if I emerged from his trunk waving some kind of weapon.

Alas, I could see no sign of anything that would make a good weapon — no wrenches or tire irons. There was a tarp, which I tucked in around Rob to keep him warm. I checked his pulse, which was still steady. As I did, I noticed that there was also a metal can of kerosene at the very back of the trunk.

"My head hurts," Rob said suddenly. Relief flooded my mind — surely it was a good sign if he was well enough to speak. I glanced over my shoulder and found that

Werzel didn't seem to have noticed.

"Shh," I whispered. "Don't talk."

"But my head hurts."

"I know," I said. "I'm going to get help as soon as I can. For now, the less you talk, the less your head will hurt."

"Okay," Rob said.

He closed his eyes again. I breathed a sigh of relief. The less Rob talked, the less likely it was that Werzel would decide to whack him again. And if Rob stayed conscious, there was a slim chance he could help me engineer our escape.

Not a chance I could count on, though.

"Hurry up," Werzel said. "Get in and drive."

I got in, hoping it wasn't a mistake. The keys were in the ignition. Werzel slid into the back seat. I started the car and felt immediately and irrationally better. Werzel still had that nasty little gun pointed at me, but I had over a ton of lethal metal under my control. Surely I could find a way to turn the tables on Werzel. Newscasters were always proclaiming that cars were more deadly than guns.

"Where are we going?" I asked aloud.

"Shut up and drive."

CHAPTER THIRTY-ONE

Easier said than done. The Shiffleys had more than enough to do keeping the streets clear. They had no reason to plow the alley behind a building that, except for tonight's performance, would be closed for the rest of the holiday season.

But unfortunately there wasn't quite enough snow to stop the Subaru. Just enough to slow us down. I took as much advantage of the delay as I could, all the while keeping my eyes open for someone — anyone — on the streets.

The Christmas decorations that had seemed so festive when I'd walked past them earlier now seemed to mock me with their cheerfulness. And where had all the hardy pedestrians gone? Clearly the shopping rush was over, and if anyone was planning to brave the snow for Michael's show, they hadn't ventured out yet. We didn't even see any of the snowplows.

"Take the next left."

The next left would be the country road that led out to our house, and eventually to the Spare Attic and Whispering Pines. Not where I wanted us to be going at all. I wanted us to stay in town, where there was at least a fighting chance of encountering someone. And where we were closer to the hospital I'd be rushing Rob to if — no, make that when, dammit! — I turned the tables on Werzel.

"Left?" I said. I tried to sound surprised and maybe even cheerful. "Onto our road? But it's a d . . ."

I let my voice trail off.

"Yeah, it's a dead end," he said. Then he laughed. "A real dead end."

"If I were you," I said, "I'd be heading away from Caerphilly. I mean really away, not just out into the countryside."

"I will be soon," he said. "Need to do a few things first."

I didn't like the sound of it. Not "We will be soon," but "I." I wanted my stint as his unwilling chauffeur to end on my terms, not his.

Relief washed over me when we got to the turnoff. Clearly the Shiffleys were rethinking their attempts to keep every road in the county plowed. Where the turnoff should have been was only a solid bank of snow they'd ploughed off the highway.

"Don't shoot the messenger," I said, as I slowed to a halt. "But I don't think we can take that turnoff."

"Don't argue with me! Keep driving!"

"I'm not arguing," I said. "I'm perfectly happy to keep driving, but I doubt if even your Subaru can get through that. Want me to go ahead and bury us in the snow?"

Werzel studied the snow bank for a while.

"Damn," he said, finally. "This really screws up my plans."

"If I were you, I'd just leave town," I said. "While the police are still busy with Norris Pruitt."

"What do you mean, busy with him? They didn't find him, did they?"

"A few hours ago."

"Lucky for me you mentioned that," he said. "That changes my plans completely."

"Just what are — were your plans?" I asked. "I realize you might not want to tell me, but I'd kick myself if I didn't ask."

After I said it, I worried that my sarcasm would anger him. But he didn't even answer for a few moments. I could see in the rearview mirror that he was frowning at the box on the seat beside him.

"Well," he said finally. "I was going to

make it look as if Norris Pruitt had killed you and your brother while trying to retrieve whatever Doleson was using to blackmail him."

"Which building were you going to torch, the Spare Attic or the Whispering Pines?"

He gave me a startled look, then relaxed.

"You saw the kerosene, right? I hadn't really decided. Maybe both. But if Pruitt's already been arrested . . . of course, I could rig something to look like a delayed fuse. You say he was only arrested a few hours ago?"

I nodded. I didn't like the way this was going.

"Do you know where?"

I was trying to think of a suitable lie — one that wouldn't result in him dragging Rob and me off to some deserted corner of town where he could carry out his revised plan without interference. But bright ideas weren't happening.

"I said where!" he said, waving the gun. I suddenly realized the truth was better than any lie I could think of.

"The stables," I said.

"What stables?"

"The college stables. That's where we're keeping the animals from the parade until the storm's past and we can get them home.

345

Norris was looking after them."

"Probably filled with nice, flammable hay," he said. "That'll do. Let's go."

I tried not to let him see how relieved I was. Short of convincing him to pull up in front of the police station and drop me off, the stables were the best possible destination. Deputy Sammy would be dropping by to see to the animals. Dropping by more frequently than needed, thanks to my hint that Rose Noire might be checking on them. For that matter, Rose Noire might well drop by to soothe the ruffled fur and feathers of the barn's inhabitants. And I was positive Clarence would look in if he was out of jail. And if Dad and Dr. Blake were in town, surely they'd check on the animals' welfare before heading over to the drama department for Michael's show. I could think of any number of people who might drop by and could help, or at least provide a distraction.

"It's close to the edge of town," I said. He'd be suspicious if I didn't put up some kind of argument. "They may not be plowing over there, either. Could be rough going."

"We'll just have to go and see. Move it."

I eased the Subaru into motion and began lumbering slowly toward the stables. Keeping my eye out for passing vehicles, of course. No need for a showdown at the stables if I could pretend to lose control of the car and spin us into the path of a patrol car or one of the Shiffleys' snowplows.

I glanced in the rear view mirror again. Werzel was staring out the window, apparently lost in thought. I didn't want him thinking. I wanted him off balance.

"So did you kill Emerson Drood?" I asked.

"Kill him? No! Absolutely not!"

"Yeah, right," I said. "That's what Doleson had on you, isn't it — that you killed Drood?"

"I didn't kill him," Werzel said. "He was already dead when I got there, so if someone killed him, it wasn't me."

"If he was already dead when you got there — then the big interview was a fake. That's what Doleson was blackmailing you about."

Silence in the back seat for a while.

"Yeah," Werzel said at last. "Far as I know, it was a suicide, but if they've decided it wasn't, they should look at Doleson. He took pictures of the body — hoping to sell them to the tabloids. And then I came along and gave him a better idea. There's a limit to how much the tabloids would pay for a shot of a small-town politico who'd hanged himself in a cheap motel room, but he knew he could milk me forever."

"He had Polaroids, right?"

"Yeah. Pictures of me going into the room, and running out, and then more pictures of the body after I'd left. And then he just sat on them."

"Until after you wrote your bogus interview."

In the rearview mirror, I could see Werzel shrug.

"The early reports said it was suicide, so I figured, what the hell. I told my editor I'd done this interview, but I wasn't sure it was tasteful, now that the guy was dead. And he fell for it. Everyone did. Got me an award — did you know that?"

"Congratulations."

"Of course, by that time, Doleson had his hooks into me," Werzel said. He was tapping the gun against his hand as if he wanted to smack something with it. "Everybody forgot about the award in a few weeks, but I still had Doleson popping up like clockwork for his payoffs."

"So what made you finally kill him?" I asked. "Did you come down planning to do it, or was that a spur-of-the-moment decision?"

No answer for a few moments, and then

he chuckled.

"Bit of both, actually," he said. "I only intended this as a scouting trip. When he found out I'd gone to work for the *Trib,* he started asking for more money. 'You're getting paid more, so I should get paid more,' was how he put it. I couldn't get him to understand that when you factored in the higher cost of living in D.C., I was earning a lot less."

I wondered if he realized how odd it sounded, the idea of discussing the cost of living with your blackmailer. As if the problem were merely the amount he was charging, not the blackmail itself.

"So you just used the parade as an excuse to come down here," I said. "You didn't know Doleson was involved."

"Not until I saw him booting your mutt out of that shed," Werzel said. "I didn't know if he'd spotted me, so I went in to talk to him and as luck would have it, I found someone had left that sharp stick lying just outside the door — well, I realized it was the perfect opportunity."

"Your idea of perfect opportunity must be a lot different from mine," I said. "I'd have thought sometime when there was no one else around to see you would be a lot more perfect. Like late at night out at the Pines."

"That's where you're wrong," he said. "A place like that is never completely deserted, and if you're spotted there, you're done for. But at your parade — that's an opportunity! Hundreds of people milling all around, and knowing Doleson, a few dozen of them were bound to have it in for him. And I'm not local, so no one would have any reason to suspect I had a grudge against the guy, and I had a perfectly legit reason for being there. So I knew as long as I could engineer getting out of the shed without being seen, I'd be home free!"

"Home free, once you got rid of a few bits of evidence," I said. "Whatever possessed you to take his picture just before you killed him?"

"I wasn't really taking his picture," Werzel said. "I knew the flash would blind him just long enough for me to get the drop on him. Of course, I didn't count on misplacing the camera before I got a chance to delete the picture. That was a problem. All fixed now, though."

He smiled and patted the pocket where he'd stashed the camera.

"Now all you need to do is get rid of the original evidence Doleson had on you," I said. "That's what's in all those boxes, right?"

"He didn't have that much on me," Werzel said. "Just this."

He held up a nine-by-twelve-inch manila envelope with "Werzel, Ainsley," written neatly along one edge. Clearly Ralph Doleson had been an organized blackmailer.

"I wasn't his only victim, you know," Werzel was saying. "He had three boxes full of envelopes. I'm keeping a few that might be useful, and the rest are going into the bonfire."

"Useful how?" I asked. "Are you planning on writing exposés, or picking up where Doleson left off?"

"That depends on the *Trib*," he said. "They're setting me up to fire me — I can tell. Sending me on nothing assignments and then complaining when I don't get a scoop. And then when I do get a scoop on Doleson's murder, they take away my byline. Well, they'll see."

I wondered briefly if the *Trib*'s editorial staff were next on his hit list. But before I could ask, we reached the barn. The parking lot outside was empty, except for Michael's truck, now covered with at least six inches of snow.

"Don't pull in very far," Werzel cautioned as I turned into the parking lot. "That's far enough. In fact, turn around so I don't have

351

to do it when I'm ready to leave."

I backed and turned until I had the car facing the exit. I did angle it to maximize the chances that he'd steer into the ditch that flanked the entrance, now visible only as a pair of slight indentations on either side of the rough track leading into the parking lot. Murderers shouldn't expect their intended victims to make it easy for them.

"Inside," Werzel said.

With Werzel keeping the gun aimed at me from a safe distance, there wasn't much I could do, so I opened the back of the Subaru, shouldered Rob again, and staggered toward the barn door. The air was so numbingly cold that even the short walk from the car to the barn set my teeth chattering. I breathed a sigh of relief when I felt the warm, welcoming air inside. Various animals stuck their heads over stall doors and I heard soft moos, baas, and whatever you call the humming noise llamas make.

Werzel looked around and shuddered as if he'd walked into a cage of hungry hyenas.

"Damn, this place reeks," he exclaimed.

Reeks? It smelled of dung and hay and the wet-wool odor of damp sheep. Maybe I was getting more used to the country than I thought. To me, the smell seemed familiar and almost pleasant.

"What a typical urban reaction to the normal, healthy smells of nature," came a voice from one of the stalls. Caroline Willner, echoing my own thoughts.

"Who the hell's there?" Werzel asked. He scuttled so he could put me and Rob between him and the voice.

"Who the hell wants to know?" Dr. Blake. Coming from the same stall.

"Meg?" Dad poked his head out of the stall in question. "Why aren't you over at the drama department? And what's wrong with Rob?"

"Come out with your hands up!" Werzel shouted.

"What the devil?" I could hear Dr. Blake mutter.

The stall door opened, and Dad hurried out. He stopped short and threw his hands up when he saw Werzel waving the gun, and was almost bowled over when Dr. Blake and Caroline Willner rushed out and collided with him. I waited, hoping someone else would emerge — Clarence, for example, or Sammy, or Seth Early. I'd have settled for almost anyone not already eligible for Social Security. No such luck.

"Back in the cell, all of you!" Werzel snapped.

"Cell?" Dad echoed. "It's a stall."

"Come out, go in — you could make up your mind," Caroline Willner grumbled.

"This is unacceptable," Dr. Blake said.

"Look, can I put Rob down?" I asked.

"Shut up, all of you!" Werzel shouted. "Into the cell — stall — now! No, wait — what's that?"

He pointed to a door at the far end of the barn that was slightly ajar.

"The feed room," Dad said. "That's where —"

"Great," Werzel said. "Better than the stall — it's got walls all the way up to the ceiling and a nice sturdy door. Into the feed room, everyone."

"Why is this man holding us at gunpoint?" Caroline asked.

"Because he's the killer," Rob said, startling all of us.

"Rob! You're all right!" Dr. Blake exclaimed.

"No, I'm not," Rob said. "My head hurts, and Meg's holding me upside down."

"It's the only way I can carry you," I said. "Despite being my brother, you're extremely heavy."

"Ha, ha," he mumbled.

"Into the feed room," Werzel said again. "Now!"

To emphasize the "now" part, he fired the

gun into the air. Or, more accurately, toward the rafters. We all flinched, and a flock of chickens who had been roosting on the overhead beams scattered in all directions. Including down, which was alarming to witness, since none of them were particularly skilled at flying. Several of them made interim stops on the walls or doors of the stalls — presumably the reverse of how they'd gotten up onto the rafters in the first place. One made a temporary landing on Dad's head before hopping down to the floor, and Caroline had to catch another plummeting hen. But apparently Werzel had missed them all. None seemed hurt, though you'd have a hard time convincing them of that — they were all running around the rafters or the barn floor squawking as if the sky were indeed falling.

"You idiot," Dr. Blake roared. "You could have killed one of those poor birds."

"He's planning to kill us," I said, as I dodged another downward fluttering hen. "Why would he worry about a few chickens?"

"Into the feed room," Werzel said. "I don't need all of you as hostages. I could make my life a whole lot easier if I finished off a few of you right now. Don't tempt me."

"Come on, Monty," Caroline said. "Let's

not get ourselves shot by this lunatic."

She marched into the feed room, taking off her cardigan as she went, as if she planned to settle in and make herself at home. Dr. Blake and Dad followed more slowly, and I trudged in last and set Rob down on the floor as gently as I could.

"If only I had my medical bag," Dad said, as he knelt down beside Rob and busied himself with an examination.

Werzel stayed at the doorway, checking the room. Apparently he liked what he saw. Dr. Blake was standing in the corner with his arms crossed, frowning thunderously at Werzel. Caroline had hung her sweater up on the wall and was sitting primly on a bale of hay.

"Okay," Werzel said. "You can all stay here. Except for you. I still need you."

He was pointing the gun at me.

CHAPTER THIRTY-TWO

Back out in the main barn, it was still intermittently raining hysterical hens, and the other animals were growing restless.

"Let's fetch those boxes," Werzel said.

The louse could at least have given me a coat.

When I came back in with the first box, I heard raised voices coming from the feed room.

"Don't be an idiot!" Dr. Blake was bellowing.

"But we have to do something!" Dad yelled back.

"Well, that's a stupid plan," Dr. Blake countered.

"Can you think of a better one?" Dad asked.

"Will you two old fools shut up so I can think!" Caroline boomed.

They continued to haggle loudly the whole time I was carrying boxes in from

Werzel's Subaru. If they really did have some kind of plan, I wished they'd keep their voices down while they were discussing it. Were any of them really that hard of hearing? Or perhaps they didn't think they could be heard over the mooing of the cows, the baaing of the sheep, and the squawking of the hens, most of whom had made it down to solid ground and were practicing wind sprints up and down the barn floor.

Werzel had me stack the boxes on the middle of the barn floor just outside the feed room door. Yes, if I were going to burn the barn down with my prisoners locked in the feed room, that was where I'd start the blaze.

I was on the last load, with the can of kerosene perched on top of the box, by the time I finally thought of a plan. I was going to pretend to be losing my grip on the box, stop to shift it, and then drop it, whirl around, and brain him with the kerosene can. Not a brilliant plan, but the best I could think of.

I was tensing to strike when I tripped over one of the hens. The box I was carrying overturned, spilling out its contents — several dozen brown nine-by-twelve labeled envelopes.

"Get up! And pick that stuff up!" Werzel

snapped.

"Okay," I wheezed, as if I'd had the wind knocked out of me in the fall. I pretended to be struggling to get up on one knee, paused as if getting my breath, and began grabbing envelopes. I noticed a familiar local name on one envelope — one of the Pruitts — and then made a determined effort not to read any others.

"Hurry up!" Werzel said.

"I'm hurrying," I said. I pretended to hurry, chattering my teeth slightly and shaking my hands to make it more plausible that I was fumbling the envelopes so badly.

I fumbled them all out of my hands when I got to the kerosene can, the better to grab it and swing as hard as I could at Werzel.

Unfortunately, I missed.

"Nice try," he said, stepping all too easily out of the way. "But I'm not — yech!"

As he stepped back, Ernest the llama spat at him — not ordinary spit, either, but the nasty-smelling greenish stuff llamas produce when they're really vexed. The horrid gob landed directly on his face. Werzel scrambled as far from Ernest as possible, reaching down as he went for a handful of hay to scrub off the llama-spit. When he stood up again, he backed up against the other side of the central aisle.

"That's it," he said. The traces of green goop still running down his face only made his smug smile even nastier. "You've outlived your usefulness. Time for — owww!"

He'd backed up against Cousin the donkey's stall. Cousin's head suddenly appeared over the stall door, and he sank his enormous yellow teeth into Werzel's upraised gun arm.

Werzel yelped and dropped the gun. I dived for it. Unfortunately, since Cousin wasn't a bulldog, he let go to try for another bite, allowing Werzel to dive for the gun, too.

We cracked skulls so hard that I saw stars. Werzel must have, too, though, and it slowed him down long enough for me to emerge with the gun.

I scrambled to my feet and backed away. After one of his police training sessions, Horace had told me how many feet away you needed to be from a running assailant to ensure that you could shoot him before he reached you. Unfortunately, I couldn't remember the exact distance — ten feet? Twenty feet? Or was that yards? All I could remember was that it was a lot farther than I would have guessed. I kept backing as fast as I could without tripping over the rampaging hens, and Werzel staggered to his feet.

"Give me that," he said, taking a step toward me.

"I don't think so." I stopped backing, put both hands on the gun, and aimed it at him.

He started backing away again. I felt relieved until I realized he was backing toward the feed room door. Did I dare shoot? If I missed, would the bullets go through the wall where they could hit Dad, Dr. Blake, or Caroline?

"Stop or I'll shoot!" I said.

He kept backing.

I pulled the trigger.

Nothing happened.

I tried again. The trigger clicked slightly.

Werzel looked puzzled.

"I could have sworn I had more bullets," he said.

"You jerk," I said. The idea that he'd held me at gunpoint for the last hour with an unloaded gun was the last straw. I switched my grip on the gun so I could use it as a club and took a step toward him.

Maybe not the smartest move. Werzel grabbed a nearby pitchfork and aimed it at me, the nasty smile returning to his green goo-stained face.

Just then the feed room door fell backward off its hinges into the feed room and Caroline Willner stepped out holding a club.

No, on closer inspection, I realized she was carrying a plaster replica of a cow's hind leg. What the —

"Take that, you fiend!" she shouted, as she cracked Werzel over the head with the fake cow leg.

The weapon crumbled, but it did the trick. Werzel staggered and fell over, and Caroline and Dad both raced to sit on him.

"Quick!" Dad shouted. "Take the pitchfork away!"

"Get some rope!" Caroline ordered.

I wrested the pitchfork out of Werzel's hand and was tying him up with a dog leash I found hanging on the wall when the door at the other end of the barn flew open.

"Hands up!"

Chief Burke and Sammy entered in a gust of snowflakes, guns drawn and pointing at us.

"About time," Dr. Blake grumbled. "Thanks, Debbie Anne. The cavalry's here."

Debbie Anne? I realized he was holding the handset of a wall phone. He put the handset back on the phone. Then he hung Caroline's sweater back over the phone and winked at me.

So that's why they'd been talking so loudly — so Werzel wouldn't hear them taking the pinions out of the door hinges and calling the police.

"These people attacked me!" Werzel shouted.

"Nonsense," Caroline said. "Arrest him for animal endangerment."

"And murder," I said. "Let's not forget murder."

"I'm innocent!" Werzel wailed.

"Shut up," Dr. Blake said, "or Caroline will smite you again."

He handed Caroline another plaster cow's leg. She scrambled off Werzel's back and stood over him, holding the leg by the hoof and tapping it gently into her left hand, as if impatient to wield it. Dr. Blake picked up the pitchfork and went to stand on the other side of Werzel, scowling with plausible menace. Werzel glanced back and forth between them, hunched his shoulders, and shut up.

Dad emerged with Rob leaning heavily on his shoulder.

"You take over, Chief," he said. "I've got to get Rob down to the hospital."

"What the hell is going on here?" the chief asked.

Dad and Rob shambled out. The others — even Werzel — looked at me. I took a deep breath.

The door slammed open again and Michael ran in, brandishing the poker from Cousin Horace's fireplace set. He'd probably picked it up in his office when he saw the signs of Rob's scuffle with Werzel. Nice to know we had the same good taste in weapons.

"Where's Meg?" he shouted. "And what happened to Rob? And what's going on?"

"It's a long story," I said.

CHAPTER THIRTY-THREE

The stables made surprisingly comfortable temporary quarters. Of course, the last few hours had been so exhausting I'd have found a concrete pavement comfortable. After we gave our statements to Chief Burke, Michael and I raced back to the drama department for the one-man show. Then we spent several hours fending off questions from family, friends, neighbors, and the press — though fortunately the only reporters still in town and not incarcerated in the county jail were the editor of the *Caerphilly Clarion* and a part-time stringer for the college radio station. It was nearly ten by the time we got back to Michael's office, and people kept dropping by to see us, so in spite of the fact that both of us were tired enough to fall asleep in one of the two-foot snowdrifts the twin storms had left behind, we took advantage of a lull between visitors to pack up our essential gear, sneak out, and hike back to the stables.

"It's the last place anyone would look for us tonight," Michael said with satisfaction, once we'd put the feed room door back on its hinges and spread out our sleeping bags inside the room. We'd thrown a blanket over some of the hay bales just outside the feed room, and were lounging there, finishing our dinner.

We'd had to take a rain check on the planned steak and shiraz but we'd unwrapped a few gifts intended for various relatives — a bottle of merlot, some gourmet cold cuts and cheeses, and four different kinds of Christmas cookies. If we all made it to Mother and Dad's for Christmas tomorrow, the intended recipients would understand why we hadn't brought their presents.

Michael had brought his iPod and a tiny set of speakers, so we had nonstop Christmas carols, courtesy of the college radio station. We lit a couple of battery-powered lanterns that the Ag Department kept around to use during power outages, and we even had our own elaborately decorated little Victorian-themed Christmas tree, stolen from the German department down the block.

"Borrowed," Michael kept insisting. "We'll

have it back long before they even notice it's gone. And it adds the perfect touch to our holiday feast."

We'd spread the presents for each other around the base of the tiny tree and hung our stockings on one of the stall doors.

We were lying in a comfortable pile of hay just outside the feed room door drinking the wine out of Michael's office coffee mugs and eating slices of cold cuts and cheese with our fingers, but it seemed like the most sumptuous feast imaginable. Of course, still being alive had just a little to do with my exhilaration.

"You can't imagine how I felt when Spike came running into my dressing room, covered with blood and barking his head off," Michael said again.

"And I did him such an injustice, assuming that the last thing he'd do was go for help."

"He's no Lassie, but he did the job."

I stuffed another bit of cheese through the mesh at the front of Spike's crate, by way of a thank you and Christmas treat, but he was so overstuffed from all the previous treats of cheese, prosciutto, and salami that he barely opened his eyes. It was the first time I'd ever seen Spike ignore food, and I was willing to bet it would be the last. In nearby stalls, Cousin and Ernest were still munching on an extra ration of oats. In fact, every animal in the barn was joining in the feast except for the chickens, who had gone back to roost in the rafters. We decided that for now they'd prefer sleep to food, so they'd be getting their Christmas treat in the morning.

"Just what was that thing Caroline whacked Werzel with, anyway?" Michael asked. "It looked like a plaster model of a cow's leg."

"That's exactly what it was," I said. "Dad was planning to make reindeer tracks in the yards of a few children — Chief Burke's grandson, and Cousin Mildred's kids. So he went over to the zoo a few days ago, made molds from one of the deer, and cast some plaster hooves."

"Cool," Michael said. "Even better than dancing on the roof with sleigh bells, and it's not every year you get snow to do it in."

"Yes, but when the snow forecast changed to feet instead of inches, he realized he needed more than just the hooves. He needed the whole legs. He decided that a cow was the best substitute available on short notice, and the only cows in town were in the college barn. Caroline and Dr. Blake came along to help him. They were making molds of the cow's legs in the stall, and using the feed room to pour the plaster and dry the legs. Lucky for me they were still at it when Werzel and I showed up."

"I'm sure you'd have found a way to foil him anyway," Michael said. "Or at least hold him off until I got here. Just one thing bothers me — was Doleson just a blackmailer, or do you think he also murdered that politician?"

"Drood? No idea. I gather the chief's going to reopen the case. See if there's any evidence to prove whether it's suicide or murder."

"Time will tell, I suppose," Michael said. "And what happens to all Doleson's blackmail files?"

"Under lock and key in the chief's office," I said. I wriggled into a slightly more comfortable spot in the hay and decided it wasn't worth the effort of reaching for another slice of ham.

"Bet a few people will get a little nervous when that comes out," Michael said, suppressing a yawn.

"I imagine anyone in those files has been more than a little nervous since the news of Doleson's death got out. The chief didn't say much about what he planned, but from what I got out of Horace, I gather that except for anything that would constitute a prosecutable crime, the rest of the files won't ever see the light of day."

"That's good. Speaking of prosecutable crimes — does the chief have enough evidence without those photos Werzel deleted?"

"Werzel may have deleted them, but as any of Rob's techies will tell you, deleted doesn't mean gone for good. The computer techs have probably already got those photos back. And I'm sure they can find some traces of blood on the lens."

"Outstanding," Michael murmured.

We listened to the carols in comfortable silence for a few minutes. "Chestnuts Roasting on an Open Fire" gave way to "O Little Town of Bethlehem." I was about to suggest that we call it a night and retire to the feed room when —

"Meg! Michael! What are you two doing here?"

I started and opened my eyes to see Dad, Dr. Blake, Caroline, Randall Shiffley, Clarence, and Mother standing over us.

"Getting away from the crowds," Michael said. "At least that was the idea," he added, sotto voce.

"What are all of *you* doing here?" I countered.

"Got to replace that reindeer hoof Caroline broke over the killer's head," Dad said.

"Reindeer hoof?"

"He means the plaster cow leg," Caroline explained. "Unless the police messed with the molds, they should still be in here."

They all trooped into the feed room where Michael and I had set up our sleeping bags. Well, most of them trooped in — the feed room was a little small to hold them all. Mother and Caroline stood outside looking on.

"Is this going to take long?" Michael asked, rather plaintively.

"Only an hour or so," Mother said.

"Isn't it going to be a little difficult to make plausible reindeer tracks in this much snow?" I asked. "I remember the last time Dad did this, there were only patches of snow, and it was pretty easy to keep from making human footprints too near the reindeer tracks. But in this much snow —"

"That's the beauty of it," Caroline said. "We're going to use the boom lift!"

"I'll put the arm out level to the ground," Randall said, sticking his head out of the door. "And move it along real slow, so they can make beautiful hoof prints ten or fifteen feet out in the middle of that unspoiled patch of snow in the town square."

"And sleigh tracks!" Clarence exclaimed. "We've got a pair of sleigh runners so we can make the sleigh tracks, too!"

"That sounds like fun," Michael said. He sounded as if he was almost tempted to help. But then he yawned prodigiously.

"James," Mother said, "why don't you do that out here?"

"Why?" Dad said, from in the feed room.

"Because Meg and Michael have had a very long day," Mother said. "And I think they would like to rest."

From anyone else, it would have sounded like a suggestion, and the plaster hoofcasters might have protested. But Mother was using the "she who must be obeyed" voice, and even Dr. Blake obediently helped pick up their gear and carry it to the far end of the barn.

"And try to be quiet," Mother said. "After all —"

"What's that?"

We all stopped and listened.

"Could that be bells?" Caroline asked.

Yes, it definitely sounded like sleigh bells going by the barn. Actually, more like over the barn.

"Who's running around with sleigh bells at this hour of the night?" Dad asked. What he really meant, of course, was, who else had stolen his idea? He dashed for the door, and the others followed him out into the snow. We could hear them stumbling about outside and shouting to each other.

"They went that way!" we heard Clarence call.

"Impossible!" Dr. Blake shouted.

"I'll have them keep it down when they get tired and come back in," Mother said. "Good night, dears."

She gave us each a kiss on the cheek and a slight but definite shove in the direction of the feed room. I noticed that our previously limp stockings were now bulging with goodies — how had she managed that in so short a time?

The sleigh bells jingled by again — this time they were definitely overhead.

"Good night, Mother," I said. "And say good night to Dad and Grandfather and Caroline and Clarence and —"

"And all the rest of the Waltons, yes," she said. "Merry Christmas to all, and to all a good night."

For once I decided to let Mother have the last word.

The employees of Thorndike Press hope you have enjoyed this Large Print book. All our Thorndike, Wheeler, and Kennebec Large Print titles are designed for easy reading, and all our books are made to last. Other Thorndike Press Large Print books are available at your library, through selected bookstores, or directly from us.

For information about titles, please call:
  (800) 223-1244

or visit our Web site at:
  http://gale.cengage.com/thorndike

To share your comments, please write:
  Publisher
  Thorndike Press
  10 Water St., Suite 310
  Waterville, ME 04901